IT WAS ALL PART OF THE MARRIAGE ARRANGEMENT—BUT FAR MORE THAN MIRANDA BARGAINED FOR

It was bad enough when Miranda's husband-in-name-only left her alone in their magnificent townhouse while he went out to enjoy the pleasures of the London night.

It was even worse when he invited a bewitching French light-o'-love from his lurid past to stay with them on an extended intimate visit.

It was thoroughly unbearable when he next introduced his gorgeous opera-singer mistress into their increasingly crowded household.

It was then that Miranda met the elegant and attentive Major von Rheinbeck—and decided that two could play at the scandalous love game. . . .

Lord Margrave's Deception

SIGNET Regency Romances You'll Enjoy

☐ **THE INNOCENT DECEIVER by Vanessa Gray.**
(#E9463—$1.75)*

☐ **THE LONELY EARL by Vanessa Gray.** (#E7922—$1.75)

☐ **THE MASKED HEIRESS by Vanessa Gray.** (#E9331—$1.75)

☐ **THE DUTIFUL DAUGHTER by Vanessa Gray.**
(#E9017—$1.75)*

☐ **THE WICKED GUARDIAN by Vanessa Gray.** (#E8390—$1.75)

☐ **THE WAYWARD GOVERNESS by Vanessa Gray.**
(#E8696—$1.75)*

☐ **THE GOLDEN SONG BIRD by Sheila Walsh.** (#E8155—$1.75)†

☐ **LORD GILMORE'S BRIDE by Sheila Walsh.** (#E8600—$1.75)*

☐ **THE SERGEANT MAJOR'S DAUGHTER by Sheila Walsh.**
(#E8220—$1.75)

☐ **THE INCOMPARABLE MISS BRADY by Sheila Walsh.**
(#E9245—$1.75)*

☐ **MADALENA by Sheila Walsh.** (#E9332—$1.75)

☐ **THE REBEL BRIDE by Catherine Coulter.** (#J9630—$1.95)

☐ **THE AUTUMN COUNTESS by Catherine Coulter.**
(#AE1445—$2.25)

☐ **LORD DEVERILL'S HEIR by Catherine Coulter.**
(#E9200—$1.75)*

☐ **LORD RIVINGTON'S LADY by Eileen Jackson.**
(#E9408—$1.75)*

☐ **BORROWED PLUMES by Roseleen Milne.** (#E8113—$1.75)†

*Price slightly higher in Canada
†Not available in Canada

Lord Margrave's Deception

by
Diana Campbell

Ⓢ
A SIGNET BOOK
NEW AMERICAN LIBRARY
TIMES MIRROR

Publisher's Note

This novel is a work of fiction. Names, characters, places, and incidents are either the product of the author's imagination or are used fictitiously, and any resemblance to actual persons, living or dead, events, or locales is entirely coincidental.

NAL BOOKS ARE AVAILABLE AT QUANTITY DISCOUNTS
WHEN USED TO PROMOTE PRODUCTS OR SERVICES.
FOR INFORMATION PLEASE WRITE TO PREMIUM MARKETING DIVISION,
THE NEW AMERICAN LIBRARY, INC, 1633 BROADWAY,
NEW YORK, NEW YORK 10019.

SIGNET TRADEMARK REG. U.S. PAT. OFF. AND FOREIGN COUNTRIES
REGISTERED TRADEMARK—MARCA REGISTRADA
HECHO EN CHICAGO, U.S.A.

SIGNET, SIGNET CLASSICS, MENTOR, PLUME, MERIDIAN AND NAL
BOOKS are published by The New American Library, Inc.,
1633 Broadway, New York, New York 10019

First Printing, April, 1982

1 2 3 4 5 6 7 8 9

PRINTED IN THE UNITED STATES OF AMERICA

FOR BOBBY

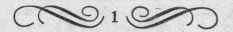

1

Miranda stopped just short of the intersection, leaned forward and peered up the main street. She could barely make out the carriage drawn up before the Knight and Dragon, but she was able to discern that it was not a public coach. Apparently Mr. Bartlett had arrived then, somewhat early at that, and Miranda heaved a sigh of relief. She was inclined to trot along to the inn, but it still lacked nearly ten minutes to one, and she thought she should not appear overly eager. She decided to review her correspondence with Mr. Bartlett in the event she had overlooked a telling point.

She began by rereading the advertisement she had clipped from *The Times*, but it was exceedingly brief. "London gentleman seeks governess," it stated. "Qualified ladies will please respond with fullest particulars."

Miranda had not, in fact, responded "with fullest particulars"; she had seen no need to reveal that she was a poor relation, educating an ever-growing flock of cousins without remuneration. She hadn't actually *lied,* she persuaded herself, glancing over the initial draft of her letter. She had said she was three-and-twenty and the daughter of an Oxford don; she had chosen not to mention that Dr. Harold Russell's death had left his only child quite destitute. She had described her five-year tenure as governess to "a squire near Horsham, West Sussex"; she had merely neglected to explain that the squire was her cousin, Thomas Cavendish. She had forthrightly listed her charges as "a girl of ten, a boy of eight and a girl of seven." Was there any reason to add that five-year-old twins, a three-year-old girl and an infant male waited in the nursery?

1

Miranda was forced to concede that the twins were the greatest single factor in her decision to seek a position. They were identical boys, inappropriately christened Mark and Luke. (Their elder brother was named Matthew, their younger, John; and Miranda feared Thomas and his prolific wife, Martha, would exhaust the New Testament before they were done.) Mark and Luke were, as Martha fondly put it, "pranksters." At the age of four, for example, they had shredded the drawing-room drapes with a kitchen knife, and only last month they had set one of the barns afire. The sudden realization that this pair of hellions would imminently graduate to the schoolroom had been sufficient to render Miranda almost physically unwell. Consequently, she had abandoned her idle, rather dreamy perusal of the advertisements in *The Times* and begun to comb the notices in deadly earnest. Upon spotting the London gentleman's advertisement for a governess, she had dispatched a response at once.

Ten days elapsed before she received a reply, and she had nearly lost hope when Mr. Bartlett's letter arrived. Miranda plucked it off the seat of the gig, noting again that it was written on heavy, expensive stationery in a fine, bold hand. But the letter, too, was quite brief:

Miss Russell,
   I trust you will forgive me when I report that I have interviewed several local respondents to my notice, this being the more convenient course. Having found none of them suitable, however, I shall meet with you Tuesday next at one o'clock at the Knight and Dragon inn in Horsham.
                                      Yours truly,
                                      Anthony Bartlett

Miranda observed, as she had upon first reading, that Mr. Bartlett had afforded her no opportunity to refuse the interview. However, since Mark and Luke had, in the interim, loosed some half a dozen frogs in her bedchamber, she was far from wishing to decline. Indeed, she had come to anticipate the encounter with almost frantic enthusiasm.

The clock in the church tower chimed one, and Miranda proceeded round the corner and up the street. She reined in behind Mr. Bartlett's carriage—a spanking new curricle, she saw now, drawn by a splendid pair of matched grays. She could not but contrast this glittering equipage to Thomas's ancient gig and piebald, half-lame mare. She wondered if her duties would require, would *permit*, her to drive such a magnificent rig through the teeming streets of London.

"Miranda!"

Richard Alcott, the landlord's son, rushed out of the inn to greet her, pausing en route to adjust his attire. Dickie, who judged himself the local arbiter of fashion, lovingly caressed his limp shirt-points and tugged at his neckcloth, which spilled untidily down the front of his waistcoat. Evidently, and erroneously, satisfied, he assumed a bright smile and strutted on up to the gig.

"Miranda," he repeated. He peered cautiously into the carriage; one of the twins' favorite amusements was to lurk on the floorboard and leap upon the necks of unwary pedestrians. Finding Miranda alone, Dickie transformed his smile to a dashing, suggestive grin. "Availing yourself of the fine weather for a little outing, are you?"

Miranda stared down at him for a moment. Dickie had been sparking her quite zealously for some six months, and Thomas had made no secret of the fact that he favored this potential connection with Horsham's prosperous innkeeper. Thomas obviously believed that Mrs. Richard Alcott would continue to serve as his unpaid governess, presumably adding her own children to the Cavendish throng in the schoolroom. The very notion hardened Miranda's resolve.

"Actually I have come to meet with Mr. Bartlett," she said coldly. "I fancy that is his carriage."

She nodded toward the curricle, and Dickie's pale, protuberant eyes widened.

"Mr. Bartlett is a friend of *yours?*" he gasped.

"Umm," Miranda grunted noncommittally. If the interview did not go well, she could perhaps more readily explain to Thomas a mysterious London "friend" than a prospective employer. She clambered out of the gig. "Please tether the horse, Dickie," she said haughtily. "I do not wish to be late."

Miranda strode across the inn yard, aware of Dickie's curious gaze upon her back, and through the front door. William Alcott stood just inside, polishing the tall mahogany clock which dominated the lobby. William and Dickie were precisely the same height, but the landlord's fondness for the offerings of his taproom had produced an enormous belly that spilled over the waistband of his old-fashioned breeches. Mr. Alcott's love of spirits had also swollen his nose to a red, bulbous appendage which seemed to positively glow as he glanced up at Miranda.

"Looking for Thomas, are you?" he growled. "He ain't here."

This was cheering news indeed, but Miranda limited her reaction to a cool, patient smile. "As it happens, I am not here to find Thomas. I have an appointment with Mr. Bartlett."

"Mr. Bartlett?" William dropped his polishing cloth. "He did say he was expecting a lady, but I'd never of dreamed it was *you*."

She must cut a very imposing figure, Miranda thought dryly; neither Dickie nor William deemed it possible that she could be acquainted with a London gentleman. "Well, it *is* I," she said aloud, "and I should very much appreciate it if you would direct me to Mr. Bartlett."

"Of course." Mr. Alcott frowned at her with reluctant, dawning respect. "I've put him in the Blue Saloon."

Earlier in the year, Dickie had determined that the Knight and Dragon required a touch of elegance and had christened its public rooms. As a result, the inn boasted, among other apartments, a Crimson Drawing Room, a Chinese Hall and a Library. The rooms bore little resemblance to their grandiose appellations; the Blue Saloon, for example, was a minuscule parlor, aptly named only because the walls, the drapes, the uphol-

4

stery and the threadbare carpet were multiple, clashing shades of blue.

William led Miranda through the dining room (now termed the Banqueting Hall) and tapped on a door just beyond. A male voice desired the landlord to come in, and Mr. Alcott threw open the door and stepped aside.

Miranda had forgotten that there was a table for two (covered by a blue cloth) in the middle of the room. As she crossed the threshold, a man rose from the chair on the far side of the table and gave her a brief nod.

"Miss Russell, I presume?"

Though Miranda had not formulated a specific image of Mr. Bartlett, she had vaguely supposed him to be a rather harried man of middle years. The reality was so unlike her assumption that she stumbled to a halt just inside the door and frankly gawked at him.

To begin with, Mr. Bartlett was young, not much above thirty, Miranda surmised. In the second place, he was quite the most attractive man she had ever encountered—tall and lean, with red-gold hair and glittering green eyes. He was wearing moss-green pantaloons, a coat of brown Bath and a white waistcoat trimmed in almond. As she studied him, Miranda speculated that he might be recovering from an illness: he seemed a trifle too thin for his clothes, and his complexion was the pale brown of a recently faded tan.

"You *are* Miss Russell?" he snapped.

He snatched up the gold-headed cane propped beside his chair and leaned upon it, enhancing Miranda's impression that he wasn't quite the thing.

"Yes," she murmured. "Yes, I am Miranda Russell. It is a pleasure to make your acquaintance, Mr. Bartlett."

"Ahem." He cleared his throat. "Would you care for some refreshment?" He waved at the half-consumed glass of ale on the table in front of him. "A glass of wine? A cup of tea?"

"Tea—tea would be fine," Miranda stammered. She observed that there was a tiny scar in the middle of his left eyebrow, lending the brow a permanent, provocative quirk.

"Some tea, please, Mr. Alcott," Mr. Bartlett instructed.

Miranda had totally forgotten the landlord, but she detected a rustle behind her as he hurried away.

"Pray do sit down, Miss Russell. And pray forgive me if I do not come round to assist you. The French provided me a souvenir several months since: a bullet in the leg. It's healing nicely, my doctor tells me, but I daresay I shall hobble about for some time to come. Please."

He indicated the chair on the near side of the table, and Miranda crossed to it and sat down. Mr. Bartlett resumed his own place and examined her quite candidly across the width of the raveling blue tablecloth. After perhaps ten seconds of scrutiny, he narrowed his brilliant green eyes, and Miranda wondered what he was searching for, what he had found.

She was not beautiful, she knew: her nose was a shade too long, her chin a bit too sharp, her mouth a little too small. She realized, on the other hand, that she had been blessed with splendid cheekbones and creamy, flawless skin. And, most arresting of all, her hair and eyes were exactly the same color—the rich, warm brown of sweet sherry. Her hair *was* a trifle untidy, of course, and her white muslin gown had long since grayed—but there was no reason for Mr. Bartlett to be one whit interested in her appearance.

"Ahem." He cleared his throat again and reached into his coat pocket, withdrew a sheet of paper and scanned it. "You state that you are three-and-twenty, Miss Russell."

"Yes. That may sound young, but I wish to assure you that I have had *considerable* experience. My father died when I was eighteen, and I was forced to move in with Thomas—er—Mr. Cavendish—" She could not continue to dissemble, Miranda decided impulsively. "You had best know at once that Thomas is my cousin. But he has made no allowances for our relationship"—quite the contrary, she thought bitterly—"and I have performed my duties *most* conscientiously. So even though I am only twenty-three, I have worked for five years, though I

6

doubt Thomas would give me a reference because he wants to keep me on, you see—"

"Are you nervous, Miss Russell?" Mr. Bartlett interrupted.

"Nervous?" In fact, she could scarcely draw breath. "Why do you ask?"

"Because you are chattering, and in my experience, women invariably tend to chatter when they are nervous. I shall not bite you; I promise you that. Insofar as your youth is concerned, I find it a distinct advantage. The ladies I interviewed earlier were far too old for the position."

"Yes, your children must be young," Miranda said. Unless he had married as a veritable child himself, they would have to be *very* young. "How old are they?"

"My children?"

"Your children."

"My children."

Mr. Bartlett took a very large sip of his ale, in the midst of which the door creaked open. William Alcott entered the room and set the Knight and Dragon's best silver tea service on the table. He poured a cup for Miranda, fussily rearranged the sugar bowl and milk pitcher and stood back, wiping his hands on his soiled breeches.

"Will that be all, Mr. Bartlett?" he asked.

"Yes." Mr. Bartlett seemed to be choking on his ale, and Miranda wondered if his wound had somehow affected his digestive system as well as his leg. "Thank you, Mr. Alcott."

William backed through the door and closed it, and Miranda tasted her tea. It was, as usual, weak and tepid, and she replaced the cup in the saucer with a sigh. "We were discussing your children, Mr. Bartlett. Their ages."

"My children's ages," he repeated carefully. Miranda was beginning to fear that his war experiences had also unhinged his mind. He delicately patted his lips with a tattered blue napkin and laid the napkin on the table. "The fact is, Miss Russell, I have no children."

"You have no children?" Miranda echoed. Was it possible that he was altogether mad? She glanced over her shoulder at the door, wondering if William or Dickie would hear her if she was compelled to scream for assistance. "Then why did you advertise for a governess, Mr. Bartlett?"

"I judged such a notice the best means of locating an educated woman."

"Ah." Miranda nodded. "You are seeking a companion then. For your wife? Is your wife an invalid? Or do you wish a companion for your mother? Perhaps you have an aged aunt or cousin, a sister with some disability—"

"You are chattering again, Miss Russell."

"So I am."

Miranda gulped down the rest of her tea and poured another cup. Mr. Bartlett drained his ale and toyed wth the empty glass.

"As it happens," he said at last, "I am looking for neither a governess nor a companion. I am seeking a wife."

Miranda strangled on her tea, showering a few drops of brown liquid on the already spotted tablecloth.

"I do apologize, Miss Russell; I fear I stated my position very badly. I do not refer to a true, legal wife, of course, but to a—how can I best explain it?"

"Pray do not tease yourself," Miranda said frigidly. "I know quite well what you mean. You are offering a *carte blanche*." She was privately astonished that a man of Mr. Bartlett's undeniable charm should be required to advertise for a barque of frailty, but perhaps he had some deficiency of character that was not readily apparent. "I am not in the least interested in such an arrangement. Good day."

Miranda rose stiffly, and Mr. Bartlett leaped to his feet as well, wincing a bit and favoring his left leg.

"Please hear me out, Miss Russell. You have gravely misconstrued my intentions. I am not offering a *carte blanche;* I wish to hire a woman to *portray* my wife. I assure you that her duties would be of a strictly—ahem—*public* nature."

Miranda glared at him suspiciously, and Mr. Bartlett flashed a winsome, rather sheepish grin.

"Very well, Miss Russell. I must own that I have got myself in a bit of a scrape. If you will resume your place, I shall tell you all about it."

He nodded toward her hastily abandoned chair, and Miranda hesitated. She had already reckoned Mr. Bartlett a man of highly questionable morality, but she was forced to admit to an intense curiosity about his "scrape." She sat down with considerable reluctance, positioning her chair well away from the table so as to permit, if necessary, an immediate escape. Mr. Bartlett sank into his own chair and discreetly massaged his leg.

"Where to begin?" he asked rhetorically. "As you have no doubt inferred, I served in the army during the late war. I was a captain in the 43rd Regiment."

"That is most commendable," Miranda said coolly. "However, I do not perceive that your military record has any bearing upon the current discussion."

"But it does, Miss Russell. Shortly before I sustained my wound"—he assumed a martyred expression—"I was billeted with a noble French couple. The Comte and Comtesse de Chavannes. I regret to say that I did not become acquainted with the Comte: he was an extremely elderly man, and he languished in a coma throughout my stay."

"How sad," Miranda said. "But the unfortunate Comte's state of health hardly seems a matter of present concern—"

"Will you permit me to finish, Miss Russell? Why must women perennially interrupt? I was at the point of saying that I *did* become quite friendly with the Comtesse."

"How nice," Miranda said. "I suppose she looked upon you as a son . . ." Mr. Bartlett was scowling at her, and her voice trailed off.

"The Comtesse hardly regarded me as a son. Madame de Chavannes was a good deal younger than her husband." Mr. Bartlett coughed. "Indeed, she is several years younger than I myself." He coughed again and attempted to sip from his empty glass. "The truth of the matter is, Miss Russell, that the Comtesse somehow

9

conceived the notion that if she were free and our countries were not at war, I should—ahem—marry her."

"You did nothing to foster this notion, of course," Miranda said wryly.

"Ahem." Miranda wondered if a fragment of shell had penetrated Mr. Bartlett's throat. "I must own that I did, perhaps, profess a certain fondness for Madame de Chavannes. In fact, I *was* most fond of Jeanne—er—the Comtesse—but not so enamored as I may have implied." Miranda felt her eyes narrowing, and Mr. Bartlett leaned across the table. "I wish you to understand, Miss Russell, that there was nothing—improper about our relationship. That is to say, we were not—"

"Your private life is not my concern, Mr. Bartlett." Much as he despised interruptions, the drift of the conversation was rendering Miranda's cheeks quite warm. "Furthermore, I still do not see how your 'relationship' with Madame de Chavannes affects your immediate situation. The war is over, it is true, and Napoleon is safely confined on Elba. However, the Comte de Chavannes has no doubt been restored to health—"

"Quite the contrary, Miss Russell." Mr. Bartlett lowered his sparkling, emerald eyes. "The Comte died some six weeks since."

"I am sorry," Miranda instinctively murmured.

"Yes. Jeanne wrote to inform me of his death. In the same letter, she advised me that as soon as she has settled her late husband's affairs, she will travel to England." Mr. Bartlett lifted his glass again and twirled it absently for a moment. "She clearly believes that shortly after her arrival, we—she and *I*—shall be married."

Mr. Bartlett looked up, and his mien was one of such abject misery that Miranda was hard put to repress a laugh. She was, by now, sufficiently confident of his sanity that she edged her chair closer to the table and poured herself another cup of tea.

"And you wish to have a 'wife' conveniently in residence when Madame de Chavannes disembarks," Miranda suggested. "You will regretfully explain that you were already committed to the marriage before you received her letter."

"Exactly!" Mr. Bartlett slammed his glass on the patched blue tablecloth, leaned back in his chair and beamed. "Do you not agree that it is a clever solution, Miss Russell?"

"Clever but exceedingly cowardly," Miranda replied, with as much sternness as she could muster. "Why do you not simply *tell* the Comtesse that she misunderstood your—your 'relationship'?"

"That was my first inclination, of course." Mr. Bartlett flashed his fetching smile, but Miranda was not at all certain he was telling the truth. "However, I have discovered that Madame de Chavannes is merely one victim of an epidemic contagion. You may be aware, Miss Russell, that the London Season is just underway. The annual husband-hunt, I call it. I have grown to feel like a particularly delectable piece of carrion, with buzzards and vultures greedily circling my carcass. The young ladies, I must confess, are far less offensive than their mothers; I truly thought I should be pecked to shreds at a recent ball. Lady Wilkes was especially insistent—" Mr. Bartlett stopped and toyed once more with his empty glass. "Be that as it may, the obvious way to *avoid* marriage is to appear to *be* married. Do you not concur?"

"Theoretically, yes," Miranda responded. "But I daresay you will find it difficult to locate a young woman to pose as your wife for twenty- or thirty-odd years."

"But that is the beauty of my scheme, Miss Russell!" Mr. Bartlett crashed his glass on the table again. "I am not demanding twenty- or thirty-odd years. I need a wife only for the duration of the Season, two months at the outside. When the Season is over, my 'wife' and I shall appear to repair to one of my country estates . . ."

Mr. Bartlett named several of said estates, but Miranda scarcely heard him. Who *was* Anthony Bartlett? she wondered. He was clearly wealthy, and she had assumed him to be a banker, a manufacturer, some other sort of entrepreneur. Yet he had spared time from his

11

business pursuits to serve in the army, he evidently associated with peers of the realm, and he owned multiple "country estates." A mysterious man indeed.

". . . and I shall let it be known that my 'wife' has taken ill," Mr. Bartlett was saying. "There will be no need for her ever to appear in public again. Yet I shall be permanently protected: I shall have an invalid wife forever declining in Herefordshire or Berkshire or some such place."

"But when you *do* wish to marry?" Miranda was intrigued in spite of herself. "What will you do then, Mr. Bartlett?"

"That is a most unlikely eventuality." He smiled again, and his perennially cocked brow lent him a distinctly devilish aspect. "I very much enjoy feminine company, but I have yet to encounter a *particular* female who can retain my interest for more than half a year. If such a woman should appear, which I strongly doubt, I shall simply announce that my poor wife, my dead wife"—he lowered his green eyes once more—"has died. I fancy I should then be a highly eligible widower."

"I fancy you would," Miranda snapped. Though she could not have explained why, his remarks had struck a spark of annoyance, and she perversely poked about for holes in his plot. "What of your relatives, Mr. Bartlett? They will certainly wish, from time to time, to pay their respects to your 'poor, dear wife.'"

"But I *have* no relatives." He beamed again, as though he were entirely responsible for this fortuitous circumstance. "None in England, at any rate. My mother is still alive, but she remarried some years ago and resides in Jamaica. She has not visited in nearly a decade, and I am certain she never will."

"Umm." Miranda groped for another objection, but nothing came immediately to mind.

"You may conjure up any number of obstacles, Miss Russell." Mr. Bartlett spoke as if he had been reading her thoughts. "However, I assure you that I have considered them all and have found my plan to be virtually foolproof. Nor do I have the time to indulge in a lengthy — debate. I am prepared to offer you the position, and I must insist that you accept or decline at once."

Miranda gazed at her hands. Though Mr. Bartlett's scheme was patently dishonest, it did not seem in any way harmful. Well, she amended, the plot might do harm to Madame de Chavannes, but Miranda could not generate a great deal of sympathy for a woman who had dallied behind the back of her dying husband.

Of far greater import then was the potential danger to Miranda herself. If anyone were to learn of her shocking conduct, to learn that she had lived, quite unchaperoned, with a young, dashing bachelor . . . She inwardly shuddered. She would be utterly ruined—altogether banned from polite society and forever unable to contract a suitable marriage.

But who was to find out? Thomas and Martha had not visited London since their brief wedding trip a dozen years before, and, in any event, neither they nor their country neighbors would be invited to the glittering saloons Mr. Bartlett apparently frequented. It was equally unlikely that Miranda would encounter any of her old Oxford acquaintances in such surroundings. At any rate, her childhood friends posed little threat: ignorant of her recent past, they would have no reason to question her sudden "marriage" to a fine city gentleman.

And if, against all odds, she *was* unmasked? What sort of suitable marriage awaited her in West Sussex? What, in short, could she possibly lose?

That left but one major consideration, and Miranda scarcely knew how to approach it. She had never before applied for a post, and this was a most peculiar post indeed. She looked up, searching for the proper, delicate phraseology.

"You are wondering the precise dimensions of my offer." Mr. Bartlett snatched the words from her mouth. "To begin with, I shall pay you five hundred pounds." Miranda stifled a gasp; it was many times what she might earn during a full year of governessing. "When

13

the Season is over, I shall provide transportation to any site of your choice. Though I shall not demand it, I should prefer you to go abroad. To Canada perhaps or, if the war is over, to the United States. The latter is an upstart little country, but I suspect it may become a minor power in years to come. If, however, you elect to remain in Britain, I trust you would be exceedingly discreet."

Miranda nodded.

"Finally, I should, of course, furnish you a suitable wardrobe, which would be yours to keep. I am sure I need not add that your clothes would be appropriate to your role as Lady Margrave."

"Lady Margrave?" Miranda repeated sharply.

"Ahem. Yes. You will understand, Miss Russell, that I felt it necessary to act incognito. My name is not Anthony Bartlett; I am Anthony Barham, Earl of Margrave. Should you decide to refuse my offer, I hope you will regard my identity, and the subject of our discussion, as matters of the strictest confidence."

The Countess of Margrave, Miranda silently mused. She had been much given to play-acting as a child; she could recall dressing in her mother's gowns and styling herself the Duchess of Such and the Countess of So. She had already evaluated the pecuniary terms of Mr.—of Lord Margrave's offer and judged them most generous; had already recognized that emigration would provide the perfect escape in the event she was discovered. But perhaps it was this, this opportunity to live her youthful dreams, that tipped the balance.

"Very well, Lord Margrave," she said. "I accept your offer. I shall immediately advise Thomas and Martha of my departure. I collect it is customary to provide several weeks' notice—"

"No." The Earl shook his red-gold head. "There is no time for notice; Jeanne could reach England at any moment. I really must insist, Miss Russell, that we travel to London tomorrow. If you cannot accommodate such a schedule, I fear I shall have to look elsewhere."

The Countess of Margrave. "Very well," Miranda said again. "I shall be ready tomorrow."

They began to discuss the logistics, and Miranda shuddered again to contemplate what Thomas and Martha would say.

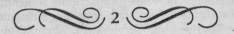

2

". . . the most flagrant instance of gross ingratitude
which I have ever experienced," Thomas concluded. He
had worked himself into a splendid rage, and he paused
to mop his fleshy, red face with a wrinkled linen handkerchief. "I can scarcely believe, after all we have done
for you, that you would leave upon half a day's notice. I
suppose we should count ourselves fortunate that you
did not simply pack your things and steal away in the
dead of night."

"After all we have done for you," Martha echoed, her
pointed nose fairly quivering with indignation. She was
a short woman and remarkably slight in view of her
five-and-thirty years and six pregnancies. "The children
will be *devastated*. The twins, especially, are *most* fond
of you."

Martha screwed up her thin, pinched face, apparently
attempting to generate a tear or two. However, her effort was rudely interrupted by the soon-to-be-devastated
twins, who galloped into the drawing room with two terrified, squealing piglets in tow. By the time Martha had
shrieked for someone! to attend the situation and Nanny
Bigg had shepherded boys and shoats alike outside,
Martha had miraculously overcome her attack of grief.

"I am certain I have never heard of your employer,"
Thomas growled. His tone implied that he was familiar
with everyone of importance in the entire British Empire. "Barton, is it?"

"Bartlett," Miranda corrected. "Anthony Bartlett." She
and Lord Margrave had agreed that Miranda must offer
a reasonable explanation of her abrupt departure, and

16

employment by the mythical Mr. Bartlett seemed as good a tale as any.

"I daresay he is a manufacturer or some such thing," Thomas sniffed. "Obviously a man of no breeding."

Thomas claimed, through his mother, a distant kinship with the Marquess of Washburn. In Thomas's mind, this vague, unproved connection compensated for his own lack of title, his unscrupulous banking practices and his dubious business pursuits.

"I suppose so," Miranda murmured. Though she had had little time to ponder her peculiar "post," she had determined, wherever possible, to avoid the telling of an outright lie.

"Well, do not come crying back to us when your position evaporates," Martha warned. "Men of business are ever at risk: wealthy today, impoverished tomorrow. When your Mr. Bartlett falls on hard times and dismisses you, dismisses you with *no notice*, you will be left entirely to your own devices. *We* have certainly done our duty by your dear mother. Do not think to prevail again upon our generosity."

"Indeed, I shall not," Miranda said fervently.

They dismissed her then—Thomas with another growl, Martha with a curt nod of her graying head—and Miranda went to her bedchamber. She was unsurprised to discover a piglet gamboling about the counterpane. She captured the little fellow with some difficulty and loosed him in the corridor, secretly hoping he would find his way to Martha's new biscuit-silk sofa.

Miranda pulled her battered portmanteau from beneath the bed and placed all her belongings inside, all except her nightgown, a fresh assortment of underclothes and the ancient blue percale frock she would wear tomorrow. She had long realized that her wordly possessions were pathetically few, but she was nevertheless astonished to calculate that her packing had required just above a quarter of an hour.

Miranda went to the door, intending to locate the children and bid them farewell, but she paused with her hand on the knob and reconsidered. If the truth were known, she was not overfond of any of the Cavendish brood, and, by now, Martha would surely have painted Cousin Miranda as a latter-day Jezebel. She crossed back to the bed, stretched out on the counterpane and gazed at the ceiling.

She imagined herself, on Lord Margrave's arm, sweeping into the Opera, the boxes abuzz with the news that "Lady Margrave" had arrived. She pictured the two of them strolling into Carlton House, His Highness's major-domo sonorously announcing "The Earl and Countess of Margrave." From the corner of her eye, Miranda glimpsed the piglet's tiny footprints all around her and hastily shut her lids. She did not believe that countesses normally slept with the livestock.

Now that her eyes were closed, Miranda's visions were considerably more detailed. She saw herself in a gown of yellow lace, waltzing through the assembly rooms at Almack's, Lord Margrave smiling down at her. The Earl's leg no longer pained him at all, and they were whirling, whirling . . . Miranda woke and detected the first gray tendrils of dawn creeping through the window.

Lord Margrave had arranged to come for Miranda at eight o'clock, but it was barely half past seven when she descended the stairs to the foyer. She set her portmanteau on the floor and cracked the front door, but the yard was deserted. Her stomach rumbling with the emptiness of her missed supper, she proceeded down the final flight of steps to the kitchen. Mrs. Stubbs, the enormous cook, was just removing several loaves of bread from the oven, and the odor set Miranda's mouth to watering.

"Good morning, Mrs. Stubbs," Miranda said.

"Miss Russell," the cook sniffed in reply. "I didn't expect to see you again. You're going up to London, I'm told. Country life wasn't good enough for you, eh?"

"I shouldn't wish to put it like that," Miranda said carefully. The old cook was noted for her fearsome temper. "But I am going up to London, yes; in fact, I shall be leaving very shortly. I was hoping to have a bit of breakfast before my departure."

"No." Mrs. Stubbs shook her head. "Mrs. Cavendish advised me that you were not to have another morsel of food from her table. Those were her exact words, miss. She was in a terrible flame as it was, and then, just before supper, she discovered that some sort of animal had got loose on her new sofa. One of the dogs, I imagine."

"I imagine so," Miranda agreed, choking back a laugh. "Well, goodbye then, Mrs. Stubbs."

"Oh, I'll give you one piece of bread," the cook said gruffly.

She cut off a heel, slathered it with butter and passed it to Miranda. Miranda wolfed it down, and Mrs. Stubbs removed and dressed the opposite heel. Miranda was able to eat the second slice with somewhat more delicacy than the first, and Mrs. Stubbs watched her, her great arms folded across her chest.

"I wish you good fortune," the cook said at last. "There was no future for you here, and they say the city abounds in all manner of wonderful things. Wonderful things and wonderful people. You might even find a husband; who knows?"

Miranda felt the tickle of a lump in her throat, and she hurriedly swallowed the last of the bread. This was no time for regret.

"Who knows?" she repeated brightly. "I might even become a countess, Mrs. Stubbs."

"Hah!" The old cook roared with laughter. "A countess; that's a jolly one, Miss Russell. Well, be off with you now."

They exchanged brief nods, and Miranda returned to the entry hall to await Lord Margrave.

At eight o'clock precisely, Miranda heard the rumble of a carriage in the drive, and she opened the door just as Lord Margrave reined in his team. Whatever his lordship's faults, and Miranda suspected they were numerous, apparently tardiness was not among them. Miranda bore her trunk into the yard, and the Earl clambered stiffly down from the seat and limped to meet her.

"Good morning," he said cheerfully.

"Good morning, Lord Margrave."

They had not previously stood side by side, and Miranda observed how very tall the Earl was. She herself was above the average in height, but the top of her head scarcely reached his lordship's chin. Margrave removed Miranda's valise to the luggage compartment and looked at her expectantly.

"Please fetch the rest of your things," he instructed. "I'm eager to be underway."

"I *have* no other things, Lord Margrave," Miranda said dryly.

"Oh?"

The Earl flashed his brilliant smile, but Miranda thought she detected a flicker of sympathy in his emerald eyes. He glanced over her shoulder.

"And we needn't wait for my loving cousins to rush out and weep upon my neck. They have made it abundantly clear that our association is permanently severed."

"But they are exceedingly curious about your mysterious employer," his lordship whispered. "They are watching us at this very instant."

Miranda whirled around and glimpsed a frantic twitch at one of the drawing-room draperies. She turned back and marched to the carriage with the dignity she felt befitting a countess, and Margrave assisted her into the seat. He climbed up beside her and clucked the horses to a start, and they cantered down the drive and into the road.

Miranda regarded the familiar landscape with an indecipherable surge of emotion—an odd amalgam of relief and excitement and fear. As Mrs. Stubbs had pointed out, there was no future for Miranda here, but the sleepy border country of West Sussex had been her world for five years. She realized, with a stab of panic, that she had cast her lot with a man of whom she knew almost nothing; the little she *did* know was hardly reassuring. She studied the Earl for a moment, peering at him sideways from beneath her lashes, and eventually cleared her throat.

"I do not wish to pry," Miranda said. "However, it occurs to me that I should have some awareness of your background, the sort of information that might arise in casual conversation. I do not wish to pry," she repeated quickly, "but I should appreciate it if you would tell me a bit about your—your *public* life, Lord Margrave."

"You really must stop addressing me as 'Lord Margrave,'" the Earl said. "We can scarcely project the image of a warm and happy marriage if we refer to one another as 'Lord Margrave' and 'Miss Russell.' My Christian name, as you know, is Anthony. Will you remember that, Miranda?"

"Yes, Anthony," she gulped.

"As to my background, I doubt you will be called upon to *provide* any information because, or so I am told, I am somewhat infamous." Anthony's grin suggested that he did not particularly object to this notoriety. "My father was the second son of the eighth Earl of Margrave, and his elder brother, my Uncle Charles, succeeded to the title. My father, for his part, inherited a good deal of the property that was not entailed, and I see no reason to deny that he was a very wealthy man."

"And then your uncle died—"

"You *must* overcome your maddening habit of interruption," Anthony interrupted. "As it happens, my father well predeceased my uncle; Papa died when I was eighteen. Two years later, as I believe I mentioned, my mother married a Jamaican planter, a Mr. Pennington. I am pleased to report that the marriage appears an extremely happy one."

Anthony lapsed into silence, but Miranda feared to venture the slightest interjection.

"Naturally my father's estates were managed by trustees until I came of age," Anthony continued, "and then I undertook their administration myself. Though I soon perceived that country life did not suit me at all, I was a model landlord for some four years. At that juncture, I could no longer bear the tediousness of my existence so I hired a number of talented bailiffs to manage my estates and purchased a commission in the army.

Gentlemen officers are often ridiculed, Miranda, but I was a splendid soldier."

Anthony Barham certainly did not suffer from undue modesty, Miranda reflected wryly.

"The rest you largely know. After five years of service, I was wounded and invalided home. Within a matter of days, Uncle Charles died unexpectedly, and, as he had no heirs, I became the tenth Earl of Margrave. Due to the combined circumstances—my wound, Uncle's death, and the fact that I had just attained thirty years of age—I elected to change the pattern of my life. I sold my commission and everything was proceeding quite well until I received Jeanne's letter."

Anthony slapped the horses to a brisker pace, as if the looming specter of Madame de Chavannes had reminded him of his perilous situation. He then turned to Miranda, and she noted again the permanent quirk of his left brow.

"Is that a war wound as well?" she asked impulsively. "The scar above your eye?"

"No." Anthony coughed. "It is a souvenir of an altogether different sort of encounter. The memento of a—ahem—*friend*."

A female friend, no doubt, Miranda thought. She supposed this "memento" had contributed to Anthony's generally dismal opinion of women.

"But what of you, Miranda?" Anthony said. "I believe your father's field was classical literature."

Miranda frowned; she had not mentioned this intelligence in her letter.

"I studied at Cambridge myself, but I recollect frequent references to Dr. Russell." Anthony seemed to possess an uncanny ability to read her mind. "I fancy he was a scholar of some renown."

"A scholar of considerable renown," Miranda confirmed, "but a man of no practical sense at all." She had never before discussed Papa's failings, had hardly dared to *think* of them; and she wondered why her tongue had suddenly run amuck. "I was left everything when he died, of course—"

"Your mother was no longer alive?" Anthony interposed.

"I *do* wish you would not interrupt me!" Miranda snapped. "No, my mother died when I was twelve, and I was the only child. As I was *attempting* to explain, I inherited Papa's entire estate, but I soon discovered that his assets and his liabilities balanced almost perfectly. After I had sold the house and Papa's library, I was able to settle his debts."

She hadn't much lamented the house, but the *books* . . . the books had been the very fabric of Harold Russell's life, and with their disposal, Miranda felt that she had irretrievably lost her father as well. She swallowed another nagging lump in her throat.

"At any rate, I had barely enough left to travel to West Sussex. To Thomas."

"And what is Mr. Cavendish's precise position?"

"He is the son of Mama's late brother. Insofar as Thomas's community standing is concerned, I suppose one might describe him as the town squire. He is the chief landlord hereabouts." Even as she spoke, Miranda realized that they had crossed the border and were well into Surrey. "He is also the local banker and owns several shops. I daresay Thomas would undertake *any* enterprise that smelled of profit."

"Including yourself."

"Myself?"

"Yes. It appears that Mr. Cavendish provided you room and board and little else." Anthony glanced at her patched blue frock, her limp straw bonnet, and smiled again; but his eyes had narrowed, and there was a grim set to his jaw. "Be that as it may, what happened next?"

"Next?" Miranda echoed.

"Yes. You came to West Sussex five years since; what has transpired in the interim?"

His question provided a nasty jolt. Miranda could not conjure up a single significant incident, and she suddenly viewed her recent existence as bleached bones, strewn upon the dead sands of a desert. The revelation was not only shocking but exceedingly embarrassing.

"Nothing has transpired in the interim," she replied stiffly. "I did not have the good fortune to become a war hero."

"Well, do not tease yourself about it," Anthony said airily. "As it happens, your background is *perfect*: orphaned daughter of brilliant Oxford don . . . Perfect!" he repeated. "We shall not have to embroider your circumstances at all."

He slapped the matched grays again, and they raced on through Surrey.

They stopped for lunch at an inn near Croydon. The landlord studied them with some puzzlement, and Miranda could well imagine that he found them a peculiar pair. Though Anthony, like Miranda, was dressed predominantly in blue, there was a substantial difference between his immaculately tailored ensemble, his snowy neckcloth, tied in a perfect Mathematical, and Miranda's disreputable attire. Apparently the innkeeper decided that the *gentleman* at least was a person of quality, for he showed them to a private room.

The landlord left them, promising to send a "splendid" meal, and Anthony propped his elbows on the table.

"We must establish the final details of our story," he said. "I believe it will be best to claim that we met in Berkshire; I visited my estate there some three weeks ago. Yes." He tapped his fingertips together. "We shall borrow from the true situation insofar as feasible: we shall say that I encountered you at the home of your cousin, whom you had served as governess for several years. I was much taken with you and paid a return visit ten days later. The servants will readily accept this sequence of events because I was—ahem—away from home two nights in the early part of last week. Having formed a violent *tendre*"—Anthony sighed dramatically —"I rushed back to Berkshire yesterday to claim my bride. In view of the suddenness of the marriage, we shall have to explain that we were wed by special license. I daresay the staff will be much relieved." He sighed again, with evident sincerity.

"Relieved?" Miranda said curiously. "Because you were married by special license?"

"Because I am *married*. Most of the servants were previously in Uncle Charles's employ, and he lived as a sedate old widower for the final decade of his life. I fear the staff has found it most trying to transfer their loyalties to a—a—"

"A rake?" Miranda prompted sharply.

She bit her lip, but Anthony merely laughed. "*I* do not classify myself a rake, Miranda; I have never intentionally harmed another human being except on the field of battle. But I shan't debate the point, for there is one last detail we must attend."

He fumbled in the pocket of his dark-blue frock coat, extracted a small box and passed it across the table. Miranda opened the box and withdrew a plain gold band.

"It is nothing elaborate, of course." Anthony sounded oddly uncomfortable. "But I fancy it will serve its purpose."

To the degree that it was unadorned, the ring *wasn't* "elaborate," but it was wide and heavy and clearly fashioned of solid gold. Miranda placed it on the third finger of her left hand, but the ring was a trifle small, and for some inexplicable reason her hands were trembling. The gold band jammed just above the knuckle.

"Here. Permit me to assist you."

Anthony reached across the table, took Miranda's hand in his own and eased the ring into place. At that very moment, the door creaked open, and a maid screeched to a halt on the threshold.

"Oh!" she gasped. "Pray *do* forgive me."

"It doesn't signify," Anthony growled. "We were married just this morning, and my—er—wife is having some slight difficulty with the fit of her ring."

"Just this morning," the maid repeated dreamily. "I wish you much happiness, sir. And missus."

She approached the table, her eyes distinctly moist, and Miranda felt a flush warming her cheeks. To her astonishment, Anthony had reddened as well, and as soon as the maid had arranged their plates on the table, he fairly dove into his roast beef and boiled potatoes.

Anthony was an excellent driver, and by three o'clock they had reached Knightsbridge. Anthony slowed the grays to a trot, and they threaded their way through a stream of fashionable carriages pouring into and out of Hyde Park. They traversed Hyde Park Corner and entered Piccadilly, where they soon encountered a high-flyer phaeton traveling in the opposite direction. The driver saluted Anthony with his whip, and his female companion peered curiously down at Miranda. Miranda suffered another twinge of panic: she would soon be required to *meet* such people, to speak with them, to *be* the Countess of Margrave. She looked at Anthony, and he, as though he had again perceived her thoughts, gave her a cheerful wink. Rake or no, Anthony Barham was scarcely a pillar of stability, but Miranda found his gesture strangely comforting.

They turned into Berkeley Street, cantered along the southern side of Berkeley Square and continued into Charles Street. Anthony halted the carriage some half a dozen doors beyond the square, and Miranda stared at the house. It differed from the neighboring residences in that it had no pilasters; it was in the Roman Renaissance style, with tabernacle windows above a rusticated arcade.

Anthony climbed down from the curricle seat and immediately snatched his cane, which had lain on the floorboard throughout their journey. He had seemed quite sprightly that morning, and Miranda collected that his leg troubled him increasingly as the hours passed. He assisted Miranda down from the seat and propelled her up the front steps, leaning heavily on his walking stick.

In contrast to the brilliant May sunshine, the foyer was dim, and before Miranda's eyes could adjust to the gloom, a spectral figure materialized in front of them.

"Good afternoon, Lord Margrave," the figure intoned.

Miranda was now able to make him out as a tall,

spare man, dressed all in black and with a startlingly profuse shock of white hair.

"Good afternoon, Horton," Anthony responded.

The butler, or so Miranda assumed, transferred his gaze to her. An expression of pained resignation crept across his features, but he granted her a cool nod. Miranda wondered just how many "friends" the Earl had entertained in his commodious London home. She felt herself blushing again and studiedly glanced about.

The entry hall was tastefully furnished with two shield-back Hepplewhite chairs, a marble-topped side table between them. There was a dining room to Miranda's left and a parlor to her right, the walls of the latter lined with books. She had vaguely supposed that Anthony's bachelor quarters would be a trifle untidy, but the rooms within her view seemed neat and spotlessly clean. His lordship must have an accomplished house-keeper, she surmised.

As if in response to this unspoken observation, a second figure floated out of the dining room. Except for the requisite differences of sex, the woman was the very image of Horton: tall, lean, white-haired and clad in a black bombazine dress of old-fashioned cut.

"*Mrs.* Horton," Anthony said brightly. "Good day to you."

"Good day, Lord Margrave." Mrs. Horton looked frigidly at Miranda and backed slightly away, as though fearing that the hems of their skirts might inadvertently brush.

"Ahem." Anthony cleared his throat. "I fancy I have a bit of a surprise. I should like to present my—ahem—wife."

He nodded down at Miranda, and the effect was much as if he had proclaimed the Second Coming. Horton's snowy brows leaped into the fringes of his white hair, and Mrs. Horton's chin dropped halfway to her shoulders. Horton appeared to recover first.

"Lady—Lady—" But he had evidently forgotten his employer's name.

Miranda felt a rush of sympathy for the old retainers,

and she ventured a smile. "I daresay it *does* come as quite a surprise," she said. "Indeed, a shock. However, I believe we shall get on famously, for I was just remarking that the house seems *exceedingly* well run."

"We shall, of course, rearrange the house to your complete satisfaction, Lady Margrave," Mrs. Horton said stiffly.

"No!" Miranda yelped. She ground her fingernails into her palms and tendered another smile. "That is to say, I was quite sincere, Mrs. Horton. I am certain I shall find *your* arrangements eminently suitable."

The housekeeper's thin face sagged with relief. "May I be the first to congratulate you, Lady Margrave? Lord Margrave?"

"The first," Horton echoed. "The marriage was rather—rather precipitous, was it not?" His piercing blue eyes stole to Miranda's waistline, then hurriedly fled to a distant corner of the foyer.

"Yes, we were married by special license," Anthony said. "Youthful passion will not be denied, eh, Horton?" Mrs. Horton emitted a small, choking sound. "Well, I believe I shall show Miranda to her room. The Yellow Chamber," he added significantly. "Please see to the carriage, Horton, and to Lady Margrave's luggage."

Horton nodded, and Anthony hobbled toward the stairs, beckoning Miranda to follow. They ascended to the first floor, which consisted of an enormous drawing room and morning parlor, both decorated primarily in tones of blue and gold. They proceeded to the second story, and Anthony led Miranda to a door at the far end of the corridor.

The Yellow Chamber was a large, bright corner room and, unlike the apartments at the Knight and Dragon, appropriately named. The bedstead was canopied and curtained in a predominantly yellow print, matching the draperies at the windows. The Brussels carpet was of a white and yellow pattern, and the settee and chairs were upholstered in yellow- and ivory-striped silk. Miranda's eyes drifted to the tall satinwood wardrobe and matching chest of drawers, the rosewood washstand and dressing table, the mahogany writing table, and she suppressed a gasp. She could not but contrast these luxurious accommodations to her tiny bedchamber at Thomas's, grudgingly furnished with a narrow iron bed, a minuscule wardrobe and an ancient, sagging desk and chair.

"This was Aunt Althea's room," Anthony remarked. "I have not—" He coughed. "That is to say, it has not been used since her death."

"You needn't explain your behavior to me," Miranda snapped. She was finding the constant references, direct and implied, to Anthony's "friends" peculiarly irritating. "As I told you at the outset, your private life is none of my concern."

She looked past him and glimpsed a door next to the wardrobe. Could her quarters possibly include a sitting room as well? She crossed to the door, pulled it open and peered across the threshold. There was no sitting room beyond but another bedchamber, larger even than her own, and done in masculine shades of burgundy, biscuit and brown.

"What is *this?*" she demanded.

"My bedchamber," Anthony replied. "Would you care to see it?"

"Indeed I should not." Miranda crashed the door to and whirled around. "I thought I had made myself quite clear on that head, Lord Margrave."

"Anthony," he corrected mildly. "And you did make your position *perfectly* clear. However, I felt it would appear exceedingly suspicious if I were to locate my beloved bride in a distant corner of the house. I assure you the connecting door will not be used. Not by *myself*, at any rate."

His green eyes twinkled mischievously, and Miranda willed herself not to flush. "Very well," she said coldly.

There was a tap on the corridor door, which Anthony had left ajar, and the Earl maneuvered it open with the tip of his cane. A footman carried Miranda's portmanteau into the room and laid it on the bed. He started out again, but he was staring so intently at his new mistress that he tripped on a corner of the rug and nearly fell. He recovered himself at the last possible instant, bowed and rushed back into the hall.

"Well," Anthony said dryly, "evidently your arrival has created a considerable furor in the household. It occurs to me that I must appoint you an abigail, and I suppose the chambermaids are already quarreling bitterly over the post. I shall confer with Mrs. Horton at once."

Anthony bobbed his red-gold head, hobbled into the corridor and closed the door behind him. Miranda looked again at the connecting door, briefly thinking to prop one of the chairs beneath the knob. But she soon reconsidered: any such obstacle would indeed appear "exceedingly suspicious" to the servants. Furthermore, she had a notion that Anthony Barham, in his own odd way, was an honorable man.

Miranda circled the room, pausing to touch the polished surfaces of the dressing table and writing table, to plump the fat silk cushions of the chairs, to caress the yellow-satin counterpane. She marveled again at the degree to which her life, if only for a month or two, had changed.

There was another tap on the hall door, but before Miranda could respond, the door flew open, and a dark young woman bounded into the room.

"I am your abigail, Lady Margrave," she announced joyfully. "My name is Cassandra, but my friends call me Cassy."

"Then I shall call you Cassy as well," Miranda said. She regarded the girl with a sense of utter unreality, reflecting that, two days since, they would have been virtual equals, might, in fact, have become friends.

"Mrs. Horton advised me that the first thing I must do is unpack for you," Cassy said.

She scampered to the bed, opened Miranda's portmanteau and withdrew the frayed muslin dress.

"Umm." She frowned. "Where do you wish me to put your gardening clothes, ma'am?"

Her gardening clothes. Miranda stifled a giggle. "In the wardrobe please," she said solemnly.

Cassy industriously hung the muslin frock in the wardrobe and plucked Miranda's black-satin Sunday gown from the trunk. The black dress was relatively respectable: Miranda had purchased it just five years before, on the occasion of Papa's funeral. Cassy was apparently unable to determine its precise function, but she removed it to the wardrobe as well. She then transferred Miranda's few items of lingerie from the portmanteau to the chest of drawers and set her stationery, her pen and her tattered copy of the *Iliad* on the mahogany writing table.

"Now." Cassy clapped her hands, as though to dislodge invisible specks of dust. "Where is your *main* trunk, ma'am?"

"That *is* my main trunk," Miranda said. "My only trunk. Everything—" She had started to say, "I own," but she formulated a hasty amendment. "Everything I brought."

"Well, that explains it then," Cassy said dubiously.

"Explains what?"

"Lord Margrave instructed me to remind you that you—yourself and his lordship—are to go to the mantua-maker's tomorrow. Promptly at two, he said. He also desired me to refresh your memory about his appointment this evening. A pressing financial matter, he said."

"Ah, yes." A "pressing financial matter" indeed!

"His lordship further stated that you are to ring for your dinner whenever you wish." Cassy indicated the bell rope beside the bed. "*I* shall bring it up, ma'am."

"Thank you, Cassy," Miranda murmured. "That will be all."

"Yes, Lady Margrave."

The abigail curtsied rather clumsily and left the room, and Miranda sank onto the satin counterpane. Anthony's private life *was* none of her concern, and she did not care a whit about his "appointments" or his "friends." Nevertheless she thought the Earl might have granted her some consideration on her very first night in London.

Miranda felt a foolish prickle of tears behind her eyelids. She blinked them furiously away and glared once more at the connecting door.

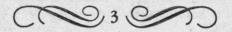

3

"I have done all I can, Lady Margrave."

Cassy's dark eyes met Miranda's in the mirror above the dressing table, and the abigail made a moue of vexation. Apparently, Miranda reflected wryly, Cassy was finding it unexpectedly difficult to serve as dresser to a woman with an almost nonexistent wardrobe. Miranda herself did not think she looked especially unhandsome: she was accustomed to the threadbare muslin gown, the wild tendrils of sherry-colored hair tumbling about her face.

"Something really should be done about your hair, ma'am," Cassy said. "While I was pinning up the left side, the right came down, and as I attempted to readjust the right, the left came all apart . . ."

Cassy rattled on, and Miranda suppressed a frown. The little maid seemed to have taken her new responsibilities a trifle *too* conscientiously. She had delivered Miranda's dinner and hovered about while Miranda consumed it, had similarly supervised her mistress's breakfast and had returned to the Yellow Chamber at one to garb "Lady Margrave" for the afternoon's excursion. The most irritating factor, Miranda conceded, was that Cassy's criticism was perfectly valid.

"Thank you, Cassy," she interrupted stiffly. "I daresay his lordship is waiting. Please fetch my bonnet."

Cassy snatched the limp straw hat off the bed and, with ill-concealed dismay, passed it to Miranda. Miranda jammed the bonnet on her head and savagely tied the strings, trying not to notice that one of the ribbons hung by the merest thread.

Anthony was indeed waiting; he was standing in the

33

street, beside the curricle, chatting with a young groom. Cassy watched as Miranda descended the front steps, much like a doting mother dispatching her rather backward daughter to a critical ball. Anthony glanced up when Miranda reached the carriage and flashed his engaging grin.

"Ah, Miranda. I was just speaking with Johnson about Daffodil." Anthony patted one of the matched bays hitched to the curricle; evidently the grays had been granted a day of rest. "We hope she is pregnant."

Must he be so shockingly frank? Miranda fumed. She managed an embarrassed smile, and Johnson regarded her with unabashed curiosity. He apparently judged her unworthy of prolonged attention, for he soon turned back to the sleek bay mare.

"Well, do keep me advised, Johnson," Anthony said. "We shall be underway now."

"Yes, milord."

Johnson handed Miranda into the carriage, and Anthony clambered up beside her, tossing his cane on the floorboard. He clucked the horses to a start, and they proceeded toward Berkeley Square.

"You slept well, I trust?" Anthony said.

Actually Miranda had tossed and turned throughout the night, her ear inexplicably attuned to the adjoining bedchamber. It had been well after dawn when she at last detected Anthony's noisy arrival and fell into a fitful sleep. But she would not, of course, confess her senseless preoccupation to his lordship.

"Quite well," she said coolly. "And I trust your *appointment* proved a success?"

"A grand success," Anthony replied. "I played macao at Brooks's and emerged nearly five hundred pounds to the good."

Miranda could not conceive why he felt compelled to offer what she was certain was a fabrication, but she elected not to pursue the matter.

They cantered along the eastern side of Berkeley Square, turned into Bruton Street and entered Conduit Street. They passed the noted tailor Weston and Meyer, patronized by both His Highness and Mr. Brummell, and stopped in front of a small establishment several doors away. Evidently Anthony's leg scarcely pained him at all today, for he swung his walking stick jauntily to and fro as he led Miranda into the elegant interior of the shop.

"Lord Margrave!" A diminutive, gray-haired woman scurried from behind a *bonheur-du-jour* desk and rushed forward to greet them. "I thought I had explained—"

"Never mind, Madame Leclair," Anthony hastily interposed. "I should like to present my—ahem—wife."

"Your—wife." Madame Leclair spoke with only the barest French accent, but she echoed the word as if it were an esoteric English noun she had not previously encountered. "Lady—Margrave." Her eyes traveled expertly from the dented crown of Miranda's bonnet to the soiled toes of her shoes. "Lady Margrave," she repeated dubiously.

"As I fear you can observe for yourself, Miranda has lately lived under the most deprived of circumstances." Anthony emitted his dramatic sigh. "She served her cousin as governess for some years, and Mr.–er–Smith neglected her most shamefully. She will require an entire wardrobe, Madame Leclair."

"An entire wardrobe." Madame glowed like one of the recent victory illuminations. "That can certainly be arranged, Lord Margrave."

Before Miranda's wondering eyes, Madame Leclair was transformed into a veritable dervish of activity. She dashed into the rear of the shop and reemerged almost at once with three assistants in tow. Even as the assistants stacked endless bolts of fabric on a display table, Madame began leafing through a great bound book of drawings.

"We shall do this one in the blue jaconet, Lord Margrave," she chattered, beckoning Anthony across the room. "This in crape, over a sarsnet slip. Black?"

"White," Anthony said.

"White, of course. Now, the peach satin." Madame fingered one of the bolts. "Is it not *perfect* for this?" She jabbed one of the drawings. "My latest, my *boldest* design, Lord Margrave."

"Perfect," Anthony agreed.

They continued to converse, and Miranda gazed at her ancient slippers. Though she knew nothing of fashion, she bitterly resented their interchange; they seemed to regard her as a helpless infant, being outfitted for her own christening. She glanced up and glimpsed a bolt of yellow lace. It looked vaguely familiar, and she recalled her half-dream, remembered herself floating through the assembly rooms at Almack's in just such a fabric.

"I should like a gown of yellow lace as well," Miranda said firmly.

Anthony and Madame started with surprise, as though they had altogether forgotten her presence.

"Yellow lace." The seamstress tapped her teeth with the tip of her pencil. "I suppose it *would* become you, Lady Margrave."

"Well, let us see," Anthony proposed.

He eased the lace from beneath a bolt of primrose satin, a length of apple-green mull, and strode to Miranda's side. He draped the fabric round her waist, then pulled it tight just below the bust. Miranda found his nearness, the brush of his long fingers, peculiarly disturbing, and she resisted an urge to jerk away.

"*Most* becoming," Anthony pronounced.

"Most becoming, indeed," Madame Leclair concurred.

The dressmaker scrawled another note on her pad and eagerly assessed the magnitude of the order. "Six walking dresses," she announced, "six evening dresses and a carriage dress. Now if I may measure her ladyship . . ."

Madame whipped a tape from the pocket of her skirt and applied it to various portions of Miranda's anatomy, pausing from time to time to scribble figures on her pad. When she wrapped the tape around the top of Miranda's rib cage, Anthony intervened.

"No, I prefer the fit to be *quite* snug there, Madame Leclair." He drew up perhaps a quarter inch of tape, and Miranda winced again as his fingers danced across her back.

"That suffices for the gowns," Madame Leclair said, "but leaves the accessories. Hats, shoes, gloves, fans . . ." Her voice trailed provocatively off. "I do not manufacture such items myself, of course, but I *am* acquainted with other tradespeople in the neighborhood."

"And I have infinite confidence in your judgment, Madame Leclair," Anthony assured her. "I should very much appreciate it if you would select the appropriate accessories and forward them with the dresses. Naturally I should reward your trouble; would a ten-percent commission be satisfactory?"

"Yes, indeed." The mantua-maker glowed again, and Miranda fancied that Madame might well be in a position to retire after Anthony's order was filled. "There is, finally, the matter of—lingerie." Madame Leclair lowered her shrewd blue eyes.

Miranda was at the point of blurting out that the lingerie hardly signified since there was no one to *see* it, but she realized that any such admission would be a decided *faux pas*. She bit her lip, and Anthony nodded.

"How good of you to remind me, Madame Leclair," he said gravely. "A complete complement of lingerie then. I shall leave that to your imagination as well."

"That completes it then," Madame said happily, dashing off a few last notes. "It is always a pleasure to serve you, Lord Margrave. And *you*, Lady Margrave," she added quickly. "I am certainly delighted to have made your acquaintance."

"When will the order be ready?" Anthony inquired.

"Umm." The seamstress gnawed her lip. "As I explained earlier, Lord Margrave, this is a very busy time."

"Yes." For some reason, Anthony tugged at his shirt-points. "However, we are to attend Lady Wilkes's ball two nights hence, and I am sure you understand that Miranda cannot go in—in—"

"In rags," Madame Leclair finished, eyeing Miranda's muslin frock again. "No, indeed. Well, as you are one of my *foremost* customers, Lord Margrave, I shall deliver an evening dress and a walking dress on Saturday afternoon. The rest—" She peered down at the order, which occupied three full pages of her notepad. "The rest within the week."

Anthony thanked Madame Leclair for her consideration, and the seamstress ushered them toward the door. Miranda glanced at the ormolu clock on Madame's desk and noted that they had been inside the shop for upward of two hours. Evidently Anthony was feeling the effects of this long interval on his feet, for he leaned a bit on his cane as they walked to the carriage.

"Well," Anthony said, turning the bays about, "are you pleased with your purchases, Miranda?"

"I should scarcely call them *my* purchases," Miranda responded irritably. "Except for the yellow lace, I hardly know what was ordered. But then I collect that you are quite accustomed to dealing directly with Madame Leclair, quite familiar with the intricacies of feminine finery. Indeed, I believe Madame Leclair indicated that you are one of her *foremost* customers."

"An exaggeration, no doubt," Anthony said airily. "Though I do feel that a new gown always makes a thoughtful gift. Do you not agree, Miranda?"

"More to the point, milord, do your *friends* agree?"

Miranda bit her lip again; she could not imagine why she was baiting him in this spiteful, childish fashion. But the Earl, as usual, merely smiled.

"Happily, they do, and I am certain you will be pleased as well. Madame Leclair is *most* talented."

"Umm," Miranda grunted.

She was utterly at a loss to account for her ill humor, but her mood, whatever its genesis, was in no way improved by Anthony's cheerful, tuneless whistling. Miranda maintained a stiff silence as they trotted back to Charles Street and, as soon as Anthony had assisted her from the curricle, stalked toward the house. But the Earl, his limp notwithstanding, overtook her at the top of the stairs, and they were standing side by side when Horton threw open the door.

"Lord Margrave!" The butler's tone approximated a discreet wail. "A—a guest arrived in your absence, sir."

"Oh?" Anthony peered into the street as though to

confirm that, except for his own curricle, it was empty. "Did he leave a card, Horton?"

"No, sir. That is to say, the guest insisted on waiting."

"Oh?" Anthony said again. He stepped forward, but Horton moved to block his way.

"It is a *woman*, sir!" the butler hissed. He cast Miranda a stricken look and began literally to wring his pale, gnarled hands. "I attempted to explain that her visit was somewhat—inconvenient and that I should advise you of her call. But she declared she had nowhere else to go, and *then*, sir—"

"*Antoine? C'est toi, Antoine?*"

Horton shuddered but apparently elected to submit to this latest, cruelest stroke of fate. He backed into the entry hall, and Miranda and Anthony trailed after him. Miranda had just made out a towering mountain of luggage, rising precariously from the marble floor of the foyer, when a figure darted out of the parlor.

"*Antoine!*" she shrieked. "*Cher Antoine!*"

The figure hurled herself into Anthony's arms, nearly bowling him over, and Miranda stepped hastily away. As Horton lowered his horrified eyes, Miranda collided with the great pile of baggage, and a valise slipped off the top and crashed upon her foot. Horton recovered himself sufficiently to rush to her assistance.

"It is no one I have encountered before, Lady Margrave," he whispered apologetically, plucking the offending valise off her foot. "I am certain there has been a fearful error." The woman began showering Anthony's face with kisses. "Well, perhaps not an *error*," Horton amended, "but she is, no doubt, an old friend of his lordship's, come for a brief visit." He replaced the valise on the stack of luggage, and a slightly larger case tumbled to the floor. "Well, perhaps not a *brief* visit. As I was at the point of telling Lord Margrave, I was astonished when she instructed the hackney driver to bear in her bags . . ."

The butler whispered on, but Miranda scarcely heard him. Anthony had stood his "old friend" slightly away, and Miranda studied her as surreptitiously as possible. She was a tiny creature, barely reaching the Earl's shoulder, and her immaculately curled blonde hair, her enormous blue eyes, lent her a distinctly dollish aspect. Horton had fallen silent, and the woman's trill of animated French, Anthony's delighted laughter, seemed to reverberate off the walls. Miranda sensed the butler's curious gaze upon her and realized that "Lady Margrave" could not continue to endure this humiliation.

"I fancy I do not have the pleasure of the lady's acquaintance," she said coolly.

"So you do not." Anthony fumbled with his neckcloth, but it was in hopeless disarray. "This, Miranda, is Jeanne, Comtesse de Chavannes. Whom," he added pointedly, "I believe I told you of."

"The lady who was so kind to you in France!" Miranda feigned appropriate surprise and granted the Comtesse a pleasant nod.

"And this, Jeanne"—Anthony groped for his neckcloth again—"is my—my wife."

"Ta—femme?"

Madame de Chavannes's eyes widened, and she clenched her tiny fists. Miranda wondered whether the Comtesse was preparing to burst into tears, attack Anthony or, possibly, assault Miranda herself. As she braced for this latter eventuality, Madame emitted a delicate moan and collapsed in a graceful heap on the foyer floor.

Anthony sighed. "Please fetch the restoratives, Horton."

"Yes, sir."

Horton sighed as well, and Miranda surmised that this was not the first such emergency the harried butler had confronted. Horton retreated down the stairs to the under story, and Anthony sadly shook his head.

"It is just as I feared. She took the news very badly indeed."

The Comtesse groaned again, stirred, thrust one shapely ankle out from beneath the hem of her skirt.

"I daresay she will recover soon enough," Miranda said dryly.

Horton returned with reinforcements, in the form of Mrs. Horton, and the housekeeper knelt beside Madame and waved a vinaigrette under her nose. After a final moan, the Comtesse's eyes fluttered prettily open, and she allowed herself to be maneuvered into a sitting position. Horton proffered a glass of brandy, which Madame gulped down with astonishing ease.

"*Ta femme,*" she murmured weakly. "*Tu comprends, Antoine, que je suis stupéfaite . . .*"

They spoke together in French for a time, and Miranda reflected that Anthony had not adequately defined his precise intentions toward the poor, jilted Comtesse. Now that Madame had been informed of the Earl's precipitous marriage, was Miranda to slink quietly to her bedchamber? She was pondering just this course when the Comtesse gave her a tremulous smile.

"*Je m'excuse, Madame Margrave, mais—*"

"I do not speak French," Miranda interrupted curtly.

Harold Russell had taught his daughter to read both Latin and Greek, but Miranda did not suppose either Anthony or the Comtesse would be suitably impressed by her dogeared copy of the *Iliad*, the only one of Papa's books she had managed to salvage.

"No?" Madame de Chavannes raised her pale eyebrows. "I was saying that I apologize, Lady Margrave," she continued, in excellent English. "I am sure you will understand that I found Antoine's news quite astounding. I wish you *much* happiness, of course."

"Of course," Miranda muttered.

"Well," Anthony said brightly, "I daresay you are famished after your long journey, Jeanne. Fortunately, I requested an early dinner this evening, and I trust it can be served in half an hour's time. Can it not, Mrs. Horton?"

"Yes, Lord Margrave."

The housekeeper rose and marched grimly down the steps, and Miranda fancied she detected a disbelieving shake of her prim, white head.

"That will give the ladies a few minutes to refresh themselves," Anthony continued. He beamed at

Miranda, beamed at the Comtesse, who was still sitting on the foyer floor. "Please have Madame de Chavannes's bags sent up, Horton."

"Yes, sir. Er—to what room, sir?"

"The Blue Chamber," Anthony replied.

The Earl extended his hand to Madame and began to lift her off the floor, and Miranda turned and hurried up the stairs. She slammed the door of her bedchamber with considerably more force than she had intended, but curiosity soon impelled her to crack it open again. Anthony and the Comtesse had just reached the landing, and Miranda watched as the Earl led Madame to a room at the opposite end of the corridor. Apparently he proposed to maintain the appearances at least—

"Is something amiss, Lady Margrave?"

Miranda whirled around and discovered Cassy standing beside the wardrobe, feather duster in hand.

"No! No, I thought I had dropped something in the hall."

Miranda hurriedly closed the door, proceeded to the dressing table and removed her bonnet. Cassy helped her to "refresh" herself insofar as possible, tugging at Miranda's hair for some ten minutes before she shook her head in despair. Miranda then suggested that she might wish to change into her black gown, but Cassy shook her head again.

"It is dreadfully old-fashioned, ma'am, and really best suited to a funeral, if I may say so."

On this happy note, Miranda descended to the dining room. Anthony had not changed for dinner either: he was clad in the black pantaloons, the smoke-gray frock coat, frogged in charcoal silk, which he had worn that afternoon. The Comtesse, however, had exchanged her brown bombazine carriage dress for a stunning evening gown of blue net. It was not at all appropriate for mourning, Miranda remarked grouchily to herself, and cut so low in the front as to verge on the indecent. A footman set a steaming bowl of mulligatawny before her, and Miranda tore her eyes from Madame's generous, and generously exposed, bosom.

Anthony took two or three swallows of his soup, laid his spoon aside and cleared his throat. "I am certain I speak for Miranda as well as myself when I regret the unhappy—misunderstanding which has occurred. I can well conceive your shock."

"It was a terrible shock," the Comtesse agreed. She had wolfed down her soup with blinding speed and now tilted her bowl so as to retrieve the last golden drops.

"Naturally we wish to make amends," Anthony said.

"That is most kind of you," Madame sighed.

The footmen removed the soup bowls and delivered the second course: salmon and turbot set in smelts. The Comtesse attacked her fish as if she feared, given any mercy, they would swim off the plate.

"I shall reimburse your passage and finance your return transportation," Anthony continued.

"That is very kind," Madame reiterated. "But I do not wish to return to France."

"Not at once, of course," Anthony said soothingly. "You must certainly rest for a day or two before undertaking such an arduous journey—"

"*Non.*" The Comtesse spoke through a mouthful of turbot. "I do not plan to return to France *jamais*. Ever."

There was a moment of shocked silence, to which the Comtesse seemed blissfully oblivious. She stabbed and consumed half a dozen chunks of fish and washed them down with a greedy gulp of champagne.

"Ever?" Anthony repeated at last.

"*Non.*"

Though Miranda would not have deemed it possible, the tiny woman had cleaned her plate. She patted her lips with the snowy linen napkin and drained her wineglass. The footmen, after debating with their eyes the proprieties of the situation, evidently elected to defer to the guest. They whisked away the fish plates and champagne glasses, proffered an entree of mutton and veal and poured generous glasses of dark, heavy claret.

"*Non,*" Madame said again, after the footmen had retreated. "As you know, Antoine, I am very fond of the Englishmen." Anthony strangled on a piece of veal.

"And though you, *méchant*, have broken my poor heart, perhaps I shall meet another nice man. It is the *Saison* in London, is it not? The time for finding husbands?"

Anthony coughed and sipped his claret. "It is the Season, yes. But I should think, Jeanne, that you would be far more likely to locate a *compatible* husband among your own countrymen."

"*Non.*" The Comtesse shook her delicate, blonde head. "My countrymen, against all *raison*, would judge me deficient in respect for dear Gervais, so recently departed, whom I adored *passionnément*, but I cannot spend all my youth in reverence of the *mémoire* of *cher Gervais . . .*"

The Comtesse paused to bolt down the remainder of her meat, and Miranda performed a wry mental translation: Madame's compatriots might find six weeks of mourning for "*cher Gervais*" a trifle scant. Whereas, in England, no one need know that the daring blue gown was decidedly premature.

"Therefore," the Comtesse concluded, swallowing a final morsel of mutton, "I feel it in my best interest to remain in London, and I accept your gracious invitation."

Miranda could not recall that any invitation, gracious or otherwise, had been extended, and she waited for Anthony to set Madame aright. To her horror, the Earl nodded.

"Very well, Jeanne; you are welcome to stay with us—with Miranda and myself—as long as you like. For our part, we shall certainly strive to present you to all the suitable young men of our acquaintance. Shall we not, Miranda?"

"In—indeed," she stammered.

"*Au subjet de cela, Antoine . . .*"

For the first time in the course of this astonishing conversation, Madame de Chavannes betrayed a flicker of embarrassment. She finished her claret, and one of the footmen refilled her glass.

"On that head, I must advise you that I am compelled to wed a man of considerable wealth. *Cher Gervais* had numerous children from his first marriage, and, as a result, he left me very little. By the time I expended a few paltry *sous* to replenish my wardrobe, I found myself with nothing in reserve. You do comprehend?"

"Perfectly." Miranda observed a slight twitch at the corners of Anthony's mouth, but he sought immediate refuge in his claret. "We shall keep that qualification in mind, shall we not, Miranda?"

"Yes," she murmured.

"Ah, you are so good to me, Antoine. And you, Lady Margrave." The Comtesse transferred her great blue eyes to Miranda and smiled. "May I say that you are a most pleasant surprise? It would have been all too easy for Antoine to marry a woman of great beauty but no warmth. Instead, I see, he has wed a homely girl, a plain girl, with much sweetness of nature."

Miranda dropped her wineglass, and a footman rushed forward to mop the red pool off the tablecloth. The servants hastily presented slices of gooseberry pie, accompanied by glasses of Tokay, and Madame permitted herself two portions of each. The Comtesse then announced that she was *"très fatiguée"* and begged to be excused. She tendered a dazzling smile, rose and, rather unsteadily, made her way to the foyer. As soon as Madame's uneven footsteps had faded from Miranda's hearing, she looked furiously at Anthony.

"What an idiotish thing to do!" she snapped. "As if our situation were not sufficiently complicated without a permanent guest living under our very roof."

"Under *my* very roof," the Earl corrected mildly. "And I could not but feel that it was the proper course, Miranda. The poor woman is obviously impoverished; indeed, she appears to be literally upon the brink of starvation."

"I daresay she would not be in such perilous straits had she not frittered away her last 'paltry *sous*' upon her wardrobe. A wardrobe which occupies, by actual count, ten cases."

"Why does that distress you?" Anthony asked. "It should not, you know. Jeanne's beauty is her sole asset, one upon which she is compelled to capitalize quite desperately. Perhaps it is difficult for a clever woman such as yourself to understand such limitations."

"The more so since, as Madame de Chavannes pointed out, *I* am decidedly homely."

She had not intended to say it, and she belatedly bit her lip. There was another twitch about Anthony's own mouth, and Miranda picked up her knife, thinking she might well kill him if he laughed. But he did not.

"I am certain Jeanne's remark was in the way of a compliment," the Earl said. "She no doubt wished to imply that you seem the domestic sort—"

"And what did she wish to imply by the word 'plain'? Was she referring to the way I—I manipulate my tableware?" Miranda flung down her knife.

"I do not know," the Earl said gently, "but I encourage you to disregard it. You are a very handsome woman, Miranda."

"Of course." Miranda was thoroughly ashamed of her foolish outburst, and she ventured a tremulous smile. "Very handsome indeed. Even Cassy has abandoned hope; she commented just this morning that something should be done about my hair."

"Even the rosebush must occasionally be pruned," the Earl said. "That necessity in no way detracts from the beauty of the rose."

Miranda had never fancied his lordship to be the poetic sort, and she thought he must be jesting. But she did not want to know if he was, indeed, mocking her, and she continued to stare at the spotted tablecloth.

"As it happens," he continued, "I am compelled to agree with Cassy. Consequently, I have engaged a *coiffeur* to attend you just prior to Lady Wilkes's ball. I trust you have no objection."

Miranda experienced a stab of the same resentment she had felt at Madame Leclair's, entertained the same angry notion that Anthony Barham, though in a most impersonal fashion, had appropriated her body. She glanced sharply up, mustering a protest. But the Earl wore a most peculiar expression—a look both speculative and oddly warm—and the words died in her throat.

"No," she murmured, "no, that would be fine."

"Excellent." Anthony tossed his napkin on the table and rose. "If you will pardon me then, Miranda, I have an imminent appointment."

Their momentary intimacy, if it had existed at all, was abruptly shattered, and Miranda felt an unreasonable wave of disappointment. "At Brooks's, no doubt," she suggested acidly.

The Earl frowned. "Perhaps I *shall* go to Brooks's," he said, as though he were musing aloud.

He bowed, his red-gold hair glowing briefly in the candlelight, and limped out. As soon as the front door had closed behind him, Miranda crept up the stairs to her bedchamber.

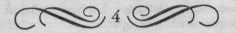 4

"You look *famous*, Lady Margrave! Absolutely *ravishing!*"

Cassy shook her head, as though unable to credit the testimony of her own eyes, and Miranda, gazing into the mirror above the dressing table, was forced to concur in the abigail's unspoken astonishment. She did not believe she would have recognized her reflection had she encountered it on the street. Monsieur Henri had cut her hair quite short in front, parted it in the center and arranged it in loose ringlets over her ears. The back, left much longer, he had braided and wound round the crown of her head. The new *coiffure* had somehow shortened her nose, rounded her chin and rendered her longish neck positively swanlike.

Cassy minutely adjusted one of the sleeves of Miranda's gown and stood back with a sigh of ecstasy. Madame Leclair's man had delivered the mantua-maker's "boldest" creation that afternoon: a peach-satin confection with white vandykes at the bust and a white *rouleau* round the hem. Miranda was inclined to pinch herself to ensure she wasn't dreaming; instead, she gingerly touched one of the elegant curls.

"Don't disturb your hair!" Cassy reprimanded sharply. "It is *perfect*, Lady Margrave. I shall be very careful with the headdress . . ."

The little abigail, biting her lip with concentration, set the white-satin *toque* gently on Miranda's head and fussed with the ostrich-feather plume. "There," she breathed. "Now we shall put on the jewelry."

"I *have* no jewelry," Miranda said dryly, returning slightly to earth.

48

"Oh?" Cassy arched one dark brow. "Well, you will be the loveliest lady at the ball even so," she insisted.

There was a tap on the corridor door, and Cassy rushed to respond. Miranda, with a final look at the alien creature in the glass, rose and had just turned around when Anthony strode into the room. He halted abruptly at the edge of the Brussels carpet, his green eyes widening.

"Miranda?" he said at last. He stared at her for a moment more. "I fear I did not adequately compensate Monsieur Henri. You look quite—quite stunning."

It was a rather backward compliment, but Miranda felt herself coloring nevertheless. "You look very well, too," she murmured.

She had tendered the remark automatically, but she realized, upon consideration, that the Earl did cut an exceedingly handsome figure in his evening clothes. The swallowtail coat made him appear even taller and leaner than he was; and the breeches and striped stockings, which looked so absurd on Dickie Alcott, displayed Anthony's long, slender legs to maximum advantage.

"Stunning," Anthony repeated. He continued to study her and frowned. "However . . ." He snapped his fingers and limped back into the hall.

Miranda gazed at her white-satin slippers, wondering what new deficiency Anthony had perceived. He hobbled back into the bedchamber almost at once, bearing a small wooden chest, which he deposited on the dressing table. He opened the chest and began combing through it.

"The Barham jewels," he explained. "In view of the suddenness of our—er—marriage, I fear I overlooked them. These should do." He withdrew a string of perfect pearls and a pair of matching earrings. "If you will assist Lady Margrave with the earrings, Cassy, I daresay I can manage the necklace."

He fastened the strand deftly round Miranda's throat, and for a moment she nearly forgot that it was part of the charade—this casual presentation of the family jewelry. Then Anthony winked at her in the mirror and rested his hands on her shoulders while Cassy fumbled with the earrings. His fingers seemed very warm, uncomfortably warm, and Miranda gritted her teeth.

Cassy finished her ministrations at last and ushered them into the corridor, chattering that they would be *quite* the most fetching couple at the assembly and might well be mistaken for *royalty*. Madame de Chavannes was awaiting them at the top of the stairs, and she favored Miranda with a look of utter amazement.

"Lady Margrave?" she gasped. "You look very—very *different*."

The Comtesse scowled and tugged the neckline of her black-crape gown a trifle lower, and Miranda felt this was the highest praise to which she could possibly aspire.

It should have been a short drive to Lady Wilkes's residence in Duke Street, but their passage was impeded by a veritable sea of carriages backed up well into Grosvenor Square. Anthony soon lost patience with their creeping progress and advised Pollard, the coachman, that they would walk the remainder of the way. Johnson, clad in livery for the occasion, assisted them out of the landau, and they traversed the final quarter-mile on foot.

The house resembled nothing so much as a castle under storm. Anthony shepherded Miranda and the Comtesse through the milling throng on the exterior steps, murmuring occasional greetings to Lord This and Lady That. Eventually they squeezed through the front door and began toiling up the stairs to the second-story ballroom.

"I do believe Lord Margrave is escorting *two* women this evening," a voice behind them hissed disapprovingly.

Miranda felt herself blushing again, but the Earl seemed not at all discomfited.

At the second-floor landing, a butler was announcing the arriving guests to her ladyship, but when the latter spotted the Barham delegation, she scurried unceremoniously forward to greet them.

"Lord Margrave!" she trilled. "What a great pleasure it is to see you!"

"It is always a pleasure to see *you*, Lady Wilkes," Anthony responded gallantly. "May I say that you are looking particularly handsome this evening?"

Her ladyship batted her eyes and wiggled a bit. She was an exceedingly heavy woman, and Miranda feared she might burst out of her gown, into which she appeared to have been sewn.

"I trust you will not object that I brought a friend?" Anthony nodded toward Madame. "This is the Comtesse de Chavannes, who was most kind to me just prior to my recent misfortune in France." He assumed his martyred expression.

Lady Wilkes granted the Comtesse a cool nod and began to glance about. "Now where is Pamela?" she said. "As you know, Lord Margrave, it is her come-out, and I've no doubt she is *besieged* with suitors. Ah, *there* she is!"

Her ladyship waved and beckoned to a rather horse-faced girl who was standing quite alone at the edge of the dance floor, toying with an ivory fan. Upon receiving her mother's signal, Lady Pamela Fenton waddled eagerly toward them, her double chin bouncing perilously near her diamond choker.

"Pamela, my dear, you remember Lord Margrave, of course. And this is Madame de Chavannes, a *remote* acquaintance of his lordship's from France. And this . . ." Lady Wilkes frowned at Miranda as though she were observing Lord Margrave's other companion for the first time.

"This," Anthony supplied, "is my wife."

"Your *wife?*"

Her ladyship fairly screeched the words, and Miranda heard a collective gasp from the crowd behind them. The gasp was immediately followed by a buzz of conversation: "*Margrave?*" "Very sudden, I fancy; I encountered him at General Dawson's just last week . . ." ". . .don't recognize the girl *at all* . . ."

Lady Wilkes drew herself up, and Miranda detected a

slight ripping sound as one of her ladyship's seams gave way. "I am delighted to make your acquaintance, Lady Margrave," she said stiffly. "Now, if you will excuse me, I *do* have other guests. Come, my dear." She flounced off, Lady Pamela shuffling obediently behind her.

Anthony ushered Miranda and the Comtesse into the ballroom. The orchestra was just tuning up, and Madame declared that, prior to the dancing, she believed she might enjoy *un petit* glass of champagne. Anthony directed her to the refreshment parlor adjoining the ballroom, and the Comtesse drifted away.

Miranda had scarcely begun to recover from the dreadful scene on the landing when she found herself and Anthony surrounded by a horde of well-wishers and curiosity seekers. Anthony presented "my wife" to Sir Harry Mildmay, to the Duchess of Oldenburgh, to a seemingly endless stream of lords and ladies, of generals and colonels and captains. Miranda nodded and smiled until her neck ached and her lips grew stiff, and Anthony, all the while, related the tale of their remarkable courtship.

"I was utterly *bouleversé,*" he proclaimed cheerfully. "I little dreamed to discover such a treasure buried in the wilds of Berkshire and disguised as a governess at that. But as soon as I had glimpsed dear Miranda, I could not rest until we were wed." Anthony threw an arm about her shoulders and drew her possessively against him, and Miranda managed another tight smile. "Miranda's father was quite renowned in his field," Anthony continued. "Dr. Harold Russell. Perhaps you have heard of him, Lord Carruthers?"

Not only had he *heard* of Dr. Russell, Lord Carruthers replied; that excellent and dedicated physician had treated Lady Carruthers during a major illness several years previously. "Saved Sophia's life, he did," his lordship added mournfully.

Lord Carruthers bowed and staggered off, leaving Anthony and Miranda suddenly alone. The Earl looked down at her and flashed his fetching smile.

"May I compliment your dazzling performance, my

dear?" he said in a low voice. "I must own that you have exceeded my most optimistic expectations."

Miranda found his scrutiny oddly unnerving. "Then I am a living tribute to the arts of Madame Leclair and Monsieur Henri, am I not?" she rejoined brightly. "Perhaps one *can* make a velvet purse of a sow's ear, milord."

"You were never a sow's ear, Miranda." That peculiar, speculative light had crept into his eyes again, and Miranda felt her cheeks begin to color. "In any event, I do not refer entirely to your appearance, though it is most gratifying. No, I daresay you have charmed the entire assembly."

"With the notable exception of Lady Wilkes," Miranda pointed out dryly.

Anthony laughed, then leaned abruptly on his cane and bit his lip.

"Let us sit down," Miranda suggested. "I'm afraid your wound is paining you."

"My wound is *not* paining me," Anthony said, through gritted teeth. He nodded toward a passing couple, shifted position and winced again.

"Why do you scruple to admit it? Do you believe that one small weakness renders you less a man?"

"We will not discuss my wound." His face had gone quite pale. "I loathe infirmity of any sort, and I refuse to be made out a cripple."

"What an absurd thing to say! You are far from being a cripple, and it would not signify if you were. You could have no leg at all and remain the person you are."

"Indeed? And what person is that, Miranda?"

For a moment she thought he was bantering, but his eyes were narrow, almost wary, and she had the sense that she had waded into a tiny stream only to find the water well over her head. She glanced hurriedly over his shoulder and beheld a figure bearing down upon them.

The approaching gentleman was quite attractive, Miranda remarked—tall and lean like Anthony, with strawcolored hair and pale blue eyes. However, there seemed something slightly strange about his bearing, and as he reached them, Miranda realized that his exceedingly high and lavishly starched shirt-points, his neckcloth tied in a complicated Oriental, had virtually immobilized his head.

"Ah, Margrave," he said. "Is it a wild rumor I'm hearing or did you think to perpetrate a prank? *On dit* that you have *married*."

"As indeed I have," Anthony said coolly. "May I present Lady Margrave? This, Miranda, is Sir Humphrey Hammond." There was a frosty gleam in Anthony's eyes, and Miranda guessed that Sir Humphrey was not one of the Earl's especial favorites.

"Lady Margrave." Unable to turn his head more than a few degrees, the baronet rotated his entire body sideways and bowed stiffly from the waist. "She's handsome enough," he added crudely, "but then I'd have expected no less, Margrave."

"I am delighted that my selection warrants your approval," Anthony snapped. "Now, if you will pardon us . . ."

He took Miranda's arm, but at that moment the orchestra struck up a waltz, and Sir Humphrey moved smoothly to bar their way.

"Is your leg still troubling you, Margrave?" the baronet inquired. "As I recollect, you languished off the floor during the last assembly, playing the wounded war hero and enjoying a good deal of sympathetic attention. Will you be able to dance this evening?"

"I fear not," Anthony growled.

"Then I shall be delighted to stand up with Lady Margrave."

Before either of them could demur, Sir Humphrey seized Miranda's elbow and steered her onto the floor. Miranda, sensing that it would be quite improper literally to tear herself from his grasp, allowed the baronet to take her in his arms. Since Sir Humphrey's attire effectively prohibited him from looking down, he pulled Miranda indecently close and spoke directly into her ear.

"I am puzzling as to where I have seen you before,"

the baronet commented. "Was it Drury Lane or Covent Garden?"

"Neither," Miranda responded, vainly attempting to loosen his iron grip. "I arrived in London only three days since, and I have not yet had an opportunity to attend the theater."

"I did not suppose I had glimpsed you in the *audience*, Lady Margrave. I assumed you had performed on one or the other stage."

"Well, your assumption is altogether incorrect," Miranda said coldly. "I have never been an actress, Sir Humphrey. Prior to my marriage, I was a governess."

"That is the tale Margrave is putting about, of course, and I can well understand his eagerness to establish your respectability. But you may be frank with me, Lady Margrave; I assure you that I am a man of discretion."

Miranda judged him, to the contrary, quite the most reptilian individual she had ever encountered, and she jerked furiously backward. "And *I* assure *you* that I *was* a governess. I should like to add that, had you been one of my charges, Sir Humphrey, I should have *attempted* to instruct you in the rudimentary principles of courtesy."

The baronet, far from displaying any symptom of embarrassment, threw back his head and laughed. He lowered his head again, and Miranda was pleased to note a grimace of pain as his shirt-points fairly pierced his cheeks.

"I admire your spirit, Lady Margrave, and I shall own that you *could* have been a governess. One never knows where Margrave's preferences may lead him. In fact, now that I think on it, he has lately forsworn actresses. He has, instead, demonstrated a marked affinity for songbirds, has he not?"

"I do not have the remotest idea what you are talking about," Miranda said frigidly.

"Oh, come now, Lady Margrave. You cannot be ignorant of your husband's liaison; Signorina Savino is appearing at the King's Theatre even as we speak. I personally count her a soprano of extremely limited talent, but perhaps that is attributable to her background. I have it on excellent authority that Signorina Savino is actually a Miss Mary Anne Stephens, the daughter of a Welsh collier. I quite believe the story, for I daresay Margrave is rather chary of genuine Italian *prima donnas* after his *contretemps* with Madame La Rosa."

Miranda realized that she should terminate this shocking discussion at once. But, her numerous protestations notwithstanding, she was exceedingly curious about Anthony's private life, and she bit her tongue, hoping Sir Humphrey would continue his narrative. The baronet did not disappoint her.

"*On dit* that Madame La Rosa broke an entire decanter of Chianti over Margrave's head. Fortunately, his lordship escaped the assault with a single cut above his eye. This was some years ago, of course, before Margrave purchased his commission. But I fancy the encounter left him with scars beyond that in his brow, for he has subsequently avoided hot-blooded ladies of Latin extraction."

Her curiosity satisfied, Miranda belatedly decided to administer the setdown Sir Humphrey so richly deserved. "This is a most improper conversation," she said icily. "I do not wish to discuss my husband's alleged *amours*, past or present."

"They are scarcely *alleged*, Lady Margrave, though I suppose his lordship is behaving with temporary circumspection. He may portray the dutiful husband for some weeks, some months, but he will eventually revert to character."

"You speak from experience, no doubt," Miranda said acidly.

"Indeed I do not, for I myself am not married. Consequently, when you find yourself alone, Lady Margrave—abandoned for nights on end, as surely you will be—I shall be happy to serve as your companion. As it happens, I live quite near you, the first house on Bruton Street off Berkeley Square. I am at your disposal; you need only send a card."

"That is very kind of you, Sir Humphrey," Miranda choked.

To her inexpressible relief, the music stopped, and the baronet, with obvious reluctance, released her. Miranda waited for him to escort her from the floor, but, to her dismay, Sir Humphrey remained in place as the orchestra tuned up for the next set. In desperation she peered about and spotted the Comtesse fairly weaving from the refreshment parlor into the ballroom.

Miranda glanced sharply back at Sir Humphrey. He was, as she had previously observed, attractive; he was clearly of the *haut ton;* and, in view of his splendid address, he was apparently wealthy. The fact that he was endowed with a singularly unpleasant personality qualified him still further as the perfect suitor for Madame.

"I should like to present you to a very dear friend of mine, Sir Humphrey," Miranda cooed. "The Comtesse de Chavannes, recently arrived from France."

"A countess, you say?" The baronet beamed and fussily patted his neckcloth. "Naturally I should be *delighted.*"

He was adjusting his shirt-points as Miranda led him across the floor.

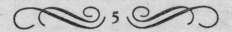

5

The eastern sky was splashed with pink when the landau drew to a halt before the house in Charles Street and Anthony escorted Miranda and the Comtesse inside. Evidently her companions were as exhausted as she, Miranda surmised, for the three of them ascended the stairs in silence and separated, with only the briefest of nods, on the second-floor landing. Miranda wanted nothing so much as to collapse into her canopied bed, but as she opened the door of the Yellow Chamber, Cassy leaped from one of the chairs and scurried forward to meet her.

"Forgive me, Lady Margrave; I was just napping a bit. But I'm quite refreshed now, I'm happy to say, and I shall help you change."

Miranda sank resignedly into the bamboo-legged chair in front of the dressing table, and Cassy carefully removed her mistress's *toque* and began to fumble with the clasp of the necklace.

"Did you have a lovely time, ma'am? Of course you did; I daresay you stood up for every set."

She very nearly had, Miranda reflected: she had spun through innumerable waltzes and quadrilles, endless boulangers and quick steps, with a dizzying succession of partners. Few of them had been sufficiently impressive that Miranda could recall their names, but Cassy's dark eyes, glowing in the mirror, demanded a response.

"Actually I did dance quite a lot," Miranda said. "And toward the end of the ball, I waltzed with the Duke of Clarence."

"His Royal Highness!" Cassy squealed. Miranda

winced as the abigail tugged energetically at one of the pearl earrings. "Did I not predict it, ma'am? Did I not say that you would be captivated by royalty?"

Miranda decided not to correct Cassy's memory and/or syntax. She further elected not to disclose her observation that His Royal Highness was a stout, balding, very ordinary man with a rather coarse sense of humor and a limited measure of intelligence.

"Indeed you did, Cassy," she said solemnly.

"And did the Comtesse have a good time?" Cassy pronounced it "comb-*tess*."

"I believe so," Miranda replied, flinching again as Cassy attacked her other earring.

In fact, this had been the most pleasurable aspect of Miranda's own evening: Madame and Sir Humphrey seemed to have developed an almost embarrassingly warm relationship. From the moment of their introduction, the Comtesse and the baronet had remained together—entwined quite shockingly on the dance floor or chatting, their chairs drawn immodestly close, on the perimeter of the ballroom. To Miranda's astonishment, they had visited the refreshment parlor only once, and Madame de Chavannes had left the assembly in remarkably sober condition.

"I think she did," Miranda reiterated. "Indeed, I believe the Comtesse has found a"—she gulped—"a charming suitor." It would do no harm for the servants to gossip about, tacitly to encourage, the budding *tendre*.

"It's so *romantic*," Cassy breathed, kneeling to remove Miranda's slippers. "And his lordship? I fancy he was *bursting* with pride. He must have had a *splendid* time."

Miranda frowned into the glass, for she did not believe Anthony had had a "splendid" time at all. Following his compliments early in the evening, he had appeared to fall into an inexplicable ill humor. He had spent the better part of the evening limping about the fringes of the ballroom, frequently pausing to glower at Miranda and her partner of the moment, and he had maintained a chilly, moody silence during the intermissions. Nor had he uttered a single word during the drive home. Cassy stood up, and Miranda managed a noncommittal smile.

"I fear his lordship's leg was paining him," she dissembled. "He is unable to dance, you know . . ." She allowed her voice to trail regretfully off.

"What a shame," Cassy clucked. "But all the more reason to rig you directly out, eh, ma'am?" It was a moment before Miranda perceived the abigail's meaning; when she did, she felt a hot flush staining her cheeks. "If you'll just raise your arms, Lady Margrave, we'll have you ready in a trice."

Miranda permitted the little maid to strip off her gown, and Cassy hurried to the wardrobe and scampered back with the revealing lace ensemble which Madame Leclair's man had delivered that afternoon. Yesterday afternoon, Miranda amended, and trust a Frenchwoman to reorder her client's priorities in just this fashion. Cassy pulled the scanty nightdress over Miranda's head and assisted her into the matching peignoir. Miranda stole a glance at her mirrored reflection and blushed again.

"You look altogether fetching, Lady Margrave," Cassy proclaimed. "Shall I knock on his lordship's door as I leave?"

"No! No, that won't be necessary, thank you, Cassy."

"Very well." The abigail bobbed her clumsy curtsy. "Good night then, ma'am."

"Good night."

Cassy retreated into the corridor and closed the door. Miranda removed the delicate peignoir, laid it gently over a chair, extinguished the candles and crawled into bed. Tired as she was, she was no longer sleepy, and she gazed at the ceiling. The shadow of the tree beyond the window was dancing over her head, writhing in the pale, gray light of early morning, and Miranda closed her eyes.

The ball had been most instructive, she thought. Though no one else at Lady Wilkes's assembly had been so inexcusably, so abominably, rude as Sir Humphrey, several of her other partners had made veiled references to Anthony's most recent liaison. Indeed, the Duke of Clarence himself had jocularly commented that he was "delighted to meet the governess who has stilled the nightingale." His Royal Highness had then guffawed in self-appreciation, his multiple chins trembling above his neckcloth.

The "nightingale" had *not* been stilled, of course, Miranda reflected bitterly; she was certain Anthony had visited Signorina Savino on at least two occasions since Miranda's arrival in London. Furthermore, the nuances of Anthony's conversation with Madame Leclair had now become abundantly clear: his lordship had ordered new clothes for his barque of frailty, and the mantua-maker had reminded him that there would be a delay, that this was "a very busy time." For appearances' sake, Anthony had nevertheless pressed Madame Leclair to expedite a few articles of clothing to replace Miranda's "rags."

Well, she was concerned with appearances as well, Miranda concluded furiously, jamming her fingernails painfully into her palms. As "Lady Margrave," she would not allow her "husband" to dangle his affairs under her very nose, to flaunt his nightly excursions. Miranda's eyes flew open, and she lifted her head and peered at the connecting door. It was entirely possible that Anthony had already crept out of the house to rendezvous with his diva. She could readily check his lordship's whereabouts, of course: she had only to steal to the door, ease it open, peek inside.

But that would be quite absurd, she decided, growing sleepy again. She had no reason to care about the appearances after all; when this silly charade was over, she would emigrate to Canada, where no one had ever heard of Lord Margrave or Signorina Savino or Madame Leclair. Miranda's head fell back to the pillow, and she pulled the bedcovers up to her neck and tumbled into blackness.

It was nearing one when Miranda woke and rang for Cassy. The faithful abigail had apparently been awaiting her mistress's summons, for she bounded into the room some five minutes later. Though it was well past the luncheon hour by country reckoning, Cassy bore a steaming cup of breakfast chocolate, which she thrust into Miranda's hands.

"As soon as you have finished, we shall get you dressed, ma'am," Cassy announced, proceeding to the wardrobe. "Will you have your new walking dress?"

She withdrew the last of Madame Leclair's offerings: a petticoat and robe of white jaconet topped by a canary-colored spencer. Though Miranda did not intend to appear in public this day, she could not bear to squelch the abigail's enthusiasm. And, she silently admitted, she, too, was beginning to develop a fondness for her luxurious new apparel.

"Very well," Miranda agreed.

She drained her cup and climbed out of bed, and Cassy trotted eagerly to her side. The little maid helped Miranda into the various garments, then fussed endlessly with the scalloped edges of the robe. When every scallop was arranged to her satisfaction, Cassy shoved Miranda most unceremoniously into the bamboo-legged chair, and Miranda stifled a smile as the abigail started tugging at her hair.

But Cassy was a surprisingly accomplished *coiffeuse*, Miranda soon conceded: she speedily repaired most of the damage wrought by the *toque* and by Miranda's restless sleep. Miranda critically studied her reflection and judged that she looked nearly as well as she had upon the completion of Monsieur Henri's professional ministrations. Cassy had just twisted the last of the front ringlets into place when there was a knock at the door. Cassy rushed to answer it, and Horton bowed from the threshold.

"Forgive me, Lady Margrave," the butler intoned, "but a gentleman has arrived. I have shown him to the drawing room—"

"The Duke of Clarence, I'll wager!" Cassy clapped her hands, and Horton looked at her with stony disapproval.

"His Royal Highness himself; did I not prophesy that he'd come calling, ma'am?"

"It is not the Duke of Clarence," Horton said frigidly. "The gentleman is a Sir Humphrey Hammond. He initially asked for Madame de Chavannes, but when I advised him that the Comtesse was away from home, he requested to see you, ma'am. If you do not choose to receive him, I shall inform him that you are indisposed."

Miranda bit her lip. She certainly had no desire to entertain the odious baronet; on the other hand, she could ill afford to commit an unpardonable *faux pas*. She wished she had thought to inquire about such matters, wished Anthony had thought to instruct her . . . Anthony.

"Please summon Lord Margrave, Horton," she said briskly. "I believe he is well acquainted with Sir Humphrey, and he will decide whether we are to receive him or not."

"Umm." Horton cleared his throat. "As it happens, ma'am, Lord Margrave departed with Madame de Chavannes. I couldn't possibly say when they might return."

The butler lowered his eyes, and Miranda gritted her teeth against a flush of humiliation. Appearances be damned then; if Anthony could disport about the city with his dollish, blonde *amie* . . .

"I shall be delighted to receive Sir Humphrey," she snapped. She rose, regally, she hoped, stalked out of the Yellow Chamber and flounced in Horton's wake along the corridor and down the stairs.

Sir Humphrey was seated on the pale blue couch in the drawing room, and he came very slowly to his feet when he spied Miranda and Horton at the archway. Miranda might have added this apparent breach of courtesy to the already lengthy catalog of Sir Humphrey's sins had she not observed that the baronet's pantaloons were so tightly fitted that they must cause him considerable discomfort.

"Good afternoon, Sir Humphrey," she said, suppressing a giggle.

"Good afternoon, Lady Margrave. May I say that you are looking exquisitely handsome today?" His shirt-points and neckcloth were quite as starched as those he had worn the night before, and, in view of the additional difficulty posed by his pantaloons, he was able to effect only the tiniest of bows.

"Thank you," Miranda said gravely. "Would you have some tea sent up, Horton?" The butler retreated down the hall, and Miranda turned back to the baronet. "Please resume your seat," she suggested.

Sir Humphrey cautiously lowered himself to the sofa again, paled with momentary pain and squirmed into a relatively comfortable position. Miranda, stifling another laugh, took one of the blue-and-gold chairs just opposite the couch.

"I am sure Madame de Chavannes will be *exceedingly* sorry to have missed you," Miranda commented.

"No more regretful than I myself," the baronet grunted. He negotiated a final, discreet wriggle, and his face sagged with relief. "Though I must own, Lady Margrave, that I am not altogether disconsolate to have found you alone. I should have sent a note round at any rate to thank you for presenting me to Jeanne."

So they were on Christian-name terms already, Miranda thought gleefully. She was hard put to repress a triumphant grin, but she managed a warm, decorous smile.

"No thanks are necessary, Sir Humphrey," she said, "for I assure you that my motives were purely selfish." This, at least, was true. "I perceived at once that you and—er—Jeanne would get on famously, and, frankly, I have been extremely worried about the poor girl. We are quite close—"

"Indeed?" Sir Humphrey interrupted, gingerly extending his long right leg. "I was under the impression that you and Jeanne had met but a few days since."

"As we did," Miranda hastily concurred. "But some—some friendships seem to develop instantaneously. Do you not agree, Sir Humphrey?"

"Indeed I do." The baronet attempted to nod, but his

64

chin abruptly collided with his neckcloth, and he peered down his nose at the shiny toe of his right Hessian. "And *I* wish to assure *you*, Lady Margrave, that my affection for Jeanne in no way diminishes my admiration for yourself." He lifted his pale blue eyes to hers. "As I indicated last evening, I should be honored to serve as your companion whenever, and as often as, the circumstances may warrant."

Fortunately Miranda detected a rattle at the archway before she could respond. She glanced up, beheld one of the footmen standing at attention in the corridor and eagerly beckoned him into the drawing room. He placed the silver tea service on the table in front of the sofa, set out the teapot, the sugar bowl and milk pitcher, the delicate china cups and saucers and departed. Miranda took her time pouring the tea, eliciting Sir Humphrey's preferences, adding the appropriate condiments, stirring. When she had strung out her tasks as long as she could, she passed the baronet his cup and sipped from her own.

"Well," she said brightly. "Though I have not yet been out, I trust it is a lovely day."

"A beautiful day," the baronet confirmed. "I noticed that your flowers are blooming, Lady Margrave, as are mine. I should like to think that the fruits of spring are in the way of a happy omen, a symbol of our blossoming friendship. Which, as I recall, we were discussing before the tea arrived."

Whatever Sir Humphrey's deficiencies, stupidity was not among them, Miranda realized grimly. He was a clever, determined man, and in view of her plans for him and the Comtesse, she dared not risk offending him.

"What a lovely sentiment, Sir Humphrey," she murmured. "I fancy we *shall* see a good deal of one another as your courtship of Jeanne progresses."

Had she gone too far? Apparently not, for the baronet merely smiled. "I fancy so," he agreed. "And, in any event, I suspect we shall meet frequently during the upcoming festivities."

"Festivities?" Miranda echoed. "I fear you have the advantage of me, Sir Humphrey."

"I was referring to the visit of the Allied Monarchs. The Czar and the King of Prussia are scheduled to arrive within a fortnight, and *on dit* that Marshal General Blücher will grace our shores at the same time. I am confident that His Royal Highness will entertain our late allies most lavishly and that all the best people will be invited to participate." Sir Humphrey's smug grin left no doubt that any roster of "the best people" included, was perhaps headed by, the baronet himself. "So I should hope to encounter you often, Lady Margrave."

"I hope to encounter you as well," Miranda said politely.

"Encounter Sir Humphrey where?"

Miranda had not heard Anthony's approach, and she started and spun her head toward the drawing-room archway. The Earl's red-gold hair was rather windblown, and his casual disarray might have lent him a boyish aspect except that his green eyes were glittering quite frostily.

"Ah, Margrave." Sir Humphrey rose with a leisure beyond that dictated by his attire. "Your charming wife and I were just discussing the imminent visit of the Allied Monarchs. I was remarking that I fully anticipate that soon we shall all be invited to Carlton House."

"I have *already* been invited to Carlton House," Anthony said coolly.

"Indeed?" The baronet's face colored most alarmingly, and Miranda feared he was at the verge of an apoplectic seizure. "Well, I daresay the cards are being delivered piecemeal . . ." He took refuge in a fit of coughing.

Miranda was wondering how this dreadful *contretemps* could be resolved when Madame de Chavannes sailed past Anthony and into the saloon. The Comtesse flashed Sir Humphrey a brilliant smile, daintily lifted the skirt of her gray-silk gown, rushed across the room and extended her hand. The baronet, still choking a bit, managed to bend sufficiently to kiss the air a foot or so above Madame's delicate fingers.

"Humphrey," the Comtesse sighed. "*Monsieur* Horton informed me that you had most *kindly* come to call, and I am overcome with *tristesse* that I was not here to greet you."

"Well, there was no harm in it, was there?" Anthony said smoothly. "I fancy the both of you would enjoy a drive in the park. My curricle is still hitched, Hammond, and I should be delighted to lend you the use of it for the remainder of the afternoon. To spare you from ordering out one of your own carriages, eh?"

Though Miranda would not have deemed it possible, the baronet flushed to an even deeper hue. She was still puzzling over his reaction when Anthony, in half a dozen long strides, traversed the drawing room, grasped Sir Humphrey's elbow in his left hand, seized Madame's in his right and propelled them both toward the archway.

"Do have a pleasant outing," the Earl instructed cheerfully, guiding them into the corridor. "And don't trouble yourself about the carriage, Hammond; I shall have a man watching out for your return. Goodbye then."

Their footsteps creaked down the hallway, faded down the stairs, and Anthony turned back to the saloon. His mood had evidently undergone another lightning change, for he looked quite annoyed again, and his scarred brow was probing the very fringes of his unruly hair.

"I do apologize if I interrupted a *tête-à-tête*," he said frigidly. He stalked to a small cabinet near the hearth, plucked a crystal decanter off the top, jerked the stopper out with a fearful clang and poured himself a generous portion of sherry. "However, I must request that you behave more circumspectly in the future."

"More—more circumspectly?" Miranda sputtered, almost speechless with rage. "You do me a grave insult, milord. If it was in my mind to encourage a *parti*, I assure you I would not select Sir Humphrey. I find him altogether repulsive and admitted him only because I felt you would wish him to be treated in a courteous manner. Apparently I was wrong. Good day."

Miranda bolted from her chair and had nearly reached the archway when Anthony waylaid her.

"Forgive me, Miranda. Come, let's sit down. Would you care for some sherry?"

"No," she muttered.

She was still fairly quivering with anger, but she allowed Anthony, noticeably limping now, to lead her back to the couch. The Earl collapsed onto the blue-silk upholstery, briefly biting his lip and massaging his leg, and Miranda sank reluctantly down beside him.

"Forgive me," Anthony repeated. "It occurs to me that I was most remiss in not warning you against Hammond and his ilk. He is what we in London term a dandy, a—"

"I know what a dandy is," Miranda snapped. "Though it may seem incredible to you, rumors of civilization have penetrated to Sussex."

"Of course." The ghost of a smile tickled the corners of his mouth, but his amusement merely exacerbated Miranda's annoyance. "More to the point, Hammond is a fearsome gossip. Worse than a gossip," the Earl amended. "Hammond is the sort who would readily *invent* a tale if he believed the story would enhance his tenuous position in society. He might, for example, claim a—er—an intimate liaison with the Countess of Margrave based on just such scanty evidence as your private meeting today."

Anthony smiled condescendingly, and Miranda nodded. "I understand," she said sweetly. "And I'm much relieved."

"Relieved?" Anthony's eyebrows darted up his forehead again.

"Yes, for I can only assume that Sir Humphrey *invented* his lurid tales of you. He told me, for instance, that a certain Madame La Rosa once attacked you with a decanter of Chianti. Of more recent vintage, if I may be permitted a pun, Sir Humphrey reported that you are exceedingly friendly with Signorina Savino, a soprano at the King's Theatre. Sir Humphrey went so far as to add that the Signorina is actually a Welshwoman of rather humble origins. Sir Humphrey has a vivid imagination, does he not, milord?"

"Mary Anne." Anthony gulped down the rest of his sherry and coughed.

"I believe that *was* the name Sir Humphrey employed! Mary Anne Stephens, as I recollect."

Anthony stared at his empty glass, lifted it, twirled it in his long fingers, as though it were the crystal ball of a gypsy fortuneteller. "I shan't deny it," he said at last. "It is true that Mary Anne and I were—friends for some time. But that should scarcely overset you, Miranda, for I am sure you left more than one suitor languishing in Sussex."

He transferred his green eyes to her, and his abrupt counterattack rendered her once more wordless. She visualized Dickie Alcott in all his ludicrous splendor and willed herself not to look away.

"I believe it would be best if we were not to pry into one another's private lives," she mumbled at length.

"I quite agree," the Earl said. "I shall simply reiterate that I should prefer you not to receive Hammond, or others of his type, alone."

Miranda glimpsed one small chink in his armor, and she could not resist a final thrust.

"I should not have been required to receive Sir Humphrey alone had you been at home," she pointed out stiffly. "Had you not been—been cavorting about with Madame de Chavannes."

"Cavorting?" To Miranda's intense irritation, Anthony threw back his head and laughed. "I should hardly term it 'cavorting,' my dear, for I had an abysmally tedious appointment with my man of business. Jeanne wished to visit a relative of her late husband's—the second cousin of the Comte's uncle or some such person—and I dropped her by en route to Mr. Oakley's and retrieved her on the return journey. 'Cavorting' indeed!"

Anthony continued to chuckle, and Miranda wondered if she was ever to score a single point against him. "I thought you were quite disinterested in business affairs," she lashed out.

"So I am." He set his glass on the table, oddly pensive. "Or was. I suddenly find myself concerned about the future. A symptom of advancing age, I suppose," he concluded lightly.

They sat in silence for a moment, and Miranda groped for a felicitous end to the conversation. "I suppose we needn't tease ourselves about Madame de Chavannes nor Sir Humphrey," she ventured at last. "They seem quite taken with one another."

"I truly pray not," Anthony said, "for the enterprise is utterly hopeless."

"Hopeless?" Miranda echoed sharply. "On the contrary, they are eminently suited. Sir Humphrey fulfills Madame's qualifications precisely. He is young and attractive—"

"Perhaps women judge him attractive," Anthony interjected.

"Intelligent," Miranda persisted, "wealthy—"

"Wealthy?" Anthony laughed again. "Hammond doesn't have sixpence to scratch with. During the Season he lives with his uncle, Viscount Crowley, on Bruton Street; the rest of the year he drifts amongst various relations and friends and acquaintances of friends. He always has a roof over his head and food in his belly and wins enough at Watier's to pay his tailor. But that is all. He recently smashed up one of Crowley's carriages, and his uncle has since denied him access to the stables. A painful setdown for Hammond, I fear."

And the reason for the baronet's acute embarrassment, Miranda thought. "Yet you lent him your curricle and one of your teams," she said aloud.

"I can afford the risk, for I am considerably wealthier than Viscount Crowley." Miranda briefly believed the Earl was serious; then he flashed his engaging grin. "And perhaps I, too, entertained the temporary notion that Hammond and Jeanne might reach an understanding. But the enterprise is, as I said, quite doomed."

Anthony flexed his left leg, and a shadow of pain flickered across his face.

"Your leg is troubling you again," Miranda murmured.

His mouth hardened, as though he intended to deny it, then he sighed. "A bit," he confessed. "I believe I shall summon Johnson to rub it down. It is rather humbling to be kneaded and prodded like an ailing horse, but Johnson seems the only person who can give me relief. Unless you would care to try, my dear?"

"Indeed not!" Miranda gasped.

But the Earl was jesting again, and that infuriating hint of laughter teased his mouth as he stood, bowed and limped out of the saloon.

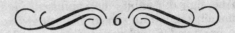

6

It was nearing six when Cassy came to the Yellow Chamber to announce the household's evening itinerary.

"The Comb-*tess* and Sir Humphrey returned about half an hour ago," she reported. "I say, he *is* a handsome fellow, is he not? And so elegantly dressed!"

"Indeed he is," Miranda choked.

"Well, at any rate, Madam dee—dee—" But the pronunciation was utterly beyond her, and the abigail shook her head. "Madam said that she and Sir Humphrey are to dine at his uncle's. Lord Crowe, I believe she said."

"Viscount Crowley," Miranda corrected absently.

"I suppose he may be there as well," Cassy agreed. "In any event, his lordship—Lord Margrave, that is—remarked that as he himself is to be away from home this evening—he must see a man about some country property, he said—there seemed little reason to serve a formal meal in the dining room. Consequently his lordship suggested that you, ma'am, take dinner in your room, and he asked me to bring it up. Which I shall do whenever you wish."

"I'm not hungry," Miranda snapped.

"Nevertheless you must fortify yourself if you're to be out dancing till dawn with *dukes* and such," Cassy said sternly. "So I shall fetch your dinner up at half past the hour." Cassy's tone allowed for no further argument. "Shall I help you change in the interim, ma'am?"

"No, thank you," Miranda muttered.

"Very well. I shall be back shortly then."

Cassy sailed into the corridor and closed the door, and Miranda glared after her. What sort of fool did Anthony take her for? she wondered furiously. Less than a week since, he had cheerfully confessed to a total lack of interest in the administration of his estates. Did he honestly expect Miranda to believe that he was now attending multiple business meetings within the same day? He had, almost boastfully, claimed that rural life did not suit him at all; did he truly hope to persuade Miranda that he was eagerly shopping for yet another piece of "country property"? She snatched her hairbrush off the dressing table and flung it at the connecting door, but fortunately it landed well short, with a harmless thud, on the edge of the Brussels carpet.

Miranda stole rather sheepishly across the room, stooped and retrieved the brush. Anthony was a clever man, she conceded, idly removing a few sherry-colored hairs lodged amongst the bristles. He had deftly converted the discussion of his relationship with Signorina Savino to a conversation about Miranda's mythical Sussex *partis*. He had thereby avoided an outright lie, a claim that the liaison had been terminated, and had equally dodged a frank admission that the *affaire* continued. Which, of course, it did. And in the midst of his dissimulation, Anthony had found the nerve, the sheer, unmitigated gall, to accuse *her* of improprieties! Miranda stalked back to the dressing table and slammed her hairbrush back upon the gleaming rosewood surface, fervently wishing that her target were, instead, the Earl of Margrave's tousled, red-gold head.

On the following morning, Cassy again plucked the white-and-canary walking dress from the wardrobe, reminding Miranda that she had exhausted Madame Leclair's limited introductory offering.

"I do not wish to wear the same gown two days in succession, Cassy," she said. "I should prefer the old muslin, please."

Cassy frowned but apparently decided to defer, for once, to her mistress's peculiar whims. She helped Miranda into the stained and threadbare frock, suppressing a shudder of distaste, then insisted that she must, at least, redress her ladyship's hair. She seated

73

Miranda in the dressing-table chair and began dismantling the complex *coiffure*.

"Madam Dee came home about eleven," Cassy said. She had evidently adopted this appellation in lieu of Madame's impossible name and title. "That is, I fancy it was about eleven because it was well before his lordship arrived, and the clock was just chiming midnight when *he* appeared."

Did Cassy never sleep? Miranda wondered grouchily. "And how did he seem?" she asked aloud.

"Sir Humphrey?"

Actually Miranda had intended to inquire about Anthony, but it belatedly occurred to her that she should be well, should be *intimately* informed as to the Earl's physical and mental state. "Sir Humphrey," she nodded.

"*Don't* move your head, ma'am," Cassy reprimanded sharply. "Well, Sir Humphrey seemed all aglow, as did Madam Dee. I do believe they are over head and ears in love; is it not wonderful? I daresay there will be a wedding before the leaves fall."

Wonderful indeed, Miranda thought morosely. Cassy's enthusiasm had brought another complication to mind: Miranda's ill-timed kindness to Sir Humphrey. When Madame learned the truth about her penurious suitor, she would jilt him posthaste, and the baronet would conveniently forget that Miranda's encouragement had been that of a matchmaker. He would redouble his pursuit of "Lady Margrave," and she would be hard put indeed to fend him off. Miranda ground her fingernails into her palms, cursing the impulse that had got her embroiled in this morass.

"Be still, ma'am!" Cassy pleaded. She bit her lip with concentration and teased the last curls into place. "There. Is it satisfactory, your ladyship?"

"Quite so," Miranda automatically responded. In fact, she decided upon inspection, the little maid had wrought a distinct improvement. The style, though similar, was not so severe as Monsieur Henri's creation, and it somehow rendered Miranda's face smaller, more delicate. "It is really very lovely, Cassy," she added.

"Well, *you* are very lovely, ma'am."

Miranda had never regarded herself in this light, and she searched the abigail's eyes for some hint of servile flattery. But Cassy seemed altogether sincere, and Miranda felt herself coloring a bit.

"Thank you," she murmured. "That will be all, Cassy. I shall follow you down, for I wish to bring up a few books to occupy my—er—spare time." Of which, she suspected, she was likely to have a good deal over the coming weeks.

Miranda entered the book-lined parlor without great optimism, expecting to discover that Anthony's library, like Thomas's, consisted largely of dogeared scholastic relics. She was forced at once to own herself mistaken: though the Earl's shelves contained the anticipated complement of well-thumbed classics, they were also crammed with recent novels and poetry and social commentary. The selections of his late uncle, no doubt. She plucked down *Pride and Prejudice* by Miss Austen, a new edition of Lord Byron's poems and Mr. Smith's treatise on the *Wealth of Nations*, which she had long intended to read. Indeed, she was already leafing through the latter as she drifted back into the entry hall, and she was not aware of voices until they fell silent.

"Lady Margrave!"

Sir Humphrey negotiated one of his awkward bows, and Miranda's eyes traveled from him to Anthony. The Earl was rotating a tall beaver hat in his long fingers, and she wondered whether he was returning from an excursion or at the point of setting out.

"What an exceedingly fortuitous circumstance!" Sir Humphrey continued. "Horton had no sooner gone to announce my arrival to Jeanne than Margrave came in."

Returning then, Miranda noted. Anthony had probably departed in the small hours of the morning to visit the Signorina.

". . . an opportunity to express again my appreciation for his kindness in placing his curricle at my disposal," the baronet was saying. "It was of enormous assistance

75

to me because my uncle has experienced some recent— ahem—difficulty with one of his equipages."

Another maddening smile hovered at the corners of Anthony's mouth, and Miranda looked hastily away.

"I am sorry to hear that, Sir Humphrey," she said.

"Now, to augment my delight," the Baronet flew on, "I encounter you as well, Lady Margrave. But pray do not feel constrained to entertain me, for I see that you are preparing to—to—"

Sir Humphrey's voice trailed off, and he examined Miranda's disreputable gown with growing shock. After some deliberation, he was apparently unable to conceive of any human activity which could possibly justify so wretched a garment, and he nervously caressed his own starched and snowy shirt-points.

"As it happens, Sir Humphrey, I am feeling extremely unwell," Miranda said. "I was seeking amusement"—she displayed the books in her arms—"and naturally I did not wish to wander about in my dressing gown."

"Naturally," the baronet agreed. "But how *sad* that you are not the thing, Lady Margrave. I fear you will be unable to attend the assembly at Almack's this evening."

Since Anthony had not mentioned an assembly at Almack's on this or any other evening, Miranda gazed studiedly at the toes of her grayed and tattered slippers. Fortunately Horton bustled down the stairs before she was compelled to formulate an answer.

"Madame de Chavannes will receive you directly, sir," the butler said. His tone suggested that the Comtesse's judgment was woefully flawed. "I shall show you to the drawing room."

Sir Humphrey bowed, insofar as he was able, to Miranda, to Anthony, and followed Horton up the stairs. When they had disappeared, Anthony emitted a low chuckle.

"Excellently done, my dear. I perceived only this morning that we could scarcely continue to parade you about in a single evening dress. Consequently, I consulted with Madame Leclair this morning, and she has promised to deliver the remainder of our order on

Thursday. But that leaves several days, of course, and your claim of illness was *perfect.*"

"And it lays the groundwork, does it not, milord?" Actually Miranda had not considered the future ramifications of her "illness" until this very instant, but it would do no harm for Anthony to believe that she, too, suffered a surfeit of cleverness. "In view of Sir Humphrey's loose tongue, everyone in London will soon be aware that poor 'Lady Margrave' is not in the bloom of health. It will come as little surprise when she disappears forever into the country, perhaps to that very 'country property' you are so busily evaluating."

"Umm." Anthony coughed and seemed to twirl his beaver hat a trifle more industriously. "Very shrewd indeed, Miranda, though I really detect no need to rush the matter."

"No need?" Miranda echoed. "I beg to differ, sir. Despite your glum predictions, it appears that Sir Humphrey's courtship of the Comtesse is proceeding apace. And once Madame de Chavannes is safely engaged, my impersonation will become quite gratuitous, will it not?"

Miranda was speaking with considerably more confidence than she felt, and she suspected, from the sudden narrowing of the Earl's green eyes, that he was prepared to challenge her. But his words, when he spoke, were not those she had anticipated.

"Are you really so anxious to escape?"

"Indeed I am!" Miranda snapped.

"Very well," Anthony said coolly. "We shall see what transpires and discuss the subject at the appropriate time. Meanwhile, enjoy your reading, my dear." He snatched up Mr. Smith's book, then plopped it, rather more forcefully than necessary, back into Miranda's arms. "I myself find Smith's opinions most intriguing though I cannot claim to agree in every respect. Good day."

With a bow nearly as terse as one of Sir Humphrey's abbreviated efforts, Anthony turned and strode into the parlor. Miranda hurried up the stairs, dimly aware of the laughter emanating from the saloon as she sped along the corridor and up to the second story. She stretched out on the canopied bed, opened Mr. Smith's book and began to read. But it was a tedious, scholarly work, one requiring the reader's full attention, and Miranda was utterly unable to muster the necessary concentration.

Was she really so eager to escape? she wondered, laying the book face down on the counterpane. She had casually thought to emigrate to Canada, but she had not considered the specifics. Would it be advisable to change her name? And, if so, to what? Something commonplace would no doubt be best: Miranda Smith, Miranda Wilson . . .

She would also be compelled to invent a background, she realized. She would reach her destination, wherever *that* might be, as a woman of some means, means far in excess of the savings of a governess. Should she claim to be a wealthy widow? The daughter of a peer? A manufacturer's heiress?

It occurred to her that any such fabrication would represent another, perhaps a permanent, impersonation, and she experienced a flutter of panic, a sense that she had forever lost her true identity. There was, furthermore, the question of those left behind. Anthony had blithely insisted that there would be no difficulty, and Miranda was forced to concede that the *ton* would rapidly lose interest in an invalid "Lady Margrave." But what of the servants? Horton and his wife could probably be persuaded that her ladyship had been dispatched to an institution of some sort, but Cassy? Miranda believed the little abigail had developed a genuine affection for her mistress, an affection that Miranda entirely reciprocated. Cassy might well demand to accompany Lady Margrave, would certainly press to visit her.

But that was the Earl's problem, Miranda concluded; her problem was to determine who she was next to be. *Lady* Miranda Smith, the widow of an obscure viscount or baronet? *Miss* Miranda Smith, daughter of same? *Mrs.* Miranda Smith? She felt another stab of panic and determinedly retrieved Mr. Smith's book. Perhaps, she thought dryly, she would claim a relationship to him.

Perversely, now that Miranda's own emotions were mixed, Sir Humphrey's wooing of the Comtesse did appear to be progressing full tilt. On Tuesday morning, Cassy delivered—along with an enormous breakfast of eggs, bacon and warm bread—news of the courtship.

"It's small wonder you're sick, Lady Margrave," the abigail chided, watching critically as Miranda picked at her food. "You scarcely eat enough to keep a bird alive. You should take a lesson from Madam Dee. *She* was up at the very crack of dawn, she ate a great, healthy breakfast, and she and Sir Humphrey took a splendid picnic to the country. His lordship lent Sir Humphrey his curricle again, and they set out *hours* ago."

"And what is his lordship doing?" Miranda asked, hoping to distract Cassy while she pushed her untouched eggs to the edges of her plate.

"Lord Margrave ordered out the landau and went to confer with Mr. Oakley about the country property."

"Indeed?" Miranda said coldly.

She dismissed Cassy and, having given up on Mr. Smith (now her tentative grand-uncle), plunged into *Pride and Prejudice*.

Cassy's Wednesday report was similar.

"Sir Humphrey is escorting Madam Dee round the town," the abigail announced. "They are going to the Wax Museum and the Botanical Gardens and, if there's time, to Hampton Court. Meanwhile, his lordship has taken Mr. Oakley to the country to view the property under consideration."

Miranda returned to Miss Austen's novel, darkly speculating on Anthony's next ruse. Perhaps, in light of Sir Humphrey's situation, the Earl would claim to require a new carriage and would pretend to venture to Hatchett's day after day. As soon as the fictional carriage was under construction, his lordship would discover a need for additional horses and would feign regular visits to Tattersall's. After that there would be grooms to hire, livery to order . . . Miranda glowered at the printed page, suspecting that Anthony could compose a considerably more imaginative tale than could the sheltered daughter of a Hampshire rector.

By Thursday afternoon Miranda had finished the novel and Lord Byron's volume of poetry, and she crept back to the parlor to exchange the books for new selections. She had just borne her choices—another of Miss Austen's stories and two Gothic tales by Horace Walpole—into the foyer when the front door opened. Fearing that Sir Humphrey and the Comtesse had returned from their excursion to Astley's, Miranda raced toward the stairs, but Horton's voice caught her up.

"Ah, Lady Margrave! I daresay you will be delighted to learn that your order from Madame Leclair has arrived." The butler's keen blue eyes darted the length of Miranda's ancient dress. "Delighted," he repeated. "If you have no objection, I shall instruct the footboys to take the delivery directly up to your bedchamber."

"Yes, thank you, Horton," Miranda murmured.

Even as she spoke, three footboys panted through the door, boxes stacked fairly to their chins, and began laboring up the steps. Miranda was preparing to follow when Anthony sauntered into the entry hall, an additional box tucked under each of his arms.

"Good afternoon, my dear." The Earl essayed a bow, and his beaver hat slipped down over his eyes. He set his burden on the marble floor and removed the hat. "Good afternoon," he said again. "It's fortunate I happened along, is it not?" He gestured to the boxes.

Cassy, Miranda's primary source of intelligence, had not seen his lordship this morning, and Miranda thought it entirely possible that he had "happened along" following an overnight visit to the Signorina.

"Fortunate indeed," she said frigidly.

"I suggest you investigate your new clothes at once so as to determine your attire for the immediate future. We are to attend a ball at Lady Clayton's tonight and an assembly at Admiral Spencer's tomorrow evening. Or have I reversed them?" Anthony frowned, and Miranda noted again that his scarred brow always remained slightly above the other. "Never mind; I fancy they are all the same in the end."

The footboys puffed back down the stairs, and Horton instructed "one of you" to fetch up her ladyship's final boxes, an assignment that prompted a bitter, albeit wordless, quarrel. At length the smallest of the trio, a lad named Bill, was glared into submission by the other two. He wearily retrieved the packages Anthony had dropped; and with a curt nod to the Earl, Miranda trailed him to the second story.

Cassy was already unpacking Madame Leclair's offerings, her fingers flying through paper and string, and she issued an unsolicited appraisal of each creation. The pink satin was "stunning," she said, "though I am not sure pink is really your color, ma'am." The white crape was "exquisite, but I believe I might have done the trim in brown rather than black." The little abigail would only concede that the silk plaid was "unusual," and she did not care for the apple-green net "at all."

"This is by far the best of the lot," Cassy concluded after she had unloaded the last box. She displayed the yellow lace, and Miranda silently concurred. "We shall wear that tonight, eh, ma'am?"

"I think not, Cassy. I should prefer to save it for a special occasion."

Miranda wondered, rather grimly, just what the "special occasion" might be. An Indian festival deep in the Canadian wilderness perhaps? At any rate, she and Cassy agreed upon an alternative selection, and the abigail, insisting there was no time to waste, scurried downstairs to order up her ladyship's bath.

Lady Clayton's and Admiral Spencer's entertainments were, as Anthony had predicted, "all the same"—so similar that Miranda was subsequently hard pressed to distinguish between them. On both occasions, she stood up for virtually every set, but she was quite unable to remember her individual partners, to separate the lords from the honorables, the generals from the captains. As she pondered the matter at Saturday breakfast, she frowned at the two notable circumstances which did come to mind.

First, the Comtesse and Sir Humphrey had conducted themselves most indelicately: strolling about Lady Clayton's ballroom hand in hand, arm in arm; whirling through Admiral Spencer's saloon chest to chest and cheek to cheek. Of perhaps greater significance, Madame had permitted herself only a few scant glasses of champagne. The Comtesse was, in short, on her very best behavior; apparently she was circling in for the kill.

Second, almost all of Miranda's partners had inquired solicitously after her ladyship's health. Miranda had vaguely claimed to be "somewhat better" and "slightly improved," all the while owning a debt to Sir Humphrey's busy tongue. Anthony really should pay the baronet for his trouble, she thought irritably, scowling across the table.

The Earl had inexplicably commanded a formal meal in the breakfast parlor this morning, and now, evidently misinterpreting Miranda's expression, he flashed his wry smile.

"They *were* rather dreadful, weren't they?" he said. "Lady Clayton has been widowed for some years, and Admiral Spencer recently lost his own wife. I have begun to pray that they will wed and hold a mutual assembly next Season, thereby sparing the nation *two* such dismal events."

"Umm," Miranda growled.

"At any rate, I believe you will find this evening's ball considerably more lively. Mr. Turner, the host, owns half the Midlands, but that, of course, does not excuse his innate lack of breeding." Anthony grinned again. "Mrs. Turner has attempted to compensate by becoming a patroness of the arts. I am told that she frequently–ahem–*entertains* the aspiring painters and writers under her protection, but who am I to cast a stone?"

"Who indeed?" Miranda snapped.

"I beg your pardon?"

"Nothing," she mumbled.

"I do fancy it will be amusing. Well, good morning, my dear."

Anthony rose and hobbled out, and Miranda choked down the tepid dregs of her coffee.

Miranda was thoroughly out of sorts by the time they reached the Turner's garish new mansion in Portman Square. They had stopped for Sir Humphrey en route, and he and the Comtesse had spent the remainder of the journey giggling and pawing at one another, the latter none too discreetly. To make matters worse, Miranda's new black-kid slippers were painfully tight, and she thought she might well be as crippled as Anthony before the night was over. The landau drew to a halt, and Miranda winced as Johnson tugged her out and set her throbbing feet upon the cobblestones.

Miranda grew somewhat more optimistic when they entered the top-floor ballroom, for it did appear that the Turners' assembly would be, if nothing else, unusual. Mr. Turner was a tall, graying man clad in elegantly tailored evening clothes, but his commanding demeanor was abruptly dispelled when he heartily welcomed them to "me home." Mrs. Turner, a dark woman of indeterminate age, was wearing a shocking gown of crimson satin and resembled, in Miranda's opinion, nothing so much as a Spanish dancer. The receiving line at Mrs. Turner's right comprised some half dozen of her current protégés—a motley assortment of wild-eyed, oddly attired, but uniformly young and handsome, men. The hostess presented her "brilliant," "marvelous," "splendid" talents, and Miranda solemnly shook each proffered hand.

"There are also a number of established artistic and literary figures in attendance," Mrs. Turner bubbled. "This, for example, is Dr. Mead. Of Oxford."

Miranda's hand was already outstretched, and she willed herself not to snatch it back. Mrs. Turner was explaining that Dr. Mead was a professor of English literature, but Miranda was well aware of his position. Dr. and Mrs. Mead and Papa and Mama had been fast friends before Mama's death. Of far more serious consequence, Thomas had been a student of Dr. Mead's.

Though Miranda had not seen the couple for some years, she had written them a note just prior to her departure from Oxford. She was maddeningly unable to recall the precise details of her message, but surely she had described her arrangement with Thomas.

"Lady Margrave," the professor intoned. He dropped her hand, smiled, wrinkled his shaggy, white brows. "I fancy we have met before, have we not?"

"I—I can't imagine where," Miranda stammered. "I arrived in London only recently."

"It would not have been in London, for I rarely come to town myself. No, I thought to have encountered you at Oxford. Perhaps you had a brother there?"

"I regret to say that I have no brothers."

"A cousin then?" Dr. Mead's frown deepened. "You look exceedingly familiar, Lady Margrave."

"I fear I have a very common sort of face," Miranda said prettily. "If you will excuse me, Dr. Mead, I believe there are others eager to make your acquaintance."

Miranda rushed past Mrs. Mead with the barest of nods and stopped just beyond the reception line. Anthony was chatting quite animatedly with the professor and his wife, and the Comtesse stood, with visible impatience, behind him. Miranda clutched her hands to stop their trembling and leaped nearly to the ceiling when Sir Humphrey tapped her shoulder.

"I wish to speak with you, Lady Margrave, and I believe we might best aspire to privacy on the dance floor."

Without awaiting a response, the baronet steered Miranda past a score of waltzing couples and took her in his arms. Miranda's feet, forgotten during her terrifying encounter with Dr. Mead, had begun to ache again, and she was scarcely able to limp along in rhythm to the music.

"I must say, Lady Margrave, that you do not seem up to the mark at all. I had initially supposed that you might be suffering from consumption, but I now collect you are in the gout."

"Gout?" Miranda echoed indignantly.

"Yes. Your feet are swollen, and you can hardly walk. I advise you to consult a physician at once."

"Excellent advice, Sir Humphrey, but I am frankly reluctant to seek a medical opinion." Miranda sighed. "My health, as you know, is—delicate."

"I do know that." The baronet, insofar as his shirt-points would allow, nodded. "It makes my task all the more difficult, Lady Margrave."

"Your task?" Miranda repeated.

"Yes. I wished to inform you first that Jeanne and I have decided to be married. I am sure you will understand that it is a matter of necessity. My—ahem—expectations have been somewhat—ahem—disappointing, and Jeanne, in addition to her many charms, is a very wealthy woman."

Miranda stopped in mid-note, and Sir Humphrey trod upon her left foot. She gritted her teeth against a moan of pain, and the baronet urged her back into motion.

"I anticipated your shock, Lady Margrave, and I want to assure you that my marriage will not impede our own relationship. Quite the contrary, I daresay: husbands tend to regard unwed men with keen suspicion, do they not?"

"I believe they do," Miranda murmured.

"I was confident of your concurrence. We shall talk again after a—ahem—a decent interval, eh?"

Fortunately the music ended before Miranda could answer, and Sir Humphrey led her off the floor. The Comtesse was seated in one of the many chairs dotting the perimeter of the ballroom, carefully nursing a glass of champagne, and she rose as they approached. Sir Humphrey kissed Madame's cheek resoundingly, then bowed away.

"Humphrey." The Comtesse shook her head. "Did he tell you of our engagement?"

"Yes. Yes, he did."

In fact, Miranda was still reeling with the shock of the news, though scarcely the shock Sir Humphrey had anticipated. Despite her antipathy to the Baronet, she was quite horrified that Madame de Chavannes had so blatantly lied to him, had so coldly misrepresented her financial circumstances. Miranda wondered if she should have enlightened Sir Humphrey and reminded herself that it was not yet too late.

"Humphrey is not *parfait*, of course," Madame continued, "but rich men seldom are. *N'est-ce pas?* An impoverished woman must sacrifice something to wed one of the wealthiest men in England."

"How true." Miranda swallowed an insane howl of laughter. They had mutually deceived one another, and that, as Madame would have phrased it, was *parfait*. "May I tender my congratulations, Jeanne? May I call you Jeanne?"

"*Certainement.*"

The Comtesse beamed and waved at her fiancé, who was bounding back across the room, and Miranda hastily excused herself.

Miranda stood up for the ensuing sets with Mr. Turner, who regaled her with an extremely immodest account of his industrial empire, and Admiral Spencer, who delivered an equally smug report of his exploits in the recent war. Fortunately Miranda heard little of either narrative, for her mind was whirling with the events of the evening. She danced the final waltz before intermission with one of Mrs. Turner's protégés, an adolescent painter who made it abundantly clear that he would not at all object to a new patroness, particularly not to one so young and comely as the Countess of Margrave. As the music finished, Miranda realized that her feet had degenerated to fiery lumps of agony, and she was compelled to lean quite heavily on Mr. Hickman (or was it Wickman?) as he escorted her from the floor. Anthony limped forward to meet them, looking exceedingly displeased, and Mr. Hickman/Wickman hurried away.

"Would you care to sit down?" the Earl inquired coldly. "I fancy so, for you appear exhausted."

He indicated a nearby pair of chairs, and Miranda glanced toward them and glimpsed Dr. Mead peering at her myopically from across the room. The professor fumbled for his quizzing glass, and Miranda spun around.

"I wish to leave," she hissed. "At once."

"Leave?" Anthony drawled. "How can you leave when it is not yet eleven and you are having such a splendid time? I do believe you have entertained more partners than any other female here. Indeed, I fear the assembly might halt altogether with your departure, in which event our hosts would be highly overset."

"Tell them I am ill," Miranda whispered. "In fact, that will prove an excellent ploy . . ." But she had not yet advised Anthony of her intention, had hardly confirmed it herself, and she stopped. "I shall meet you at the street."

Miranda hobbled down the stairs and lurked nervously in the shadow of a tree outside the house. Despite her caution, Pollard apparently spotted her, for the landau had just clattered up to the door when Anthony emerged. The Earl's mood seemed, if possible, to have deteriorated, and he propelled Miranda roughly to the carriage.

"This is most embarrassing," he snapped, as the landau got underway. "Mrs. Turner was obviously affronted, and I had to arrange alternative transportation for Hammond and Jeanne. On the whole, a disgraceful performance, my dear. One I trust you will not soon repeat."

"I shall not repeat it," Miranda promised, "for this, milord, is the last act of the play." Having pronounced her decision, she drew a deep, ragged breath. "I am sure you will agree that it is time for our charade to end."

"End?" Anthony sounded genuinely puzzled, and as they passed beneath a street lamp, Miranda observed the uneven quirk of his brows.

"Yes." Miranda was sitting across from the Earl, and she moved to the edge of the seat and lifted one tutorial finger, realizing that she looked like the governess she so recently had been. "First of all, Sir Humphrey and Jeanne are engaged; I presume they related their happy intelligence to you?"

"Indeed they did." Anthony's lips quivered with one of his half-smiles. "I should adore to be a mouse in the wall when they set out to count their money and discover they haven't a farthing between them."

"That is beside the point," Miranda said severely. She held up another finger. "In the second place, I was very nearly unmasked tonight. Dr. Mead knew my parents, knew Thomas, knew me; he dandled me on his knee when I was a child."

"Which, if I may point it out, was a goodly number of years ago. You parried the professor quite admirably; I've no doubt he is persuaded that he made an error."

"That is beside the point," Miranda repeated stubbornly. "Do you not see that the longer this—this farce continues, the greater the chance of complications?" She stabbed a third finger into the air. "Furthermore, I have laid ample foundation for my disappearance. Even before this evening's—*performance*, there were a hundred people in London prepared to attest to my ill health, and my premature departure tonight will simply heap fuel upon the fire. I have, in short, performed my duties, performed *beyond* my duties, and I propose to leave tomorrow."

"I see." Anthony plucked off his *chapeau bras* and twirled it upon the tip of one long forefinger. "It occurs to me that, with your entire new wardrobe safely in hand, you are unseemly eager to terminate our agreement."

"That has absolutely nothing to do with it—"

"You were hired for the duration of the Season," Anthony interrupted coolly. "You were not hired to serve until Jeanne found a husband or until you encountered a doddering Oxford don at a ball—"

"Reduce my pay then!" Miranda snapped. "What is fair, milord? Four hundred pounds? Three hundred? You name the figure; I am merely attempting to protect the both of us from further unpleasantness."

The door handle rattled, and Miranda became belatedly aware that the carriage had stopped. Johnson opened the door and assisted her out, and she was relieved to note that her feet had grown quite numb. She rushed up the front steps, idly observing that the house was unusually well lit, and struggled for a moment with the doorknob. Anthony had just reached her side when Horton threw open the door.

"Lord Margrave! Lady Margrave! I have wonderful news! Mrs. Pennington arrived in your absence!"

Miranda did not recognize the name, and she stole a sidewards glance at Anthony, wearily supposing that Mrs. Pennington was another of his multitudinous inamoratas.

"Just under an hour ago," Horton continued. "She was quite exhausted, of course, and has retired. But I am delighted to say, sir, that your mother seems in excellent health."

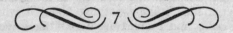

7

"I personally prefer the gray, ma'am, but I fear you would find it a trifle uncomfortable because it promises to be a very warm day. So perhaps you should wear the blue jaconet though I must say I think the trim altogether too fancy—"

"Oh, for heaven's sake, Cassy," Miranda snapped. "Pick one or the other; it doesn't signify."

The abigail's arms drooped, and the hems of both walking dresses brushed the Brussels carpet. "I realize you are overset about meeting your new mother-in-law," Cassy said stiffly. "But you really needn't take it out on me, ma'am."

"I'm sorry," Miranda mumbled. "You are quite right about the gowns, Cassy; the jaconet would be more suitable."

She slipped out of her peignoir, and Cassy helped her into the blue muslin. The little maid was correct about the trimming as well, Miranda decided; the elaborate white flounces round the bottom did seem a bit excessive. Miranda sighed, and Cassy seated her at the dressing table and began to repair her hair.

"There is no reason for you to be nervous," Cassy said forgivingly. "Mrs. Pennington is a lovely woman."

"You've met her?" Miranda frowned, vaguely recollecting that Anthony's mother had resided abroad for many years.

"This morning." Cassy nodded. "Mrs. Pennington required some assistance with her toilette, and as *I* am an experienced dresser, Mrs. Horton desired me to attend her."

"I see." Miranda bit back a smile.

90

"She's a most handsome lady. She much resembles Lord Margrave, or he her, as the case may be. And she's *thrilled* about the marriage, ma'am; you need have no fear on that account. She said it was the grandest surprise of her life. 'I knew nothing about it when I set out,' she said, 'and I could hardly contain myself when Horton told me that Anthony had wed at last.'"

Cassy rattled on, and Miranda gritted her teeth. She could scarcely credit her ill fortune, could scarcely conceive that she had been thwarted within twenty-four hours of escape. Well, perhaps forty-eight, she conceded, for Anthony had not yet been convinced of the wisdom of her departure. But she would have persuaded the Earl; she was certain of that. Anthony was a reasonable man, and he would soon have recognized that they were tempting fate. As it was, fate, in the form of Mrs. Pennington, had dramatically outmaneuvered them.

But maybe it was not yet too late. Miranda's eyes narrowed, and Cassy, evidently misinterpreting her mistress's piercing gaze, hastily rearranged one of the front curls. She could still send word that her mysterious "illness" had worsened, that she was quite unable to leave her bed. In which event, Mrs. Pennington would demand to see her ailing daughter-in-law at once and might well insist on nursing her through the remainder of the Season. The Season! Miranda was suddenly struck by an appalling thought. Having traveled all the way from Jamaica, Mrs. Pennington was unlikely to return in the immediate future. It was, in fact, entirely probable that Anthony's mother would stay on for some months, indefinitely extending Miranda's impersonation. Miranda felt her jaw sag, and the mirror confirmed her utter dismay.

"Is it still not satisfactory, ma'am?" Cassy asked anxiously. "I have done the best I can."

"It is fine," Miranda muttered, barely glancing at her perfectly coiffed hair. "I am a trifle overset after all."

And that, she concluded grimly, was certainly the greatest understatement of her life.

Miranda marched boldly down the stairs and across

the dining room, but her tenuous courage evaporated just outside the entrance to the breakfast parlor. She plastered herself against the dining-room wall and peered cautiously through the archway. She could not see Anthony from her vantage point, but she could hear his voice, and Mrs. Pennington, clearly visible in one of the side chairs, was smiling and nodding.

Miranda was forced to own Cassy right again, for the Earl and his mother looked a great deal alike. Mrs. Pennington seemed tall, though it was difficult to tell, and her face, at least, was lean—sharp boned and hollow cheeked like that of her son. Her coloring predicted Anthony's a quarter-century hence: her red-gold hair was threaded with gray, lending it a slightly pinkish hue, and her eyes had faded from emerald to the paler green of the sea. Said eyes flickered abruptly toward the archway, and Miranda, fearing she had been detected, hurried on into the room.

"And here she is now!" Anthony rose from his place at the head of the table, limped to Miranda's side and threw an arm about her shoulders. "Did I not tell you she was lovely, Mama?"

Without warning, the Earl lowered his head and touched his mouth to Miranda's own. The shock of it rendered her quite breathless, and as she struggled for air, her lips parted a bit. Anthony, with his free arm, drew her against him, and Miranda suppressed an urge to tear herself away. Eventually he released her, looked down at her, and Miranda could not judge whether his expression was one of satisfaction or surprise.

"Here she is," he repeated. "Miranda."

"Mrs. Pennington." Miranda's voice was inexplicably hoarse, and she cleared her throat. "I'm delighted to make your acquaintance."

"We shan't have that at all." Mrs. Pennington waved an admonitory finger. "No, indeed; you must call me—" She wrinkled her brows, which were still precisely the same red-gold as Anthony's. "You must call me 'Mother Elizabeth,'" she declared at last.

Miranda thought this form of address best suited to an

abbess, which Anthony's mother—clad in a far-from-demure gown of primrose mull—clearly was not. But Miranda was still oddly breathless, her mind strangely clouded, and she elected not to argue.

"Mother Elizabeth," she murmured.

Anthony guided Miranda to the chair at the foot of the table. Perhaps she *was* ill, Miranda decided, for her knees were exceedingly weak. She poured herself a cup of coffee, noting that the spout of the silver pot clattered against the rim of her cup.

"You do not yet seem quite the thing, my dear," Elizabeth clucked sympathetically. "Your adorable little maid informed me that you had been confined to the house for several days earlier in the week. Naturally I was in hopes you might be in a delicate condition." Elizabeth beamed, and Miranda narrowly managed not to strangle on her coffee. "But Anthony advises me that it is a trifle early for any such joyful circumstance."

"Early, yes," Anthony agreed airily, "but we certainly shan't waste any time in that endeavor, Mama. I fully anticipate we shall present you a grandchild in the very near future. Eh, my love?"

His lordship beamed as well, and Miranda shot him a furious glare down the length of the table.

"I can scarcely credit the testimony of my own senses," Elizabeth said happily. "Frankly, my dear, I had quite given up on Anthony; I feared he would remain an incorrigible rake the rest of his days. I believe it simply serves to prove that a good woman, the *right* woman, can work wonders upon a man. Nevertheless the change is utterly astonishing. When Anthony told me of his wedding gift to you—" Elizabeth gasped and clapped one hand over her mouth. "Oh, dear; it was supposed to be a surprise, wasn't it?"

"There's no harm in it, Mama," Anthony assured her. "Miranda had already got wind of it."

"Got wind of what?" Miranda asked suspiciously.

"I have bought you a country home, my love; I made the final arrangements yesterday. I fancy it represents a perfect compromise. It is located in southern Hertfordshire, near enough to London that we can come to town as often as we please, yet far enough to offer the benefits of privacy and country air. I daresay it will become our primary residence, and it will certainly be a splendid location for the raising of a family."

"Do you see what I mean, my dear?" Elizabeth said rhetorically. "I can hardly believe that my son has developed a fondness for the country, discovered the joys of family life . . ."

Elizabeth plucked her napkin off her lap and dabbed for a moment at her eyes, and Miranda suppressed an inclination to hurl her coffee cup at Anthony's head.

"Well," Elizabeth sniffled, "I believe I had best complete my unpacking. Once I am settled, my dear, you and I shall become *thoroughly* acquainted."

"Settled" had exceedingly ominous implications, Miranda thought grimly, but she tendered a tremulous smile. "Yes, Mother Elizabeth," she murmured.

The three of them rose, Miranda struggling up a bit tardily, and Anthony escorted his mother to the archway. Elizabeth tripped on into the dining room, and Anthony turned and flashed his most engaging grin.

"If you will excuse me, my love, I still have some plans to make in regards to the Hertfordshire property—"

"How dare you!" Miranda screeched.

"Miranda, please." Anthony hobbled to the foot of the table and thrust her back into her chair. "You really must try to be more discreet, my dear." He pulled one of the side chairs to the corner of the table and sat down. "Now, quietly, my love, pray tell me what distresses you."

He had laid his hand not an inch from hers on the linen tablecloth, and, beneath the table, their knees were nearly touching. Miranda recollected the shocking moment he had seized her in his arms, taken shameless advantage of his mother's presence to make a most improper advance. But the Earl's maddening half-smile was playing at the corners of his mouth, and Miranda vowed not to reveal how violently his kiss had overset her.

94

"You know quite well what distresses me," she hissed. "If I may borrow your words, milord, your recent performance was entirely disgraceful. I neither know nor care why you elected to purchase property in Hertfordshire, but I object most strenuously to your claim that it was a wedding gift to me. And insofar as your absurd chatter about 'presenting' grandchildren and 'raising a family' is concerned, you cannot be so obtuse as to fail to perceive that you have immeasurably complicated our situation; and I can only presume that, from some perverse motive which totally escapes me, you deliberately set out to do so." It was probably the longest sentence Miranda had ever pronounced, and she was compelled to pause for breath.

"My motive was not in the least perverse," Anthony said mildly. "Though I regret to say it, it is quite likely that this will be Mama's last journey to England. I saw no harm in persuading her that her dreams have been realized, in sending her home with happy memories and bright expectations."

"Speaking of expectations, milord, just when do you expect your mother to return to Jamaica?"

"Ahem." Anthony coughed and flicked an imaginary speck of lint from the immaculate lapel of his azure frock coat. "Mama did indicate that she might wish to stay on as late as Christmas."

"Christmas!" Miranda yelped.

"Shh! Please, my dear, discretion. I am confident that we can devise some sort of arrangement. Mama will no doubt want to visit relatives—"

"I thought you *had* no relatives," Miranda interrupted.

"Ahem." Anthony coughed again and fumbled with his snowy neckcloth. "I am, as I said, certain we can reach a mutually satisfactory agreement. I shall, of course, increase your remuneration commensurate with your additional length of service. And, as it does appear that you will be required to continue in my employment beyond the end of the Season, you will certainly need further clothes. I suggest you repair to Madame Leclair's tomorrow and order a dozen new gowns." Miranda scowled. "Two dozen?"

It was patently a bribe, but Miranda glimpsed no avenue of escape. None, at any rate, that would not break Elizabeth's maternal heart and, at the same time, create a sordid scandal amongst the London *ton*.

"Very well," she said coldly. "But I warn you, Anthony, that I plan to leave at the earliest suitable opportunity."

"Yes, yes." The Earl patted her hand, and Miranda snatched it away. "I knew you would behave in a sensible manner, my love."

"And stop calling me 'my love,'" Miranda snapped.

"Yes, my love."

Anthony rose, bowed, limped out, and Miranda flung her napkin in his wake.

Miranda had intended to take immediate advantage of his lordship's calculated generosity, but she woke on Monday morning to the drum of rain upon her windows and, when she peered out, beheld a thoroughly dark and dismal day.

"And cold, ma'am," Cassy informed her, clearing away Miranda's breakfast tray. "I daresay you will be quite comfortable in the gray."

The abigail assisted Miranda into the Circassian-cloth walking dress, propelled her to one of the chairs, seated her and tucked a blanket round her knees.

"There. Would you care for something to read?" She plucked one of Mr. Walpole's books off the mahogany writing table and placed it in Miranda's hands. "I really must advise you not to go out, for this is just the sort of day to send you into a relapse. Indeed, Mrs. Pennington is *most* concerned about your health. 'Miranda doesn't actually seem a delicate girl,' she said, 'but—' What was the term she used? 'High-strung'; that was it. 'She appears to me to be exceedingly nervous and high-strung,' Mrs. Pennington said. 'Of course I understand, twice over, the trials of a bride—'"

"That will be all, Cassy," Miranda said firmly.

"Yes, ma'am."

Cassy curtsied out, and Miranda opened the book. Within an hour, she was unquestionably shivering, whether as a result of the horrors of *The Castle of Otranto* or the damp chill of the room she could not be certain. There was a knock on the door, and Miranda smashed the book shut, painfully crushing one of her forefingers between the covers.

"Come in, Cassy," she quavered.

The door creaked slowly inward, and Miranda's eyes began to water with terror. Perhaps Anthony had chosen the most expeditious, most "sensible," most final means of ending their charade.

"It is not Cassy," Elizabeth said cheerfully, peeping round the door. "I thought to avail myself of the wretched day for a little chat." She closed the door and started across the room, stopped and examined Miranda with shock. "But you look altogether distraught, my dear. I should hate to learn that Anthony is—is mistreating you."

Elizabeth's pursed lips left no doubt as to the nature of the mistreatment she envisioned, and Miranda felt her cheeks coloring. "No—no, nothing like that," she stammered. "I was just reading the most frightful book." She hastily set Mr. Walpole's dreadful tale on the carpet.

"Anthony did mention that you are an avid reader." Elizabeth perched on the edge of the canopied bed. "But I am naturally eager to know *all* about you, and I collected, after last night, that I should have to seek you out if we were ever to have a private moment." Elizabeth frowned. "I was not aware until the dinner hour that there is another woman in residence. I must own that I find the situation a trifle peculiar."

"Yes," Miranda agreed. "Er—no. That is to say, Anthony met Jeanne—the Comtesse—while he was serving in France, and she was very—kind to him. When she subsequently lost her husband, he felt duty-bound to take her in. Temporarily, of course."

"Anthony." Elizabeth fondly shook her head. "The dear boy has always been magnanimous to a fault. I should have surmised the circumstances at once, for it is quite apparent that Anthony has forgone all forms of improper behavior."

Miranda wondered what Elizabeth's reaction would be if she were to learn that her "dear boy" was conducting a torrid *affaire* with an opera performer. "Quite," she choked aloud.

"And Sir Humphrey?" Elizabeth asked. "It appears that he and Madame de Chavannes are rather—fond of one another." She frowned again, apparently recalling the giggles and gropings which had punctuated the meal from first course to last.

"Yes, they have just become engaged," Miranda said. "It was an exceedingly rapid courtship."

"Much like your own." Elizabeth smiled. "Anthony informs me that he was utterly *bouleversé,* and I can only assume that the attraction was mutual."

"Uh—yes," Miranda said.

"I believe he indicated that the two of you met in Berkshire? Where you were employed as a governess?"

"Uh—yes."

"Do not hesitate to confess it, my dear, for tending children is a highly respectable profession. Indeed, I must own myself most relieved; I often entertained fears that Anthony might become embroiled with an actress or some such person. How very fortunate that he did not."

"Fortunate," Miranda echoed weakly.

"You were employed by your cousin, were you not? A Mr.—" Elizabeth wrinkled her red-gold brows.

Miranda hesitated. Might Anthony have told his mother at least a portion of the truth? In view of the Earl's propensity, and glib facility, for invention, she suspected not. "Smith," she supplied, remembering the name his lordship had so casually tossed to Madame Leclair.

"Yes, that was it. Mr. Smith. I understand your life was not entirely happy."

"Not entirely, no," Miranda confirmed dryly.

"Well, that is all in the past," Elizabeth said kindly. "I

have every confidence that you and Anthony will spend long and joyful years together. And *fruitful* years," she added, gazing significantly at Miranda's waistline.

Miranda flushed again and quelled an urge to cross her arms protectively over her stomach. "I do pray so," she muttered.

"Well." Elizabeth glanced brightly about the room. "The house has not changed in the least since poor Althea's death. Have you noticed, my dear, that the counterpane is a bit threadbare?" Elizabeth indicated a minuscule tear tucked well out of sight behind one of the draperies.

"No, I had not," Miranda said.

"If I may be perfectly frank, it is symptomatic of a general deterioration throughout the premises. I could not but observe, for example, that the drawing-room upholstery is *quite* faded. I never did share Althea's taste, and now that her dreadful blues are going to gray, the effect is really most unpleasant. In short, my dear, I must counsel you to redecorate the place from top to bottom."

"Redecorate?" Miranda gasped. "I—I do not disagree with your judgment, Mother Elizabeth, but I do feel that any such undertaking would be decidedly premature."

"Nonsense. A woman must take these matters firmly in hand. I can scarcely describe the execrable condition of dear Harry's house when I arrived upon the scene. I was naturally reluctant to imply any criticism of Harry's late first wife, but I forced myself to plunge in at once, and the result was well worth my efforts."

"I'm sure it was," Miranda said, desperately groping for a courteous, credible escape. "But you had had years of experience, Mother Elizabeth—"

"And I shall be delighted to assist you; indeed, I was hoping you would ask. We shall begin shopping for furniture and fabrics immediately, and I daresay the house will be entirely refurbished well before Christmas."

"Immediately," Miranda gulped. "Do you not think it would be best to wait until after the Season? Yes, the Allied Monarchs are arriving momentarily." She seized upon the first excuse that came to mind. "I believe Anthony and I shall be *quite* occupied during their visit."

"You're such a clever girl, my dear," Elizabeth said approvingly. "You're quite right: London is altogether dead in the late summer, and we shall be able to do this house and the Hertfordshire property simultaneously. And I daresay we shall negotiate a few bargains in the process. Oh, it will be splendid fun!" Elizabeth consulted her watch and rose. "Well, I fancy it is time for lunch. Will you join me?"

"Thank you, no," Miranda mumbled. "I am not hungry."

"Nevertheless you must eat; you are entirely too thin for child-bearing. I shall instruct your abigail to bring up a tray. Good day, my dear."

Elizabeth fairly danced out of the room, and Miranda stared miserably after her. Christmas? Christmas was better than six months away, six interminable months of "furniture and fabrics" and "splendid fun," six months of daily physical inspection.

Miranda retrieved her book and soon decided that, relative to her own circumstances, Mr. Walpole's castle was a very cheerful place.

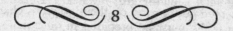

8

The rain ended in mid-afternoon, and twilight brought a twinkle of stars. Miranda was sufficiently confident of the weather to announce at dinner that she would make her journey to Madame Leclair's on the morrow.

"Consequently, I shall require the landau," she concluded.

"That may prove awkward, my dear," Anthony said. "Jeanne and Hammond have requested the loan of the curricle again. Where is it you're going?" He frowned at Sir Humphrey and the Comtesse, seated unnecessarily close on the far side of the table.

"To arrange our wedding," the baronet replied. "We have determined to be wed on the sixteenth which, as it happens, is dear Jeanne's birthday."

Sir Humphrey patted the Comtesse's knee, and she fairly coiled herself about his arm. In view of their increasingly shocking behavior, Miranda judged it fortunate that the nuptials were to occur in just above a week's time.

"Congratulations," Anthony said absently. "At any rate, I have business matters to attend tomorrow, and I fear I shall need the landau myself."

"How very inconvenient," Miranda snapped. "As I recall, it was you who insisted that I was to return to the mantua-maker's. It would appear you have now changed your mind. But then it is a part of the human condition to change one's mind, is it not, milord?"

Miranda glanced meaningfully at Elizabeth, who was wolfing down her pigeon pie, and Anthony coughed.

"I deeply regret my thoughtlessness, my love. You must, of course, take the landau. May I ask, however,

101

that you schedule an early start so as to have the carriage back by noon?"

"Certainly," Miranda cooed.

She stabbed triumphantly at her own pie. If his lordship expected her to carry on their ludicrous charade for half a year, he must be prepared to offer more than a handful of new gowns.

It was, in fact, just after nine when Miranda descended the stairs, for she feared, given any opportunity, Elizabeth would elect to join her. Cassy accompanied her mistress to the door, sternly instructing her not to order another thing in pink.

"And do not permit so many flounces on the day dresses, ma'am, and remember that you look handsomer in brown than black . . ."

Miranda nodded and hurried to the landau.

There was little traffic at this hour, and they reached Conduit Street in under a quarter of an hour. Johnson assisted Miranda out of the carriage, and she was idly surprised to note another landau already drawn up in front of Madame Leclair's establishment. Johnson escorted Miranda perfunctorily to the door, then rushed back to see to Daffodil. He studied the bay mare from several angles, prodded her flanks, knelt and peered at her underbelly. Miranda, reminded of Elizabeth's passionate interest in her own procreative capabilities, blushed and proceeded inside.

The shop was empty, but a bell upon the door stridently proclaimed Miranda's entrance. She paused to finger a display gown, and a clerk scurried out from the rear of the store.

"Bonjour, Madame!"

The clerk bustled forward, chattering in French. From the few words Miranda understood (*très belle, merveilleuse*), she inferred that the clerk was eagerly recommending this particular style for Madame's consideration.

"I do not speak French," Miranda said at last. "I fancy it would be best if I could see Madame Leclair."

"Madame Leclair." The clerk shook her head and launched into a lengthy explanation. Miranda eventually

picked out the phrase *"Madame s'occupe"* and collected that the mantua-maker was busy with another client.

"Will she be long?" Miranda asked.

The clerk brightened. "Long, short, any way you want."

"I really must see Madame Leclair," Miranda sighed, "and I am in a bit of a hurry." The clerk's smile grew distinctly frozen. *"In—a—hurry,"* Miranda repeated. She had a vague theory that English, if pronounced slowly and clearly enough, was universally comprehensible. *"Now.* I must see Madame *now."*

The clerk's smile had begun to wilt at the edges, and she caressed the display gown as if for support.

"I am Lady Margrave," Miranda said. Surely the seamstress had advised her assistants that his lordship was one of their "foremost" customers. *"Margrave,"* Miranda stressed.

"Margrave! Oui, Margrave!" The clerk snapped her fingers and sped away.

Miranda crossed to the counter and absently leafed through one of Madame's sketchbooks. She found a walking dress she thought Cassy would approve—a tailored gown trimmed in simple easings round the hem—and a pelisse suitable for winter. She decided, Cassy's advice notwithstanding, to order the pelisse in black.

"Voilà!" The clerk staggered out from the rear of the shop and dumped three enormous boxes upon the counter. *"Voilà,"* she panted again. *"Les robes pour Margrave, oui?"*

"I believe you have made an error," Miranda said kindly. "I did not come to fetch any robes—er—dresses, but to order some. These are not mine."

The clerk smiled and bobbed her head. Miranda heard the demanding tinkle of the doorbell, and the clerk glanced up and nodded at the new arrival. She looked back at Miranda and smiled again.

"They—are—not—mine," Miranda insisted. She glimpsed a scrawl in the corner of the topmost box and pointed to it. "You see? These clothes are for a person named Savino."

Savino! Miranda smashed her fist into the box, and the clerk leaped instinctively to one side.

"Wrong color?" she asked anxiously. "Wrong size?"

"The wrong *woman*," Miranda said furiously.

Apparently Madame's assistant had not heard this criticism before, for she looked exceedingly puzzled and not a little frightened. Miranda's thoughts were clouded with rage, but she distantly realized that she should drop the matter at once: any further conversation, or attempt thereat, could only add to her humiliation.

"Never mind," she snapped. "I shall pursue the subject at a more convenient time."

She whirled around, and her eyes fell upon the new customer. The woman was inspecting one of the display gowns, her back to Miranda, but there was something tantalizingly familiar about her posture. It would bear the palm, Miranda thought grimly, if she were to encounter Mrs. Turner or Mrs. Mead or one of the numerous prim ladies she had thus far met in London. The client half turned, seeking a different perspective, and Miranda's heart crashed into her throat. Martha! It couldn't be, but it was—Martha Cavendish! Miranda spun back to the counter.

"Wrong *style!*" the clerk suggested triumphantly.

"Never mind!" Miranda hissed. "I shall discuss it with Madame Leclair."

"Madame Leclair," the clerk agreed at last, and, to Miranda's horror, she trotted into the rear of the shop.

Dear God! Miranda's hands had grown quite soggy, and she ripped off her gloves and shoved them into her reticule. She must escape at once, before Madame Leclair appeared, but how? Though the shop contained a profusion of mirrors, none of them provided Miranda a view of Martha, and she tried to reconstruct their relative positions. Martha, as she recollected, was near the front of the establishment, to the right of the door, and Miranda stood at the back and left. It seemed, therefore, that she could slip along the left-hand perimeter and reach the door without exposing her face or barging into her cousin.

Miranda took a deep breath and began to creep, crabwise, down the side of the room. She had previously judged Madame Leclair's shop a small one, but it seemed now to have assumed the proportions of a largish castle. She ventured a sidewards peep and gauged herself twenty feet from the door, fifteen, ten. When she reckoned the remaining distance as no more than eight feet, she elected to risk a final sprint. She turned, started to bolt and stumbled into one of the delicate chairs scattered randomly about the showroom. Miranda and the chair went down together in a hopeless tangle of wooden legs and muslin flounces.

"Oh, I *say!*" Miranda felt hands tugging at her skirt, then watched as the chair, as if by magic, rose into the air. "Fortunately it isn't damaged," Martha said.

"Thank you," Miranda choked. She averted her face and scrambled to her feet. "Thank you very much." She proceeded frantically toward the door, but she had twisted her left ankle a bit, and it buckled beneath her.

"Were *you* injured?" Martha belatedly asked.

"No. No, really I am fine." Miranda resumed her headlong flight as best she could: STEP-step, STEP-step . . .

"But you are not fine at all; you are limping. And your bonnet is all askew; here, permit me to straighten it." Martha's thin arm snaked out and propelled Miranda about, and her eyes widened. "Miranda?" she gasped. "Is it you, Miranda?"

"Martha!" If Miranda had intended to feign surprise, she could not have been more persuasive, for her voice emerged a veritable shriek. "I did not *dream* that I should encounter you in London." This, at least, was true.

"I suppose not," Martha said coolly, "for Thomas and I were always reluctant to go on holiday." She jerked Miranda's leghorn hat unceremoniously into place. "I am happy to say that our circumstances have improved immeasurably, for we have found a *competent* governess to assist Nanny with the children."

"How nice," Miranda mumbled. "Well, I'm afraid I must be off—"

"Though I must own that Mrs. Dutton is our second replacement. The first was a local girl, Catherine Stark. Perhaps you remember her?"

"I believe so," Miranda muttered. "But I fear I really should be underway—"

"Catherine proved altogether unsatisfactory," Martha sighed. "She was totally unable to get on with the twins; why I cannot imagine."

"No, indeed," Miranda said. "Well, it was lovely to see you, Martha—"

"Mrs. Dutton, however, is perfect. It is an enormous relief to Thomas and me to have *confidence* in our employees. Nevertheless I was astonished when Thomas proposed quite suddenly—Saturday, I think it was, or was it Friday?—proposed, as I say, quite suddenly that we journey to town. 'We haven't been to the city for years, my dear,' Thomas said, 'and I daresay a holiday would benefit the both of us.'"

"As I am sure it will," Miranda said. "And do extend my fondest regards to Thomas." She negotiated a desperate step or two toward the door.

"But what are *you* doing here, Miranda?" Martha performed a swift but keen inspection, and Miranda hoped her collision with the chair had rendered her suitably untidy. "I daresay you are on an errand for your mistress. Mrs. Burton, is it not?"

"Yes," Miranda murmured. "Well, good day, Martha, and pray do remember me to Thomas—"

"Lady Margrave!" Madame Leclair sailed from the rear of the shop, her tape measure fairly flapping in the breeze. She granted Martha a cool nod, then transferred her attention back to Miranda. "Please accept my most humble apologies, Lady Margrave."

"Lady Margrave?" Martha peered around and apparently confirmed that no third person lurked behind the draperies. "Lady Margrave?" she repeated wonderingly.

"I am given to understand that there was some slight confusion," the mantua-maker continued smoothly. "My assistant somehow conceived the notion that these gowns were yours." Madame whisked the offending boxes out of sight beneath the counter. "They are not, of course, and I do trust you will overlook the error. Now, how may I serve you, Lady Margrave?"

"Lady—Margrave." Martha had gone quite pale.

"You are alone today?" Madame Leclair inquired. "I regret that the Earl could not accompany you."

"The—Earl," Martha echoed. "The—Earl." Her eyes widened again, but she looked, this time, as though she were waking from an exquisite dream. "Miranda!" she squealed.

"You are acquainted?" The mantua-maker bounded forward, clearly warming to her heretofore anonymous new client.

"Lady Margrave is my cousin!" Martha ecstatically confirmed. "My very own, very dear cousin!"

"You are Mrs. Smith then," Madame said dubiously.

"No, Mrs. Cavendish." Martha seized Miranda's hands and rushed on. "But why did you not tell us, Miranda? Mrs. Stubbs recounted your remark about becoming a countess, but she thought, we *all* thought, you were jesting. Whyever did you fabricate a tale about Mr. Burton and being a governess and all of that?"

"That," Miranda gulped. She cast frantically about for a credible explanation. "Anthony, the—the Earl, that is, wished to inform his mother of our marriage first, and she was on her way to England at the time; in fact, she arrived just three days since—"

"And I've no doubt you would have advised us of your happy news posthaste." Martha squeezed Miranda's hands until the knuckles cracked most alarmingly. "I always knew you would be a splendid success, Miranda. I have often said to Thomas, 'Thomas,' I have said, 'a girl of Miranda's beauty, Miranda's cleverness, is destined to be a splendid success. Indeed,' I said, 'indeed, it is entirely possible that Miranda will end up a countess!' "

Martha flung Miranda's hands joyfully away and clapped her own. "Oh, I can scarcely wait to meet the Earl, and I fancy Thomas will be as thrilled, nay, *more* thrilled, than I. Unfortunately Thomas is attending some sort of business meeting today, but we shall *definitely* call tomorrow. Just where are you residing?"

Miranda glimpsed a slender ray of hope and put her newly inventive mind to work. Perhaps she could manufacture a fictional address that would keep the Cavendishes wandering aimlessly about throughout their stay in London.

"Charles Street," Madame Leclair supplied helpfully. "Number eight."

"Eight Charles Street." Martha clapped her hands again. "We shall certainly be there tomorrow, Miranda. In the interim, you *must* advise me as to the latest fashions."

Before Miranda could demur, Madame steered them both to the counter and eagerly opened her sketchbooks.

The morning seemed endless, but it was, in truth, not yet noon when the landau returned to Charles Street. Though Miranda had ordered the full two dozen gowns proposed by his lordship, she felt herself quite inadequately compensated for her trials, and she slammed the front door with a resounding crash.

"Ah, Miranda." The Earl sauntered out of the parlor. "You are exceedingly punctual, my love. Did you have a pleasant excursion?"

"I had a *miserable* excursion," Miranda snapped. She became belatedly aware that Horton had materialized in the dining-room archway, and she granted the butler a frigid smile and yanked Anthony back into the parlor. "I encountered *Martha!*" she hissed.

"Martha?" His lordship frowned, evidently attempting to recollect if he had a "friend" of this name. Eventually he shook his head with some relief. "Who is Martha?"

"Martha Cavendish, my cousin. The one who saw me off to London not a month ago. Saw me off to be a *governess*, if you recall."

"I am sure you advised her that even a governess requires the odd new dress or two."

"I had no chance to advise her of anything because Madame Leclair was brightly addressing me as 'Lady

108

Margrave' and regretting that 'the Earl'—my adoring husband—could not be with me."

"Well, do not tease yourself about it," Anthony said airily. "I shouldn't suppose you will meet up with her again."

"Oh, but I shall, milord, and you as well. Martha is coming to call tomorrow, with Thomas in tow. Perhaps you see, now it's too late, the complications I tried to warn you of." Miranda realized that she was being a trifle unfair, but she had to blame *someone* for her wretched predicament. "I believe I neglected to mention an additional complication. Your mother insists that she and I are to redecorate the house. Houses, I should have said: this one, the Hertfordshire property; maybe she will decide to redo everything before she is through."

"Mama does have excellent taste," Anthony said blithely. "And I daresay my various homes could bear a bit of improvement."

He was utterly, maddeningly unconcerned, and Miranda felt her temper, which had hung by the merest thread, altogether snap.

"There is one other matter I wish to bring to your attention, milord," she said furiously. "I experienced a second unwelcome surprise at Madame Leclair's this morning when her assistant presented me three great boxes of gowns. I now lament that I did not open them so as to determine *Signorina Savino's* preferences and size."

"They are ready then," Anthony said cheerfully. "I must ask Madame Leclair to deliver them."

"Would it not be simpler if you were to deliver them yourself?" Miranda spat. "On one of your daily visits to the Signorina?"

"Daily visits?" Anthony raised his brows, and his scar disappeared beneath the red-gold fringe of his hair. "As it happens, I have not seen Mary Anne since your own arrival in London, my love. I ordered her gowns weeks since, and Madame Leclair informed me, due to the exigencies of the Season, that they would not be finished for some time. Now that they are, there seems little reason to cancel the order, which I should be compelled to pay for at any rate. Consequently, I shall, I repeat, instruct Madame to deliver them at once."

"You might also *instruct* Madame Leclair to *instruct* her assistants to exercise a great deal more caution in the future. I fancy you are not the only client who is outfitting a barque of frailty as well as a wife."

"I fancy not." There was a familiar twitch at the corners of his lordship's mouth. "One might almost suspect, my dear, that you are jealous of Mary Anne."

"That is quite the most absurd notion you have ever conceived," Miranda said icily. "However, I warn you, milord, that if our ridiculous charade is to continue, as, in view of your deplorable planning, apparently it must, I will not be held up to ridicule. You recently counseled me to exercise discretion, and I strenuously recommend that you follow the same advice."

Miranda whirled about and stalked out of the parlor. She thought she detected a low chuckle behind her, but she refused to titillate the Earl's perverse sense of humor by turning back to look.

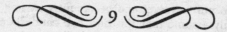

Not knowing the precise hour at which to expect her cousins' unwelcome call, Miranda instructed Cassy to wake her at eight, and she was dressed and coiffed by nine.

"Now you must allow yourself ample time to prepare for the reception this evening," Cassy admonished, fussing with the peach-gauze trim round the bottom of Miranda's skirt. "And do you not think you should wear the yellow lace, ma'am? Surely this qualifies as a special occasion: an evening at *Carlton House!*" The abigail straightened and regarded her mistress with glowing, pleading eyes.

"I daresay it does, Cassy," Miranda agreed. "Very well, the yellow lace it is."

"Oh, *splendid*, ma'am!" Cassy clapped her hands. "I shall see it's ready and arrange for your bath. You may leave everything to me, Lady Margrave."

The little maid skipped gaily into the corridor, and Miranda walked to the window and peered out. But she could not see the street from her vantage point, and she decided she would simply have to wait until Horton advised her of the Cavendishes' arrival. She sank into one of the striped-silk chairs and attempted to finish *The Castle of Otranto*; but her mind soon began to wander, and she laid the book aside.

Was it possible that Anthony, as he claimed, had not seen Signorina Savino since Miranda's arrival in London? She could conceive no reason for the Earl to lie about the situation, and it would certainly be characteristic of his lordship to cast aside a paramour with no more thought, no more regret, than a frayed and graying neckcloth.

And he had apparently been truthful about the numerous appointments required to inspect and secure the Hertfordshire property.

That was another mystery: why would Anthony choose to purchase yet another country estate? Miranda could only assume that the Earl had candidly confessed his concern about the future as well, and the Hertfordshire property no doubt represented an excellent investment. Anthony, of course, had elected to embellish the circumstances of the acquisition for Elizabeth's benefit.

Elizabeth! Miranda snapped her fingers. She must ensure that her "mother-in-law" not encounter Thomas and Martha, and there had been no opportunity to discuss the matter yesterday. Miranda believed his lordship should be the one to invent a suitable tale for his mother, and she leaped up, hurried into the hall and tapped on Anthony's bedchamber door.

"Lady Margrave." Parker, Anthony's valet, frowned. "Did I fail to hear you at the connecting door?"

"Uh—no," Miranda mumbled. "I was just coming up the stairs, and it occurred to me that I must speak with his lordship."

"Well, I regret to say that he is away from home, ma'am. He has gone to Guthrie's to get his ensemble for the evening. I could not say when he might return."

"I see. Thank you, Parker."

Miranda slipped back to her own room, heaving a sigh of relief. There was every hope that Thomas and Martha would come and go before Anthony finished with his tailor. Her cousins would be bitterly disappointed, of course, and Miranda would be compelled to fabricate an excuse to keep them at bay for the remainder of their holiday. Perhaps she should say that she and Anthony were departing tomorrow for the country; yes, that would be perfect. Miranda was dismayed to realize that she was perspiring quite profusely, and she patted her face with one of her new linen handkerchiefs before she sank back into the chair.

Miranda had just completed Mr. Walpole's book and slammed it closed with a final shudder when Cassy bounded through the door. Miranda nearly started out of her seat, and Cassy skidded to a halt at the edge of the Brussels carpet.

"Oh, I am sorry, ma'am. I should be more careful to knock; Mrs. Horton is always reminding me of that. At any rate, *Mr.* Horton sent me up to advise you that you have callers. A Mr. and Mrs. Cavendish. They *say* they are your cousins."

Cassy's lips thinned with disapproval, and Miranda was briefly tempted to send Thomas and Martha away. If the necessity arose, she could later insist that her servants had erred. . . . She shook her head.

"They are *not* your cousins?" Cassy said joyfully.

"Yes, they are," Miranda sighed. "Please desire Horton to show them to the drawing room, Cassy. I shall be down directly."

Miranda spent a full five minutes fumbling with the *rouleaux* around her sleeves and another five repairing her immaculately coiffed hair. Eventually she perceived that the longer she delayed, the greater the likelihood of Anthony's return, and she dragged herself to the saloon.

"Miranda!" Thomas jumped to his feet and rushed to the archway, tripping over his old-fashioned, ill-fitting top boots. "My dear, darling girl!" He planted a damp, fervent kiss in the vicinity of her right temple. "We planned to be here earlier; indeed, we have been underway for upwards of an hour. But the traffic is beastly; it seems the entire populace has taken to the streets in hopes of glimpsing His Royal Highness or Their Majesties or one of our brave Allied generals. It is a magnificent day for England, is it not?"

Thomas stood her slightly away and beamed down upon her. "And how magnificent *you* look, my dear! I always suspected that a ravishing beauty lurked just beneath your motley old gowns and bonnets."

Miranda decided not to point out that her "motley" attire had been entirely due to Thomas's clutch-fisted ways. "You look quite well, too, Thomas," she said. In fact, he looked as he had since late adolescence: plump, florid and balding.

"And where is the Earl?" Thomas peered eagerly over Miranda's shoulder.

Miranda essayed another sigh. "Unfortunately, Anthony is out," she replied. "He had a number of errands, chief among them a visit to Guthrie's."

"Guthrie's," Thomas echoed approvingly. "My tailor as well." He tugged up his sagging pantaloons, minutely narrowing the gap between them and his waistcoat, which was several sizes too snug. "And when will he be back?"

"Not for hours, I should suppose." Miranda mournfully shook her head. "I am certain he will be caught up in the traffic as well, and he was *so* anxious to meet you."

"We shall wait then," Martha said brightly, burrowing into the blue-silk sofa.

"Wait," Miranda gulped. "I fear that would be inconvenient, Martha. Anthony, when he does return, will need to dress for the reception; I myself was at the point of doing so when you arrived." Miranda hoped neither of her cousins would note that the mantel clock was just striking noon. "I should naturally adore to invite you back tomorrow, but, as it happens, Anthony and I are leaving for Hertfordshire—"

"Miranda?" Anthony strode through the archway, vainly attempting to reorder his windblown, red-gold hair. "Horton informed me that your cousins had come, and I am *delighted* not to have missed them. Mrs. Cavendish?" He swept an exceedingly courtly bow, and Martha sprang up, snagged her toe in the hem of her skirt and narrowly missed a headlong dive over the table in front of the couch. "Mr. Cavendish?" The Earl extended his hand.

"Your Grace," Thomas murmured, reverently and incorrectly. Miranda thought for one awful moment that her cousin intended to kneel and kiss Anthony's outstretched fingers, but Thomas confined himself to seizing said fingers in both of his own pudgy hands. "I can scarcely express *my* delight in making your acquaintance. Though, I must own, I feel I have known

114

you for years; my close relative, the Marquess of Washburn, speaks of you often and fondly."

"Indeed?" Anthony said jovially. "How peculiar that Washburn has never mentioned your connection to me. I fancy he has grown a trifle forgetful in his dotage, eh, Mr. Cavendish?"

"I fancy so." Thomas dropped Anthony's hand and jerked up his pantaloons again.

"Well, we shall certainly remind Lord Washburn of his oversight tonight, shall we not, Anthony?" Miranda's voice was alarmingly shrill. "I was advising Thomas and Martha, just prior to your arrival, that we must be preparing for the Regent's reception."

"The reception?" Anthony frowned at the clock, his scarred brow darting down his forehead. "The reception is hours away, my love; surely we have time for a cup of tea. See to it, please, Horton." Anthony nodded toward the archway, and, as often happened, Miranda became aware of the butler's presence only as he scurried away. "Though I daresay you would prefer something a bit stronger, Mr. Cavendish. A glass of sherry perhaps?"

"A spot of sherry would be most welcome indeed if it would pose no trouble." Thomas trailed the Earl to the cabinet near the hearth, and Miranda glared furiously after them. "I am particularly pleased to meet up with you today, Your Grace, since Miranda informs me that you are departing for Hertfordshire tomorrow."

"Hertfordshire?" Anthony glanced lazily round at Miranda, and she widened her eyes in frantic signal. "I believe we did discuss such a journey, but I have now decided against it. This promises to be an especially exciting Season; do you not agree, Mr. Cavendish?"

Thomas agreed most firmly, and the two men continued to chat as Anthony poured the sherry.

"He is *wonderful*, Miranda," Martha whispered. "So handsome, so charming . . ." Her voice trailed ecstatically off.

"Is he not?" Miranda snapped. She ground her fingernails into her palms, wondering what new means of torture the Earl might be devising.

"Hello?"

Elizabeth stood at the threshold, head cocked, eyes darting about the saloon. Clad in a gray and cerise gown, she resembled nothing so much as a curious robin.

"Pray forgive me. I heard voices. Naturally I've no wish to intrude—"

"Nonsense, Mama. Do come in. I am sure you will be pleased to meet Miranda's cousins, Mr. and Mrs. Cavendish. My mother, Mrs. Pennington."

There were nods and murmurs of greeting all round, after which, to Miranda's horror, Elizabeth ensconced herself firmly on the sofa.

"Mrs. Pennington," Martha trilled. "As I recollect, it was on your account that the Earl and Miranda kept their marriage a secret."

"A secret?" Elizabeth frowned. "I was unaware—"

"The news got about, of course," Anthony interrupted smoothly, "but we did succeed in surprising my mother. Did we not, Mama?"

"Indeed you did," Elizabeth agreed. "And a grand surprise it was to discover my son wed to such a lovely girl. I judge him most fortunate to have found dear Miranda, particularly in view of the circumstances." She frowned again. "I hope, Mrs. Cavendish, that you are not related to those dreadful Smiths."

"No," Miranda said hurriedly. "No, there is no connection. What *can* have delayed the tea?"

"Smiths?" It was Martha's turn to frown. "Who are the Smiths?"

"Miranda's other cousins, the ones in Berkshire. The ones with whom she was living—"

"I fear Mama is a trifle confused." Anthony fondly shook his head. "The fact is, it was a Mr. Smith, an acquaintance of mine in Berkshire, who suggested I introduce myself to Miranda. Mr. Smith had studied under Dr. Russell some years ago, and he encouraged me, should I find myself in Sussex, to seek out Dr. Russell's charming daughter."

"Sussex?" Elizabeth spoke as though the Earl had mentioned a remote outpost of the British Empire with which she was but vaguely familiar. "I am quite certain you stated that you met Miranda in Berkshire, a statement Miranda confirmed—"

"Just how *did* you meet?" Thomas interjected.

"Anthony was in Sussex to see to one of his estates . . ."

"I had traveled to Sussex to attend a boxing match . . ."

Their words emerged simultaneously, and simultaneously they fell silent. Miranda scowled at the Earl; he had got them into this morass, and he could extricate them.

"I had journeyed to Sussex to see to an estate, and I availed myself of the opportunity to attend a boxing match. It is a sport I greatly enjoy, though only as a spectator, I am sorry to say, since I suffered my wound."

Anthony assumed his martyred look, but the expression was lost on Thomas, who was now frowning as well.

"I did not realize that Your Grace owned property in Sussex," Thomas said. "And I had thought myself entirely informed as to the local landlords."

"I fear you misunderstood, Mr. Cavendish." Anthony splashed another portion of sherry into Thomas's glass, as if to imply that his lordship's guest had imbibed an excess of midday grape. "I traveled to Sussex with the intention of *purchasing* property. As you know, I selected an estate in Hertfordshire instead."

"What a pity," Martha sighed. "We might have been *neighbors.*"

"And then what transpired, Your Grace?" Thomas pressed.

"I recalled Miranda's name and sent a card, and Miranda agreed to meet me at the Knight and Dragon. I am confident that my dear Miranda will concur when I report that we developed a mutual, an instantaneous, *tendre* and decided to be married at once."

"How *romantic,*" Martha breathed.

Thomas, who was infinitesimally more sensible than his wife, continued to frown for a moment. But he apparently elected not to question his unexpected good fortune, for he soon beamed on Anthony and Miranda in turn.

"Romantic indeed," he said. "May I offer my sincerest congratulations, Your Grace?"

"You may." Anthony topped Thomas's glass again.

"I was *quite* certain that the Smiths were Miranda's cousins," Elizabeth insisted. "I was given to understand that Miranda was living in Berkshire . . ."

There was a rattle at the archway, and Elizabeth's voice trailed off. A young footman stumbled across the drawing room and managed to spill both the sugar and the milk when he set the tray on the table in front of the couch. As Miranda "helped" him mop up, she somehow dumped half a dozen lemon slices on the floor. A full ten minutes elapsed before the entire accident was set aright and the ladies were safely sipping their tea. In the interim, Anthony and Thomas had assumed the blue and gold chairs on the opposite side of the table. The Earl had brought the sherry decanter along, and each time Thomas sipped from his glass, Anthony hastily replenished it.

"What is it that brings you to town, Mr. Cavendish?" Anthony inquired pleasantly.

Sip, sip; trickle, trickle.

"Town," Thomas repeated. Whatever his faults, he was not an intemperate man, and his eyes had grown distinctly glazed. "Bushiness, Your Grashe. A conshern with which I am sure you will sympathesize, conshidering your own vasht—vasht—" But his lordship's interests were evidently so vast as to defy description.

"I *do* sympathize," Anthony said sympathetically. "Would you care for more sherry, Mr. Cavendish?"

"No!" Martha snapped.

"Yes, thank you, Your Grashe." Thomas extended his glass, and Anthony, though hard pressed to keep pace with its dipping, dancing rim, refilled it.

"However," Martha said, "now that we are here, we naturally wish to take full advantage of the city's many *activities.*" She fixed Thomas with a paralyzing stare, but he was attempting to extract a handkerchief from his pocket, apparently to wipe up the rivulet of wine he had

118

dribbled on the table. "Do we not, Thomas?" Martha said sharply.

"Yesh, my love," Thomas giggled.

Anthony plucked a linen napkin off the tea tray, dabbed up the spill and, with a kind smile, replenished Thomas's glass.

"What Thomas means to say," Martha continued, glowering at her husband, "is that we were very much in hopes of attending the Regent's reception this evening."

"Perhaps your relative, Lord Washburn, can obtain you an *entrée*," Anthony suggested.

"I did think to prey on the Marquesh, of course," Thomas said. Miranda was certain he had intended to say "prevail," though his actual usage was probably the more accurate. "However, I sheem somehow to have mishplashed his London addresh."

"That is unfortunate." Anthony shook his head. "I wish I could assist you, but I am afraid it is out of the question. In view of the large contingent of foreign guests, there were but a limited number of invitations issued. Indeed, I cannot gain access for my own dear mama."

"What a shame." Miranda's sigh sounded quite genuine, for her voice was fairly quivering with relief. "Well, as I indicated earlier, we really must be preparing for the reception." She crashed her cup into her saucer and rose. "I do hope we shall see you again before your return to Sussex. Though, in light of our very busy schedule, I fear it unlikely—"

"But it is not unlikely at all," Anthony said brightly. "As it happens, I have two extra tickets for the opera performance Saturday night. *On dit* that His Royal Highness and Their Allied Majesties will be in attendance, and I daresay the evening will be most entertaining. Will you join us, Mr. Cavendish? Mrs. Cavendish?"

Miranda surmised that her countenance must be very odd indeed, for she felt her mouth drop open with dismay and her eyes narrow with rage at nearly the same instant. Fortunately, no one seemed to notice: Martha was literally bouncing about the sofa, Thomas had almost fallen out of his chair, and Elizabeth was observing the antics of both.

"Of course we shall!" Martha squealed. "Of course we shall! Oh, I do hope Madame Leclair can complete a gown in time. The white lace would be perfect; do you not agree, Miranda?"

"Perhaps Anthony would consent to speak to Madame," Miranda said frigidly. "He has considerably more influence with her than with His Royal Highness."

"Be that as it may," Anthony said, "I believe Mrs. Cavendish may require *two* gowns, for I am confident that I can procure two additional vouchers for the Wednesday-night assembly at Almack's. But then you may be unable to remain in London for so extended a period, Mr. Cavendish; I fancy your numerous business enterprises demand constant attention."

"Conshtant," Thomas confirmed mournfully. "No, I musht certainly return to Shussex long before Wednesday—"

"Indeed you need not!" Martha screeched. "Almack's, Thomas! *Almack's!*" Miranda suspected that, quite apart from Thomas's "enterprises," Martha would allow the house to burn and the children to starve before relinquishing such an opportunity.

"Well, it is settled then," Anthony said cheerfully. "We shall see you on Saturday and again on Wednesday. I should like to request that we use your carriage as well as my own on both occasions, Mr. Cavendish. We shall have others in our party: my mama, of course, and some dear friends of ours, Sir Humphrey Hammond and the Comtesse de Chavannes."

"The Comtesse de Chavannes!" Martha, literally trembling with joy, pronounced the name much as Cassy had. "However can we repay you, milord?"

"No repayment is necessary," Anthony said nobly. "Indeed, I wish I could be of greater service to the family of my darling Miranda."

"I shall toasht to that, Your Grashe." Thomas drained his glass. "You've acquired a shplendid girl; make no mishtake about it. She was an exshellent governess, I might add, and we bitterly regretted her losh." Thomas's eyes had become a trifle moist, and he dabbed at them with the sherry-soaked napkin. "I only lament that Miranda's dear mother could not be with ush to share our happinesh—"

"I believe we had best be leaving," Martha said. "If you could but write a *small* note, milord, we shall stop at Madame Leclair's en route to the hotel . . ."

Anthony dashed a message on the back of one of his calling cards; then he and Martha assisted Thomas out of his chair. They proceeded slowly across the saloon, Thomas leaning alternately on his wife and his wonderful new cousin.

"I fear Mr. Cavendish's heavy responsibilities have temporarily bested him," Anthony clucked as they reached the corridor. "I trust he will be quite recovered by Saturday evening. And should you encounter any difficulty with Madame Leclair, pray do advise me, Mrs. Cavendish . . ."

They shuffled down the hall, started carefully down the stairs, and eventually their footsteps faded away.

"Well." Elizabeth finished her own tea and set her cup and saucer on the table. "They are a lovely couple, Miranda, though I note that Mr. Cavendish seems a bit overfond of spirits." She assumed her familiar frown. "I cannot conceive how I so totally misconstrued the circumstances of your and Anthony's meeting. I was *quite* persuaded that the Smiths were your cousins and that you were residing with them in Berkshire. Be honest with me, my dear; do you think my mind is deteriorating? I am not yet five-and-fifty, but my dear grandmother was altogether babbling before she reached her sixtieth year . . ." Elizabeth bit her lip.

"Your mind is perfectly acute, Mother Elizabeth," Miranda snapped. "I daresay Anthony's explanation was at fault. I often find his conversation exceedingly confusing."

Elizabeth was still puzzling, still frowning, as Miranda excused herself and rushed out of the room.

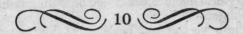

Miranda's toilette required nearly three hours, at the end of which Cassy loosed a stream of adjectives and adverbs that left her mistress's head awhirl.

"The gown is absolutely spectacular, ma'am," the abigail stated. "It suits your coloring superbly, and you look altogether dazzling in it. And your hair, if I do say so myself, is gorgeous."

Cassy was a trifle prejudiced, of course, and Miranda stood away from the mirror and critically examined her reflection. The pale yellow lace *did* complement her sherry-hued hair and eyes, she decided, and the low, tight *corsage*, done in a darker saffron shade, emphasized her smooth shoulders and seemed to augment her bosom. It had been Cassy's idea to bind the Barham pearls round Miranda's braid, leaving her neck bare, and the effect was quite dramatic. If she did not look "dazzling," Miranda thought, she looked as well as ever she had.

"We shall use the long earrings, ma'am," Cassy said, fumbling through the jewel box. "Yes, here they are; the teardrops."

She reached eagerly for her ladyship's right ear, but Miranda, after some weeks of painful experience, gently plucked the earrings from Cassy's hand and put them on herself. The little maid tugged her mistress's hands into the elbow-length white-kid gloves and at last pronounced Lady Margrave "ready."

Cassy escorted Miranda to the foyer, where, to Miranda's embarrassment, she found a veritable committee awaiting her. Horton and Mrs. Horton, Anthony, Elizabeth and Jeanne gazed simultaneously up as she

122

descended the final flight of stairs, but before any of them could acknowledge her arrival, Cassy was clapping her hands with delight.

"You look simply *stunning*, Lord Margrave!" the abigail declared. "Did you observe, ma'am, that his lordship's coat is *exactly* the color of your hair?"

As usual, Cassy's eye was true: above his white-satin breeches, Anthony wore a deep-brown coat which shimmered as he moved. The Earl strode forward to meet them, and Cassy clapped her hands again.

"You are the most *elegant* pair I have ever beheld," she breathed. "Like a vision from a dream."

"Are they not?" Elizabeth agreed. "It thrills one to imagine what *beautiful* children they will have."

Mrs. Horton blushed a bit at this shocking suggestion, but even she seemed rather awed, and the butler himself murmured that Lord and Lady Margrave were "exceedingly handsome." Jeanne remained silent for a moment, then emitted a mournful sigh.

"What a pity that we shall be unable to share your *triomphe*," she said. "Unfortunately, dear Humphrey has taken *quite* ill."

Apparently the baronet's invitation had failed to arrive after all, and Miranda surmised that he must be "quite ill" indeed. Anthony solemnly offered his hope that Sir Humphrey might soon be better, and, after adieus to all, steered Miranda to the landau. They occupied facing seats, and as the carriage got underway, the Earl examined Miranda with frank appreciation.

"You do look exquisite this evening, my love," he said. "Yellow becomes you most remarkably; how clever of you to insist on the gown."

"Do not think to turn me up sweet with your compliments," Miranda snapped. "I demand to know just what it is you're about."

"About?" Anthony echoed innocently. "I was under the impression that we were en route to Carlton House for what promises to be a glittering assembly."

"And I must own myself enormously relieved and altogether astonished that Thomas and Martha are not with us," Miranda said coldly. "Your generosity this afternoon was quite overwhelming."

"Ah, you no doubt refer to the fact that I served Mr. Cavendish a slight excess of sherry. I calculated that if your cousin's mind was a bit clouded, he might forget to pose some potentially awkward inquiries. You will recall that my strategy proved most effective: Mr. Cavendish did not pursue the circumstances of our meeting and our very swift courtship."

"Your strategy *would* have been 'most effective' had you rested the matter there," Miranda said. "However, *you* will recall that you then proceeded to invite Thomas and Martha to the opera. As if that were not sufficient, you subsequently encouraged them to extend their stay in London so as to accompany us to Almack's. So I shall ask again, milord: what are you at?"

"I saw no harm in it," Anthony said airily. "Your cousins are overjoyed at the prospect of mingling with their so-called betters; why should I not give them pleasure when I can do so at no inconvenience to myself? Furthermore, has it not occurred to you that the deeper they fall into our debt, the less the likelihood they will create any disturbance? Mr. Burke's observation to the contrary, I should not suppose the Cavendishes will turn and bite the hand that fed them."

"But you must see that their involvement renders our charade infinitely more difficult," Miranda protested. "What is to happen when I retire to the country to languish my life away? Thomas and Martha will certainly demand to visit their dear, suffering relative."

"We shall ponder that when the time is upon us."

"That is precisely my point," Miranda hissed. "I cannot conceive that there will ever *be* a convenient time for me to disappear. In view of your—your largesse, Thomas and Martha will be forever hovering in the background. How do you intend to be rid of them?"

"I shall consider that—"

"When the time is upon you," Miranda finished wearily.

Anthony flashed his engaging grin and launched into a

cheerful, tuneless whistle, and Miranda gazed at the floor of the landau. She had long entertained a notion that the Earl was deliberately contriving to complicate their situation, but she was quite unable to explain why he should choose to do so. Anthony's explanation, on the other hand, was altogether sensible, and any further objection on her part would sound extremely foolish. She contented herself with a final glare of annoyance, then stared studiedly out the window.

The streets had been unusually crowded almost from the outset of their journey, and as they clattered into Pall Mall, the crowd swelled to a veritable mob. The late editions of the papers had confirmed Thomas's report: throughout the day, the populace had congregated at the Pulteney Hotel in hopes of glimpsing the Czar; at Clarence House in hopes of seeing the King of Prussia; at Mr. Gordon's home in St. James's Park in hopes of paying tribute to Marshal General Blücher. Evidently the throng was now streaming toward Carlton House, intent on viewing not only the Allied Monarchs and military heroes but the cream of the English *ton* as well. At several points, Miranda thought they could not continue without running down a cluster of hapless pedestrians, but Pollard expertly maneuvered the carriage through the horde, and eventually they reached the huge Corinthian portico of Carlton House.

As they stepped into the entrance hall, Miranda vaguely recalled the debut she had envisioned—she and Anthony strolling into a great reception room, an attendant sonorously announcing them, His Highness bounding forward to greet them. The actual scene was a minute step above chaos: a harried footman inspected their cards of invitation and nodded them unceremoniously forward. They were immediately engulfed in a sea of frantic humanity; except for their silks and satins and jewels, the Regent's guests looked and behaved much as had the mob in the streets.

Miranda glanced at the porphyry columns, at the cornices adorned by Etruscan griffins and became aware that the crowd appeared to have formed a disorganized line, all moving in one direction. She was just beginning to speculate on where the line might be leading when Anthony introduced her to a Lord Coleraine. The three of them chatted a moment, if a conversation conducted entirely in shouts could be termed "chatting," and his lordship was swallowed up in the throng.

"Lord Coleraine is a close companion of His Highness's." Anthony spoke in a relative whisper, a tone only slightly above that of normal discourse. "He was, until recently, a Colonel George Hanger, and he was once married to a gypsy. He seems to have reformed since he inherited his brother's title."

Miranda had little opportunity to absorb this fascinating information, for Anthony soon presented her to Lord Castlereagh—a tall, gangling, surprisingly shy man—and Lord Liverpool, whose bold nose, set mouth and long, ungainly neck Miranda recognized from Mr. Cruikshank's caricatures. As Lord Liverpool bowed away, Anthony and Miranda moved through an archway, and Miranda perceived the purpose of the line. They were in the throne room, and Queen Charlotte, His Highness's mother, was holding court.

Miranda distantly noted the canopy of helmets and ostrich plumes and debated what she should say when Her Majesty engaged Lady Margrave in conversation. "What a splendid assembly, Your Majesty. The lanterns on the pillars are a lovely touch . . ." No. "I am certain you are exceedingly proud of your son, Your Majesty . . ." No; no, indeed.

As it happened, no comment was necessary, for the guests were being paraded before the stiff little Queen at the rate of some dozen per minute. Miranda scarcely had time to sweep her best curtsy, to receive a terse nod in turn, before a velvet-clad footman propelled her on. Eventually he released her, and she stopped, intending to wait for Anthony, but the relentless crowd encircled her, drove her on. By the time Anthony had paid his own respects to the Queen, his red-gold head was barely visible on the opposite shore of an ocean of waving plumes and sparkling diamonds and elegantly cut uniforms.

Miranda stood very quietly, as though she might thereby disappear. She reflected that Martha or Jeanne, either one, would take full advantage of the circumstances, would pluck at the nearest male sleeve and bat her eyes. "Pardon me, I am Lady Margrave, and I seem temporarily to have misplaced my husband . . ." But Martha and Jeanne, whatever their deficiencies, were *real*, and Miranda was not. She had never before so keenly felt her deception; had never so strongly perceived that she was an intruder. She opened her miniature ivory fan and waved it far more enthusiastically than the moderate heat of the room required.

"You do not enjoy yourself, Madame?"

"I am enjoying myself well enough," Miranda snapped. "I find the room a trifle warm."

She turned and glanced idly up. He was a tall man, dressed in a bottle-green uniform with great gold epaulets. His face was rather moon shaped, and his curving mouth was disproportionately small. He looked oddly familiar, but it was a long moment before Miranda connected him to the sketches in the evening papers.

"Your Majesty!" She gasped and dropped a deep curtsy to the Czar of Russia, nearly tumbling to the floor and half wishing she would. "I am, of course, enjoying myself *immensely*."

"Then I envy you, Madame. Lady? Mrs?" Alexander's brows darted up his very high forehead.

"Lady—Lady Margrave," Miranda stammered. "The Countess of Margrave."

"Lady Margrave." The Czar swept a courtly bow, as if she were the Empress and he a lowly footboy. "I myself judge the proceedings insufferably tedious. Consequently I indulge my—how do you say it?—my avocation?"

"Your hobby," Miranda gulped. Her mouth was so dry she could hardly speak. "And what might your hobby be, Your Majesty?"

"I greatly fancy beautiful women, and I discover the English ladies to be especially fetching. You, for example, possess coloring which is most *extraordinaire*."

"But it isn't extraordinary at all." ("Extrordnytall"; Miranda's words were falling all over one another.) "My hair is brown; my eyes are brown; I daresay you know many Russian ladies who look exactly like me." ("Zactlikme.")

"You seem nervous, Lady Margrave." The Czar's tiny mouth formed a kind smile. "Why is that?"

"It—it isn't every day one speaks to an Emperor." After the initial hesitation, Miranda thought she sounded quite coherent.

"But royal persons are often very average; if you are acquainted with His Highness, you surely realize that. No, the real heroes of the day are Marshal General Blücher and the Marquess of Wellington, who, I understand, has now been made a duke, and Platov, the leader of our own valiant Cossacks. I should like to present you to him, Lady Margrave."

Miranda was not certain who "him" was, and, at any rate, she was in no frame of mind to welcome an introduction to any of the alleged heroes. She was casting about for a polite demural when the Czar squinted over her shoulder and nodded with astonishing servility.

"But I fear any such presentation must wait, for my sister summons me." Miranda's eyes followed His Majesty's and fell upon the impossible Duchess of Oldenburgh, who was beckoning imperiously from across the room. "Pray excuse me, Lady Margrave, and never doubt that you are an extraordinary woman indeed."

The Emperor bowed away, and Miranda attempted to record every detail of their conversation, for, with appropriate amendments, she must surely relate the entire encounter to Cassy. She then looked about for Anthony, but the Earl seemed to have vanished. Not surprising: the crowd, after the obligatory introduction to Her Majesty, had apparently been left to wander quite freely about. Miranda, though she had no idea where she might be going, made her way to the far end of the throne room.

She soon reached an enormous circular dining room, and she came to a halt and gazed around in awe. The walls of the room were lined with pier glasses which seemed to turn the silver-topped Ionic columns into a forest of marble. Miranda was jostled impatiently from behind, and with a weak smile of apology she stepped inside. Refreshments had been laid out in various portions of the room, and an army of footmen rushed about with trays of champagne. Miranda accepted a glass of wine and continued to peer around. She recognized several people she had previously met but no one she cared to talk to, and she drifted out. She doubted that any person present had noted either her arrival or departure.

Miranda descended the great curving stairs to the lower floor, partly from curiosity, mostly from a desire to locate some island of solitude in the bedlam. The first room she entered she initially supposed to be a chapel, for it resembled nothing so much as a miniature cathedral, with a nave, carved pillars bordering the aisles and stained glass windows. But a nearby voice soon set her straight: "Ah, I *thought* to find His Highness in the conservatory!" Miranda glanced about, glimpsed the Regent himself, fat and resplendent in a uniform of his own design, and hurried out.

She could not later explain precisely where the library was located, but when she found it, she rushed inside with an audible sigh of relief. It was not deserted, but there were no more than a dozen guests within, and Miranda, as she always did amongst books, felt immediately at home. She was sorely tempted to dig through the shelves so as to judge the reading material currently in royal favor, but she suspected that would be unpardonably gauche, and she sank onto a settee and sipped her champagne.

She had been sitting some five minutes when she became aware that she had captured the attention of a man across the room. She identified his uniform as Prussian, and she briefly fancied that she was to have a private conversation with King Frederick William himself. However, she soon recalled from the newspaper drawings that His Majesty was a gaunt, rather walleyed and altogether unprepossessing figure. The man present, whom she studied as surreptitiously as she could, looked as a King *should*: tall, muscular, fair-skinned, blonde. He walked toward her, and Miranda observed that his eyes were quite a startling shade of blue and that he appeared to be a few years older than Anthony, five-and-thirty perhaps.

"Good evening." He stopped immediately in front of her, clicked his heels smartly together and made a small, stiff, military bow. "May I take the liberty of presenting myself? I am Major Karl von Rheinbeck."

"Major von Rheinbeck," Miranda murmured. "I am Lady Margrave." She wondered how many more times she would be compelled to repeat that fabrication. "The Countess of Margrave."

"Lady Margrave." The Major clicked his heels again. "May I join you?"

Their corner of the library was entirely empty, and the settee could comfortably accommodate herself, the Major and several others besides. In short, Miranda saw no courteous way to decline, and she nodded. Rheinbeck discreetly seated himself as far from Miranda as he reasonably could, crossed his long legs and fastened his brilliant blue eyes upon her.

"You are alone, Lady Margrave?" he inquired.

"No, no, I am not. That is to say, I am alone here in the library, but only because my—my husband and I became separated in the crowd."

"I see." Though Miranda could not be certain, she thought the Major's eyes grew a trifle darker. "If I had a wife as lovely as yourself, I should watch after her much more closely than that."

His English was excellent; he had only a very slight difficulty with his *th*'s and a faint hint of a *v* sound about his *w*'s. And Miranda nervously sensed that he was not dropping casual compliments as did Sir Humphrey or the Czar or Anthony himself.

"I fear your wife would take grave exception to your remark, Major von Rheinbeck," she said lightly.

"I regret to say that I have no wife. I have been in the army throughout my adult life, and I think my profession is not conducive to a happy home."

"I am sure my husband would agree." Miranda was not sure of this at all, but she somehow felt it important to remind the Major of Anthony's existence. "He was in military service for some years himself."

"Indeed? And where did Lord Margrave serve?"

"Where?" Miranda echoed. Another detail she had failed to explore. "His final post was in France. He was in the army before we married, you understand."

"Ah. You have been married but a short time then."

"A very short time; yes, indeed; under a month."

"Well, I wish you much happiness, Lady Margrave. I daresay your husband made an extremely wise decision when he abandoned his military career to pursue the domestic life. Now that the war is over, I myself am pondering retirement. I wonder whether I should be happy; what do you think?"

Miranda again entertained an uncomfortable notion that the Major was not engaging in idle chatter. "I couldn't possibly speculate," she said brightly, "for I scarcely know you. I can only attest that Anthony and I are exceedingly happy." She took a great swallow of champagne and promptly choked, but fortunately Major von Rheinbeck didn't seem to notice.

"Did you grow up in London, Lady Margrave?" he asked.

"No; no, I did not." To Miranda's considerable surprise, she found herself narrating a substantially truthful account of her life. She edited a few minor points, of course: in her telling Thomas and Martha emerged as the very personification of kindness, and she selected Anthony's most recent version of their meeting and courtship. But when she finished, Major von Rheinbeck knew she had been raised in Oxford, knew she had lately been a governess, knew she had "married" the Earl of Margrave after a very brief acquaintance.

The Major nodded, as though she had passed some rigid military inspection. "I guessed at your scholarly background when I found you in the library. Beautiful women are all too often empty-headed; it is a distinct pleasure to encounter the exception."

Miranda once more detected a layer of seriousness beneath his smooth banter, once more took refuge in a gulp of champagne. "And what of yourself, Major?" she inquired.

His late father had been the third Baron von Rheinbeck, the Major replied, and Karl and his elder brother Franz had been born and bred in the "small" family castle, situated not far from Berlin. Miranda, hard put to visualize a "small" castle, merely nodded. Naturally, the Major continued, his brother had inherited the title, and "as I believe often occurs in England as well," the younger son had turned to a military career. "At the risk of sounding immodest," the Major concluded, "I should like to add that I am not dependent upon my army income; I am a man of considerable means."

His comment *was* immodest, of course, and consequently unnerving because Major von Rheinbeck did not seem the immodest sort. Miranda tilted her glass to her mouth, but she had long since drained the last drop of champagne.

"I fancy we have talked long enough," the Major said, "for your glass is empty. Shall we avail ourselves of His Highness's splendid refreshments?"

Miranda thought she should demur, but she didn't wish to wound the Major. "Certainly," she murmured.

The crowd in the conservatory had swelled appreciably since Miranda's last visit, and it was with some difficulty that Major von Rheinbeck shouldered them to the nearest refreshment table. His Highness's "splendid" offerings had been quite picked over, and Miranda, who had had no dinner, swallowed three oysters, two lobster patties and several pastries, wondering regretfully what exotic treats had occupied the now empty serving dishes. The Major managed to procure each of them a fresh glass of champagne, and they retreated to a relatively quiet sector of the room.

The throng was sufficiently noisy to preclude any but the most desultory conversation, and Miranda and Rheinbeck were chatting about passing attire and personalities when they were approached by three Prussian officers, young and rather flushed with drink. The Major made appropriate introductions, but Miranda was only able to ascertain that the trio consisted of two lieutenants and a captain, and the ensuing discussion, conducted mostly in German, in no way enlightened her. She contemplated how best to excuse herself; perhaps she should simply melt into the crowd. She took one tentative backward step and collided with the Earl of Margrave.

"Anthony!" she squealed. She briefly thought to lead him away, then realized that the Prussians had fallen silent. "I should like to present Major von Rheinbeck; my husband, Lord Margrave." The Major obediently clicked his heels and bowed. "And this is, these are . . ." Her voice trailed off, and Rheinbeck supplied the names in a guttural, incomprehensible stream.

"I am delighted," Anthony drawled. "I have been searching for my dear wife upwards of an hour; little did I expect to find her entertaining the entire Prussian army."

"Oh, hardly the entire army, Lord Margrave." His charm notwithstanding, Major von Rheinbeck seemed a rather humorless man, and he had apparently, perhaps fortunately, missed Anthony's sarcasm. "These gentlemen are merely the members of my own staff. But then I daresay you are quite familiar with military organization, for your wife tells me that you yourself served in the army for a number of years."

"That I did," Anthony said coldly. "However, I am unable to enjoy the victory celebration except as a spectator because I suffered a wound in the latter stages of the war and was invalided out. You will understand that *I* did not serve in a staff capacity, Major; I was in the line."

Rheinbeck flushed a deep brick-red, and Miranda felt herself blushing as well. She could not conceive why Anthony was behaving so abominably, and she quelled an urge to correct his characteristically distorted account of his departure from the army.

"That is most unfortunate," the Major said stiffly. "Does your wound continue to trouble you, Lord Margrave?"

"Yes," the Earl snapped, "it troubles me constantly." He leaned on his cane so dramatically that Miranda feared it might penetrate the marble floor. "Indeed, it has troubled me intensely all evening, and I was seeking Miranda, seeking her *at length*, so as to suggest that we depart."

There was no suggestion about it, of course; it was clearly a command. Rheinbeck glanced at Miranda, a fleeting expression of sympathy crossing his handsome features, and Miranda managed a tremulous smile.

"Of course we shall go," she murmured. "I very much enjoyed making your acquaintance, Major."

"And I yours, Lady Margrave." He tendered his stiff little bow. "I hope to see you again before I leave England."

He seemed, as he had all evening, to be speaking at a level beyond that of normal courtesy, and as Miranda smiled again, his brilliant eyes grew oddly distant. He suddenly looked years older and, despite the presence of his admiring junior officers, utterly alone.

"Would you care to call, Major von Rheinbeck?" she asked impulsively. "We live not far away, at number eight Charles Street."

"Indeed!" Rheinbeck brightened at once. "I shall arrange a visit with great enthusiasm, Lady Margrave."

Anthony's fingers fastened painfully about her arm, and Miranda mumbled her farewells to the other Prussians. The Earl fairly dragged her up the circular stairs and propelled her roughly to the entrance. There was a considerable delay as one of His Highness's attendants summoned their carriage, a delay during which Anthony studied the columns and courtyard of Carlton House with elaborate interest. Once they were seated in the landau and the vehicle was underway, the Earl undertook a keen examination of the passing streets, which were now altogether dark and deserted.

"I do not understand why you are so annoyed," Miranda ventured at last. "It was not *I* who demanded to leave early on this occasion."

"Annoyed?" Anthony whipped his head about, and even in the darkness Miranda could see the glitter of his green eyes. "I am not annoyed, my love; I am merely speculating how best to accommodate our Prussian friends. Do you fancy the Major will come alone, or should I brace for an invasion? Shall I instruct Mrs. Horton to arrange an army mess in the drawing room?"

"Oh, for heaven's sake, Anthony. Major von Rheinbeck is a perfect gentleman, and it should be obvious to you that he is lonely. I saw no harm in inviting him to call—"

"The harm," the Earl interrupted frigidly, "is that you and I agreed to behave with maximum discretion throughout the remainder of our relationship. It *is* obvious to me that the Major is lonely and equally obvious that he would be delighted to find solace in the arms of a comely English countess. In short, my dear, your behavior this evening was far from discreet."

Miranda gazed down at her white-satin slippers and silently owned Anthony right. Her conduct *had* been indiscreet, the more so since she was well aware that Major von Rheinbeck's interest exceeded the casual. She briefly considered the possibility of rescinding the invitation, then realized that she could not get in touch with the Major even if she wished. But she would not, she vowed, admit her fault to the Earl.

"Let us not tease ourselves about it," she said lightly, looking up. "I daresay the Major will forget the invitation altogether, and I do not suppose we shall see him again."

But Anthony was already staring back out the window. In contrast to the glitter of Carlton House, the night seemed very dark, the streets very quiet, and the steady clop of the horses' hoofs very loud.

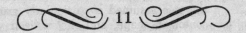

11

As Cassy helped her prepare for bed, Miranda related a considerably embellished version of her encounter with the Czar. She described His moderately handsome Majesty as a man of "godlike" looks, intimated that he had consulted Lady Margrave on several burning diplomatic issues and implied that she had behaved with perfect aplomb throughout their lengthy interview. Cassy was so entranced that she put her mistress's nightdress on backwards and, mercifully, altogether forgot to remove the teardrop earrings.

Miranda crawled into bed, but the tree was dancing on the ceiling again, and its twisted branches seemed somehow symbolic, a silent rebuke. She reflected on the tale she had narrated to Cassy. Her exaggerations were innocuous enough, of course: they had given Cassy a great deal of pleasure, and it was unlikely that the little abigail would learn of her mistress's small deceits. But it horrified Miranda that she was suddenly able to lie so readily, and she wondered how it had come about.

Miranda had always regarded herself as a person of almost painful honesty. Naturally she had engaged in the occasional social lie: she had refused to stand up with Dickie Alcott because her "feet hurt"; she had assured Mrs. Stubbs that her wretched chicken curry was "delicious"; she had extravagantly praised Martha's brown bombazine gown, which, in fact, looked like a saddle blanket. But Miranda could not recall that she had engaged in even a serious dissimulation until the day she carefully composed her letter of response to Anthony's notice. Since that time, she had lied to virtually every one of her current acquaintances, from Cassy to the Emperor of Russia.

It was easy, and infinitely comforting, to blame the Earl for her dishonesty, and Miranda did so for a moment. Then the tree assumed a particularly grotesque, particularly contorted shape, and she realized what it was that troubled her so. Insofar as she could ascertain, Anthony had never lied to *her*; it was she who had broken that last, tenuous trust. Her airy assurance notwithstanding, she did not believe that Major von Rheinbeck would forget her invitation, and she had not believed it when she said it. She had no doubt that the Major would call and no doubt why. She had lied to Anthony, and now there was but one final step: she wondered when she would begin to lie to herself.

Miranda closed her eyes, but the tree continued to writhe in her mind, and it was a long time before she fell asleep.

Miranda rose late the following morning and allowed Cassy to select her uniform of the day—a lime-green dress trimmed in emerald gauze. The abigail maneuvered her mistress into the chair before the dressing table and had just unpinned her hair when there was a knock upon the door.

"Come in," Cassy sang.

The door opened very slowly, and Horton peered cautiously into the Yellow Chamber. Finding, to his obvious relief, that Lady Margrave was not scampering about *au naturel,* he frowned at Cassy with intense disapproval.

"Her ladyship might find it more convenient if you were to *answer* her door," he said stiffly.

"Yes, sir." Cassy began brushing Miranda's hair, betraying not the slightest symptom of contrition.

"At any rate," the butler continued, "you have a caller, Lady Margrave. A foreign gentleman."

"The Czar!"

Cassy waved the brush with triumph, unfortunately neglecting first to dislodge it from Miranda's hair. Miranda winced and averted her eyes, fearing to discover that Cassy's enthusiasm had rendered her largely bald.

"Where will it end, ma'am?" Cassy asked rhetorically. "First the Duke of Clarence comes to call, now the Czar; the next thing we know the Regent himself will be pounding down the door."

"The Duke of Clarence?"

Horton's frown deepened, and Miranda bit back a correction. Cassy's misstatements were not deliberate; they were the stuff of fantasies and wishes and dreams. Totally unlike Miranda's own sordid lies . . .

"*I* do not recollect His Highness's visit," Horton said frigidly. "Nor is the present caller His Royal Russian Majesty. The gentleman is a Major von Rheinbeck." Miranda distantly noted that the butler's German pronunciation was quite as flawless as his French. "I showed him to the drawing room, but I did not, of course, state that you would receive him, Lady Margrave."

Miranda pondered the option Horton had dutifully provided. She had only to dispatch the butler to the saloon, to desire him to report that her ladyship was "away" or "occupied" or "indisposed." Rheinbeck was not a fool; he would recognize the cue and bow permanently out. But that, Miranda decided, would be to compound dishonesty with cowardice, and the Major deserved better. She must receive Rheinbeck and inform him, as gently as possible, that further calls would not be welcome.

"Please tell Major von Rheinbeck that I shall be down directly," Miranda said, as briskly as she could.

Horton nodded and retreated into the corridor, and Cassy shook her head.

"How could he forget the Duke of Clarence?" she wondered aloud. "And don't despair, ma'am; I am certain the Czar *will* come and probably before the day is over."

The little abigail fairly attacked her mistress's hair, and Miranda winced again, judging herself quite sufficiently punished for her transgressions.

As Miranda approached the drawing room, she detected a murmur of voices, and when she stepped inside, she was pleased to find Elizabeth ensconced in her customary position on the sofa. Rheinbeck leaped to his feet and negotiated his brief bow.

"Good afternoon, Major," Miranda said. "Please resume your seat, and I shall order some tea."

"I have already done so, Miranda, dear," Elizabeth trilled. "The Major and I have been conducting the most fascinating conversation; we have been comparing life in Jamaica to that in Prussia." She spoke as if the two localities were so similar as to be practically indistinguishable.

"I was at the point of asking just how long you have been in England, Mrs. Pennington." Rheinbeck had reclaimed his place on the couch, and Miranda noted that he sat ramrod stiff—shoulders back, feet flat upon the floor, palms resting on his knees.

"Under a week," Elizabeth replied. "You will understand, Major, that my visit was a surprise, but as it happened, the surprise was to myself. I had no notion that dear Anthony had wed, and you can imagine my delight when I learned of the event. I am, of course, particularly thrilled that he selected Miranda. She is not only beautiful; she is exceedingly clever as well."

Elizabeth beamed at Miranda, and Rheinbeck transferred his own startling blue eyes to the chair across the table.

"I am aware of that, Mrs. Pennington," he said, his gaze unwavering. "Lady Margrave is a remarkable woman indeed."

Miranda's cheeks grew warm, and she looked hastily down and picked an imaginary thread from the gauze round the bottom of her skirt. She sensed the Major's eyes still upon her, but fortunately his scrutiny was interrupted by the clatter of a tray in the archway. Miranda eagerly beckoned in the footman, who set the tea tray on the table. Elizabeth speedily poured and passed the cups around.

"Miranda *is* remarkable," she said, as if there had

been no lull in the conversation, "and no one appreci-
ates her qualities more keenly than myself. I am utterly
astonished by the transformation she has wrought in
Anthony. Are you acquainted with my son, Major?"

"Er—yes." Rheinbeck's face colored, and he took refuge in a polite cough.

"I presume you met him only recently, so you will find
it difficult to credit that Anthony's behavior was once
rather—rather questionable. Well, let me not hide my
teeth, Major: my son was a bit of a rake. However,
Miranda has *entirely* reformed him, and, as I am sure
you observed for yourself, his conduct is now quite
faultless."

"I did observe that." Rheinbeck choked on his tea.

"At any rate, that is all in the past," Miranda said hurriedly. "I should like to elicit Major von Rheinbeck's im-
pressions of England. Have you visited our country
before, Major?"

He had, Rheinbeck replied, but as an adolescent, and
he had noted improvements almost beyond counting. "I
need hardly point out that the circumstances of this
journey are altogether different as well," he added. "We
are truly being entertained in royal fashion, as I daresay
Lady Margrave will attest. An interesting event occurred
after your—ahem—departure last evening, Lady Margrave: there developed a rumor that the Czar has fallen
in love with Lady Jersey." Miranda was glad of Cassy's
absence; she feared the little abigail would be mortified
to learn that her mistress had been bested by an aging
Irish countess. "I fancy His Majesty is perpetrating a
prank, but one never knows."

"One never does," Elizabeth agreed. "I well recall, a
decade or more ago, rumors of the present Regent's marriage to Mrs. Fitzherbert . . ."

Elizabeth related the story and several other scandals
dating from her residence in England, and Rheinbeck
supplied two or three provocative tales of life at the
Prussian court. Miranda was quite content to remain
silent and watch the minutes tick away on the mantel

clock. After some three quarters of an hour had elapsed, the Major drained his second cup of tea and rose.

"I must beg to be excused," he said, tendering his stiff little bow. "His Majesty has asked me to wait upon him this afternoon."

"What a shame," Elizabeth clucked. "Anthony will be *so* sorry to have missed you. Well, you must simply return tomorrow, Major, and hope that he will be at home."

Miranda shot her alleged mother-in-law a look of warning, but it was far too late, for the Major was enthusiastically nodding.

"I should be delighted to return tomorrow if such a visit is convenient for Lady Margrave. At about the same hour, shall we say?"

"Yes," Miranda mumbled; "yes, that would be fine."

She summoned Horton to show Rheinbeck out, and as the two men disappeared down the stairs, turned back to the saloon. Elizabeth was sorrowfully shaking her head.

"What a lovely man," she sighed. "My meeting with the Major increases my appreciation of you manyfold, my dear. I daresay that without your influence, without your love, Anthony, too, could well have become a lonely middle-aged bachelor."

Miranda strongly doubted that the Earl of Margrave would ever be "lonely," but she judged it best to drop the matter at once. "It was very kind of you to invite the Major back," she murmured.

"I only regret that I shall not be here, for I myself plan to call on an old friend tomorrow. But I am sure you and Anthony will entertain the dear Major *quite* well in my absence."

Elizabeth flashed a sunny smile, rose and sailed out of the drawing room.

Miranda and Anthony attended a small dinner party that evening, and Miranda fully intended to mention the Major's forthcoming call. However, the precisely right opportunity did not seem to present itself, and it was not until the next noon, completely dressed and coiffed, that she at last dispatched Cassy to the Earl's bedchamber to request that his lordship be available to receive an imminent visitor. Cassy sped back with the news that Lord Margrave had departed several hours before and had not yet returned.

"But," the abigail concluded brightly, "he is expected at any moment, ma'am."

"Splendid," Miranda sighed.

Perhaps she should send Rheinbeck away after all, she thought, should instruct Horton to advise the Major that Lady Margrave had been called to the scene of a family emergency. She was pondering whether the emergency should take the form of natural death, grave illness or a fatal accident when the butler tapped on the door and announced that Major von Rheinbeck awaited her ladyship's pleasure in the saloon.

Rheinbeck was, as usual, clad in his uniform, but he had added a new flourish to his military behavior. After tendering his customary bow, the Major walked forward, seized Miranda's hand and bowed again, permitting his lips barely to brush her knuckles. He straightened, continuing to hold Miranda's hand rather more firmly than convention dictated, and gazed into her eyes. Miranda was just experiencing the first flutter of discomfiture when she heard a short, sharp cough behind them. Rheinbeck dropped her hand with indelicate haste, and they simultaneously spun toward the archway.

"Miranda!" Anthony limped into the room, leaning on his cane as though every step were excruciating beyond description. "Horton informed me you had a guest. Captain von Ritter, is it not?"

"Major von Rheinbeck," the Major corrected stiffly.

"Major von Rheinbeck, of course. I fancy I encountered you at Admiral Spencer's assembly."

"It was at His Highness's reception."

"His Highness's reception, of course; how *could* I have mistaken one of our recent heroes? I must own myself surprised to find you here, Captain; I should have supposed you would be at Ascot with the rest of our Allied guests."

"I was, in fact, invited to Ascot," Rheinbeck said, "but His Majesty excused me. I do not particularly fancy racing."

"No?" Anthony raised his uneven brows. "Perhaps you share His Russian Majesty's predilection for female—rather than horseflesh. Well, I shan't continue to intrude. Good day."

The Earl bowed pleasantly and hobbled out, and Miranda bit her lip. Anthony's remark had been altogether crude, and she scarcely knew how to begin to explain it.

"I pray you will forgive my—my husband," she said nervously. "Apparently his wound is troubling him again, and I collect he is a trifle out of sorts. Please sit down, Major. Would you care for some tea?"

"No, thank you, Lady Margrave." Rheinbeck lowered himself to the sofa and assumed his familiar rigid posture. "Actually I loathe tea. I took it yesterday only because I did not wish to offend Mrs. Pennington; she is a charming woman."

"Is she not?" Miranda's voice was alarmingly shrill. "I believe she and Anthony are a great deal alike; do you not concur, Major?"

"They *look* a great deal alike," Rheinbeck said dubiously.

"Well, be that as it may, perhaps you would prefer a bit of sherry."

Miranda bounded toward the liquor cabinet, but Rheinbeck's voice caught her up. "I do not seek refreshment, Lady Margrave. I came solely to see you."

"How very kind of you to say so, Major." Miranda took one of the chairs opposite the couch and, for good measure, eased it well away from the table. "I only regret that Anthony's physical condition has dampened the occasion."

"I wonder if Lord Margrave's condition *is* entirely physical," Rheinbeck said. "It occurs to me that he may, in fact, be experiencing some difficulty in adjusting to domestic life. Mrs. Pennington indicated that his previous existence was quite—quite colorful."

The Major's remark unquestionably strained the bounds of propriety, but his choice of words was so tactful, his expression one of such sincere concern, that Miranda could not be offended. She blushed and gazed at her shoes.

"There is also the matter of military versus civilian life," Rheinbeck continued, as though he, too, had recognized the dangerous drift of the conversation. "The situation has led me to ponder my own future most seriously. Perhaps I should be making a grave error if I were to terminate my career and retire to the country."

"Perhaps so," Miranda murmured uncomfortably.

"Though, for my own part, I believe I should find domestic life, civilian life, entirely pleasurable if I were to locate a suitable wife." Miranda felt the Major's piercing blue eyes upon her and wondered how long she could continue to stare at her white-kid slippers. "A woman much like yourself, Lady Margrave: handsome, clever, sensitive—"

"And I am sure you *will* locate just such a woman," Miranda interposed brightly. She feared that, without interruption, Rheinbeck would exhaust his entire store of English adjectives. "You have been altogether occupied with your military activities, forced to direct your whole attention to the winning of the war, and you have had no opportunity to consider marriage." Miranda realized that she was chattering, but she was quite powerless to stop. "I daresay you have met numerous ladies who would have proved *most* suitable, but distracted as you were with battle plans and such, you were unable to pursue any sort of courtship—"

"I *have* encountered numerous ladies," Rheinbeck interjected quietly. "None of them could hold a torch to you, Lady Margrave."

Miranda elected not to correct his faulty idiom. "You *think* that," she said desperately, "because, as I say, you were not *seeking* a wife at the time. It often happens, Major, that when the moment is ripe for marriage, the most unlikely person will suddenly appear ideal."

"Did you find it so when you met Lord Margrave?"

His implication was unmistakable, but Miranda decided to ignore that as well. "Not—not exactly," she replied, "but my position was entirely different. I fancy that when you return to Prussia, you will encounter an old friend, perhaps even the *daughter* of an old friend, and discover yourself altogether smitten. Speaking of which, Major, I am certain you are *quite* eager to see your homeland again. I am told it is a beautiful country."

Actually Miranda had not been told this at all, but she was frantic to change the topic of discussion.

"It *is* beautiful," Rheinbeck confirmed. "I hope you will be able to visit one day, Lady Margrave. I should also be delighted to present you to my mother, for I daresay the two of you would get on famously. I believe my mother would remind you a good deal of Mrs. Pennington."

"Are you gossiping about me?" Elizabeth peered through the archway, and Miranda nearly collapsed with relief. "I am enormously pleased not to have missed you, Major, though sorry to report the circumstances of my early return. I found my friend, Lady Thornton, to be in a shocking state indeed. Her breath positively *reeked* of spirits when I arrived, and she consumed three full glasses of sherry during my brief call. I was hard pressed to make any sense of her conversation, but it might be of interest to you, Major, that she has also heard the rumor concerning the Czar and Lady Jersey . . ."

Elizabeth rattled on—Rheinbeck offering an occasional "yes?" or "no!" or "indeed!"—and the Major soon rose and asked to be excused.

"I regret that I shall be unable to call tomorrow," he said. Miranda suppressed another sigh of relief. "However, I trust that I shall see you at the opera tomorrow evening. Good day, Lady Margrave. Mrs. Pennington."

Rheinbeck bowed and retreated, and as soon as he had started down the stairs, Miranda muttered her own excuses and hurried to her room.

Cassy, who was now persuaded that Major von Rheinbeck was the Czar incognito, had requested a few hours of freedom to visit her sister "while your ladyship entertains His Majesty." Miranda sank into the chair before the dressing table and took advantage of the unaccustomed privacy to study her countenance in the mirror.

She was not sufficiently immodest or, perhaps, sufficiently confident, to judge herself beautiful, but it was clear, whatever her attributes or lack thereof, that Major von Rheinbeck was infatuated with the mythical Countess of Margrave. And was he not the "suitable *parti*" she had awaited all her life? She briefly attempted to compare him to Dickie Alcott, but the contrast was ludicrous: the Major's physical presence, his charm, his sophistication reduced Dickie to a flat, rather cruel jest.

Miranda wondered what would happen if she were to confess her true situation to Rheinbeck. She suspected he would initially be quite shocked, but his stern, Teutonic disapproval would quickly devolve upon Anthony. He would whisk Miranda off to Prussia in the proverbial blink of an eye, and her problems would be instantly resolved. Well, not instantly, of course—problems never were—but a "small" Prussian castle was infinitely preferable to a teepee somewhere in the Canadian wilderness. And, at any rate, she would be well and forever rid of the outrageous, red-haired Earl of Margrave.

Miranda felt a peculiar chill, and she glanced at the window, but the day was sunny, and it was only a warm summer breeze that teased the curtains. She looked back at her reflection, but it seemed that her eyes had turned to green—glittering, accusing emeralds. I owe you nothing! she told Anthony's eyes, and I shall not permit you to destroy the remainder of my life.

But she decided not to confide in the Major, not just yet, and the decision rendered her oddly tired. She stood, drew the drapes against the terrible tree in the garden and stretched out on the canopied bed.

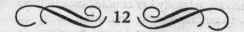

12

Cassy had scarcely begun to dress Miranda's hair when there was a knock at the door of the Yellow Chamber. Apparently recognizing Horton's discreet tap, Cassy hurried across the room to answer, and the butler granted her a cool nod of approval. He then announced that Mr. and Mrs. Cavendish had arrived and had been shown to the saloon.

"Well, they will simply have to wait," Miranda snapped. "They are quite early; we are not scheduled to leave for the opera for nearly half an hour."

"I shall so remind them, ma'am," Horton said. "Fortunately, Sir Humphrey came early as well, and I daresay the three of them can entertain themselves most admirably."

"Sir Humphrey!" Miranda shuddered to contemplate the consequences of a private conversation between the tattle-box baronet and her curious cousins. "Tell them I shall be along *at once*, Horton."

The butler bowed out, looking a trifle perplexed, and Miranda urged Cassy to finish her *coiffure* with all possible speed.

"I am doing the best I can," the abigail protested. "Though I must say, ma'am, that I think your first idea the best: to leave your cousins cooling their heels awhile. After all, you kept the *Czar* waiting ten full minutes."

In fact, almost a quarter of an hour elapsed before Miranda reached the drawing room, out of breath and with her *toque* a bit askew. Thomas and Sir Humphrey rose, the latter with his customary difficulty, and Martha lifted one gloved hand in greeting. Their pleasant, rather

147

fatuous expressions implied that nothing untoward had been said, and Miranda heaved an inward sigh of relief.

"Pray resume your seats, gentlemen," she instructed. "How lovely you look, Martha!" This was not precisely true: though the white-lace gown was, indeed, "lovely," Martha continued to look like the harried country wife she was. "I see that Madame Leclair was able to finish your dress without complication."

"Without complication but at great expense," Thomas growled. "I was just discussing the matter with Lord Hammond." Thomas seemed determined to promote the new peers of his acquaintance well above their actual stations. "His lordship had advised us that he intends imminently to wed, and I was at the point of warning him that wives are an exceedingly costly commodity."

"But well worth the investment," Sir Humphrey said gallantly, as Martha's eyes narrowed. "And I am extremely fortunate in that respect, Mr. Cavendish; my fiancée is a woman of considerable means."

There was a fit of coughing at the archway, and before Sir Humphrey could struggle up, Thomas bounded across the room to assist the Comtesse inside.

"Pray do forgive me," Jeanne sputtered prettily. "I fear I do not find the English climate altogether *agréable*."

Thomas escorted Madame to one of the chairs opposite the sofa, and Sir Humphrey, who had managed to attain an upright stance, performed the introductions. Miranda wondered if Thomas would be able to recognize the Comtesse when next they met; his eyes seemed riveted to the plunging neckline of her pink-net gown and the bounteous bosom it so generously exposed.

"I am exceedingly pleased to make your acquaintance, Madame de Chavannes." Martha did not sound pleased at all, and her words were punctuated with a furious glare at Thomas. "Sir Humphrey has recently informed us of your impending marriage. May I take the opportunity to wish you much happiness?"

"Thank you," Jeanne sighed. "It is, *vraiment*, a happy

ending to a strange story. Did my *chère amie* Miranda tell you that she stole Antoine away from me?"

Thomas and Martha turned simultaneously to their cousin, looking much like spectators at a tennis match.

"Yes," the Comtesse continued brightly. "I must confess that I had designs on Antoine when I traveled to England following the death of my dear husband. To my immense shock, I discovered that Antoine had wed during the few months since our previous encounter. However, as your Monsieur Shakespeare says, all is well that ends well, *n'est-ce pas?*"

"Ness pah, indeed," Thomas agreed. "But that does bring up a point, Miranda. After our conversation—Wednesday, was it not?—I remained somewhat confused about the exact circumstances of your and His Grace's courtship."

"You were somewhat confused about *everything* on that occasion," Martha snapped.

"Nevertheless I was unable to determine whether His Grace offered during your very first meeting—"

Miranda dropped her fan, and, Sir Humphrey being once more confined to the couch, Thomas scrambled to retrieve it. Miranda was desperately groping for some new and innocuous topic of conversation when Anthony and Elizabeth appeared in the archway. The Earl proposed a quick glass of sherry before their departure, but Miranda and Martha, though presumably from different motives, insisted that the group leave immediately.

When they reached the foyer, there was a lengthy debate as to how the passengers were to be distributed amongst the two carriages. Miranda was loathe to leave any of the party alone with her cousins, but it was quite impossible to suggest that five be crammed into Anthony's landau while Thomas and Martha drove alone. Eventually she decided it would be best to expose Elizabeth to her cousins' inquiries, and on the slender grounds that the landau was slightly larger than Thomas's ancient barouche, she fairly thrust her "mother-in-law" into the Cavendish vehicle.

The carriages set out in tandem, but as they approached the Haymarket, the traffic swelled. Thomas's coachman-cum-handyman, unaccustomed to the aggressive ways of city drivers, fell farther and farther behind; and Miranda and Anthony, Jeanne and Sir Humphrey had been standing outside the King's Theatre almost twenty minutes when the Cavendish carriage at last rolled up. Miranda was distressed to observe that Thomas wore a deep frown, but she soon glimpsed him tugging at his breeches and optimistically surmised that his grimace signified nothing more than physical discomfort.

Miranda vaguely recalled her vision of sweeping into the opera, but the lobby was so jammed with bemedaled officers, stately lords, bejeweled ladies and glittering Cyprians that she doubted Napoleon himself would garner more than a passing glance. They made their way to Anthony's box with some difficulty, the Earl occasionally employing his cane as a battering ram. Upon their arrival at the box, there was another debate about the seating arrangements; Miranda ultimately found herself located between Anthony and Sir Humphrey.

Miranda had hardly settled into her chair when the murmur of conversation swelled to a roar. She peered about and saw the Regent, the King of Prussia and her friend the Czar taking their own places in a box not far away. The buzz subsided, and Miranda tried to estimate just how many could be seated in the vast gallery and pit, the five tiers of boxes. Three thousand? Four thousand?

The hum ebbed again, fell almost to silence; then there was a burst of applause. Miranda, assuming that the performance was about to begin, looked at the curtain but detected not so much as a tweak.

"Good God," Sir Humphrey hissed behind his hand. "It is the Princess of Wales." The baronet indicated a box directly across from theirs, and Miranda beheld two women bustling into their chairs.

"Which one?" she whispered back. She was reluctant to betray her ignorance but intensely curious about His Highness's estranged wife.

"On the left. Her companion is Lady Charlotte Campbell. Good God," Sir Humphrey repeated, clapping his own hands with glee. "His Highness is in the briars now. *Her* Highness was not invited to any of the festivities, but the public has clearly taken her part. What do you suppose the Prince will do?"

The baronet's question was rhetorical, and at any rate, the applause had increased to such a pitch that any response was impossible. As the clapping reached the point of ovation, the Regent stood and bowed to the box on the opposite side of the theater, and the Allied Monarchs followed his lead.

"A victory for Princess Caroline," Sir Humphrey pronounced.

Was it? Miranda wondered. The Czar and the King and the Prince resumed their seats, and the applause died away, but Miranda continued to stare at the Princess of Wales. She seemed a pathetic creature: her face was rouged far too brightly, and her hair was an untidy mane of yellow curls. If the second lady of the realm could be so shamefully neglected by her husband, what hope was there for lesser wives? Miranda stole a sidewards glance at Anthony, then caught herself abruptly up. She was *not* his wife, and she must remember that, must somehow escape the great, sticky web of lies that increasingly enmeshed her.

Just as the curtain parted, Miranda detected another stir in the Regent's box and observed Major von Rheinbeck taking his seat behind the King of Prussia. He, too, began peering about the theatre, but Miranda judged it unlikely that he would pick her out, and she took the opportunity to study him. He was a fine figure of a man indeed: tall even as he sat, his blonde hair fairly glowing in the dimness.

Rheinbeck was the obvious solution to her dilemma, and Miranda speculated on what their life together might be. She did not know whether the Major possessed his own residence in Prussia; if not, he could certainly afford to construct one. Near the family castle perhaps. Though she would not have a title, Frau von

151

Rheinbeck would be a person of considerable standing in the community. If the Frau became homesick for England, her doting husband would no doubt arrange frequent return visits; in fact, they would probably travel extensively throughout Europe. If Miranda insisted, the Major would surely agree to have their children educated in Britain; their sons might well attend Oxford. At some point, Miranda would seek out the Earl of Margrave, now an aging *roué*, and present her tall, fair children to him . . .

"I believe the songbird is in rather less good voice than usual this evening," Sir Humphrey drawled.

Miranda had been attending the performance not at all, and she glanced desultorily at the stage before she grasped the import of the baronet's words.

"The songbird!" she gasped. From her opposite side, she heard a clatter as Anthony kicked his cane against the wall of the box.

"Ah, yes; I failed to recollect that you have not previously seen Signorina Savino perform. That is she, in the gold costume."

Miranda leaned forward as unobtrusively as she could. The Signorina appeared to be very dark: though it was impossible to determine the color of her eyes, her hair was as black as the coal her father purportedly mined. And she was far slighter than Miranda had imagined—short and slim and delicate. It was entirely likely, of course, that Signorina Savino dyed her hair, and her diminutive stature was no doubt exaggerated by contrast to the enormous lead soprano. It was the Signorina's turn to sing again, and even Miranda's untutored ear detected three flat notes within the first dozen bars.

"She is in *very* poor voice," Miranda commented to Sir Humphrey, with considerable petty satisfaction.

She attempted for a time to concentrate on the performance, but she had never much fancied opera. And it seemed that her lies now stalked her far and near and from every direction; from Anthony and Sir Humphrey and the rest of the party in their box, to Rheinbeck just down the way, to the Princess of Wales across the

152

theatre, to Signorina Savino wailing on the stage. Miranda felt a flutter, then a surge, of panic, and when the performance was finally over, she was dismayed to find her hands quite damp.

The crush in the foyer was even more oppressive than that preceding the performance, and by the time they reached the street, they discovered it a veritable sea of carriages. As they waited for their own equipages to appear, Elizabeth and Martha gushed about the "splendid" performance; Jeanne compared it, unfavorably, to the Paris opera company; Sir Humphrey bounded about, greeting numerous alleged "friends"; and Thomas tugged, with growing displeasure, at his breeches. Anthony said nothing but bounced his cane upon the cobblestones until Miranda was hard put to repress a scream.

The carriages rattled up at last, the barouche in front. Anthony handed his mother into the Cavendish vehicle, and Johnson assisted Sir Humphrey and the Comtesse into the landau. As the groom took Miranda's elbow, Anthony began hobbling back toward the landau, and at that moment there was a disturbance behind them.

"*Dio mio!*" A feminine shriek. "Please to let me by!"

The portion of the crowd nearest the street did, in fact, part a bit, and Signorina Savino hurtled through the breach. Miranda had a scant second in which to note that the Signorina had exchanged her golden costume for a demure gown of white muslin.

"Anthony! *Grazie Dio!*"

Signorina Savino hurled herself into Anthony's arms, and the Earl's cane flew out of his hands, narrowly missing a dignified officer of His Majesty's Navy.

"Oh, I say." Sir Humphrey thrust his head out the side of the landau.

"What is it? What has happened?" Elizabeth, who had taken the rear-facing seat of the barouche, leaped up, whirled around, lost her balance and fell atop Thomas and Martha. "Oh, dear," she lamented. "Oh, dear."

Thomas shoved Elizabeth quite unceremoniously back into place, and, trying to stand himself, nearly unroofed

153

his carriage. Martha seized Thomas's sleeve, whether in an effort to pull him down or herself up Miranda could not determine.

Signorina Savino, oblivious to the general consternation, alternately sobbed on Anthony's shoulder and whispered into his ear. Well, maybe she *wasn't* oblivious, Miranda amended: she occasionally tossed out an Italian word as if to appease the mob.

"Terribile!" the Signorina screeched. Sob, sob. *"Spaventoso!"* Whisper, whisper.

At length Anthony extricated himself from the Signorina's clutches, retrieved his cane and proceeded to the landau.

"As you have no doubt inferred, Mary Ann has encountered some difficulty." Miranda credited him with an understatement of historic magnitude. "I fancy I had best stay behind for a time."

"What is it, Anthony?" Elizabeth called. "What has happened, dear?"

"If it would not prove inconvenient, Hammond, I should like to request that you exchange places with my mother. The Cavendishes can drop you off en route to their hotel, and after Pollard has driven the rest home, he will return for me."

"Well, of course," Sir Humphrey responded silkily. "As a man of considerable sophistication myself, I naturally sympathize with your *embarras*. If I may be of additional assistance . . ."

The baronet continued to chatter as Anthony accompanied him to the barouche, and Elizabeth was no less voluble on the return trek.

"It hardly signifies *what* carriage I ride in, Anthony, but I must own myself altogether puzzled. Did this woman simply materialize from thin air? I must warn you, my dear, that indiscriminate charity is not entirely a virtue . . ."

The two vehicles got underway at last, Miranda staring stonily ahead so as to avoid the curious gaze of the crowd. From the corner of her eye, however, she caught a final glimpse of the Signorina, wringing her tiny hands and rushing toward Anthony again.

"I do not understand it at all." Elizabeth, in the rear-facing seat, had a full view of the retreating scene, and she shook her head. "I can only assume that Anthony was acquainted with the dreadful creature at some earlier period in his life. She no doubt seeks to take advantage of his celebrated generosity. Well, I shouldn't care for it if I were you, my dear; I am confident that Anthony will dismiss her in short order indeed."

"Yes," the Comtesse concurred. "She is probably an old friend of Antoine's who does not *comprend* his present circumstances. He but needs a private moment to explain the situation, and then he will send her off, *non?*"

Miranda searched Jeanne's great blue eyes for a hint of mischief, a trace of triumph, but found far worse: pity. She lowered her own eyes, and the Comtesse launched into a bright critique of Madame Alberi, the lead soprano, a dissertation of which Miranda heard scarcely a word.

Cassy was, of course, awaiting her mistress in the Yellow Chamber, and Miranda immediately excused her.

"His lordship was—er—detained at the theatre," she explained. "And as there is a matter I really must discuss with him, I shall have to remain up until he returns."

"How good of you not to insist that I stay up as well, ma'am. I shall help you into your nightclothes at once then, and be off to bed myself."

Miranda bit back a correction; it was quite natural for Cassy to assume that Lady Margrave would greet the Earl in her dressing gown. Another deceit, another lie. Miranda bit her lip again, sorely inclined to expose the whole, shoddy charade. But Cassy was already plucking at her dress, and Miranda allowed herself to be disrobed, then rerobed in the very scantiest of her nightgowns and its matching wrapper. Cassy bobbed a sleepy curtsy and slipped into the hall, and Miranda stared absently in her wake.

She really did not need to wait up for Anthony after all, she decided. To the contrary: the better course by far would be utterly to ignore the *contretemps* at the theatre. Whatever the Earl's past or present sins, Miranda was persuaded that Signorina Savino's assault had taken him entirely by surprise. Miranda was not in the least interested in the songbird's "difficulty" nor in whether and how Anthony might resolve it, and her silence would serve to demonstrate her total lack of concern. When she encountered the Earl tomorrow, she would offer a casual comment about the performance, nothing more. She tried to recall one of Jeanne's clever remarks; had the Comtesse judged Madame Alberi "short of wind" or "short of range"?

Miranda heard a clatter in the coach yard, which lay below her rear window, and hurriedly snuffed the candle on the dressing table. She leaped into the canopied bed and had pulled the bedclothes up to her neck before she realized that there was another candle burning on the writing table. Since it would not do at all for Anthony to imagine her overset, even *awake*, she bounded out of bed again, dashed across the Brussels carpet and extinguished the second taper as well. She stood for a moment, adjusting her vision to the darkness, and detected a faint whispering from the direction of the staircase.

Voices? Had the Earl taken to chatting with himself? Miranda eased her door almost infinitesimally open and laid one eye to the crack, and at that moment Anthony and Signorina Savino appeared at the top of the stairs.

Here? The Earl had dared to bring his barque of frailty *here*? There was but a single lamp in the corridor, and the long, flickering shadows it cast strengthened Miranda's impression that she had stumbled into a particularly vivid dream. Then Anthony tugged the Signorina directly through the pool of light and down the hall to the door of the bedchamber on the opposite side of his own. He opened the door and ushered the songbird inside, and the door clicked softly shut behind them.

Miranda closed her own door and leaned against it, literally trembling with rage. Anthony had a most peculiar notion of "maximum discretion," she reflected furiously. It was not sufficient that he had fetched his "friend" home; no, he must place her in the adjacent bedchamber. In short, the Earl's behavior had finally exceeded even the loosest bounds of propriety, and it was not to be tolerated.

Miranda heard a faint sound beyond the connecting door and threw open the corridor door again. She had taken a long step into the hall when she remembered the extremely revealing nature of her attire. She hurried back across the darkened bedchamber, fumbled in the wardrobe, located and donned her gray kerseymere pelisse, returned to the door. But she now thought she detected a thin shaft of light at the far end of the hall, from Jeanne's or Elizabeth's room perhaps. She would be hard pressed indeed to explain her outlandish appearance, and she decided it best not to risk observation. She closed the corridor door, marched to the connecting door and knocked as loudly as she dared.

"Miranda, my love. What an exceedingly pleasant surprise."

The Earl had removed his coat and shirt, and Miranda found his bare chest oddly distracting. His shoulders were broader than she had fancied, and there was a mat of soft, red-gold hair curling just below his throat . . .

"May I hope that you were impelled here by a sudden, an overwhelming flood of emotion?"

"Indeed you may," Miranda snapped. She tore her eyes from his chest and spotted another connecting door, identical to hers, on the opposite side of the bedchamber. The sight immeasurably hardened her resolve. "In fact, I have recently experienced a number of sudden, overwhelming emotions, milord. Though it is difficult to choose among them, I should have to place 'annoyance' and 'disgust' high upon the list. Nor do I wish to forget 'incredulity.' I can hardly conceive, after our many conversations concerning the matter of discretion, what led you to settle your paramour under this very roof. In full view of your mother, to say nothing of myself—"

"I can hardly conceive any reasonable basis for your objection," Anthony interrupted coolly. "As it happens,

Mary Anne is not my paramour, and her presence here in no way stems from our previous relationship. According to Mary Anne, Madame Alberi attacked her quite unprovokedly just prior to this evening's performance. It was not a *physical* attack, of course, though I am given to understand that Madame Alberi did throw a cosmetic jar at Mary Anne's head—"

"Well, *prima donnas* are prone to such displays, are they not?" Miranda interjected nastily. "Inclined to toss things about: jars and bottles, *decanters . . .*" She managed an evil smile.

"What is it you want to discuss, Miranda?" the Earl inquired pleasantly. "I somehow collected that you were distressed about Mary Anne. If, in fact, you wish to dredge up certain admittedly unsavory incidents which occurred in the distant past, I shall be delighted to oblige you."

He had put her on the defensive again, maneuvered her into the wrong. Miranda dropped her eyes, encountered the bare, disturbing chest, peered hastily at her naked feet, poking out from beneath the hem of the pelisse.

"In any event," Anthony continued smoothly, "at the end of the performance, Mary Anne was discharged from the company. As she was residing in quarters provided by her employer, she simultaneously lost her home. Under the circumstances, I saw no harm in offering a temporary haven; in truth, I felt it my duty." The Earl assumed his martyred expression.

"A noble sentiment," Miranda said frigidly. "However, it occurs to me that you could have discharged your 'duty' quite well by settling Signorina Savino in a hotel."

"I should naturally have explored that alternative had I not chanced to read that all the respectable hotels in the city are fully booked. I'm sure I needn't remind you that we are presently inundated with foreign visitors."

Anthony flashed a cool smile, and Miranda suppressed an inclination to suggest that the songbird would no doubt feel entirely at ease in an *un*respectable hotel.

"And just how long is Signorina Savino to stay?" she asked.

"Mary Anne will remain a few days, a week at most, while she recovers from the dismaying episode and seeks alternate employment. I perceive nothing 'annoying' or 'disgusting' about the situation, but perhaps I have erred."

"Erred?" Miranda screeched. "It is a breach of propriety shocking almost beyond imagination. Did you not pause for a single moment to consider the consequences?"

"I rarely consider consequences, my dear. If I did, we should not be conducting this conversation, should we? Have *you* never pondered the consequences to my position if our deception should be discovered?"

"*Your* position?" He was twisting everything around, and Miranda groped furiously for a rejoinder. "Did *duty* also dictate that you place Signorina Savino so cozily at hand? I note that her bedchamber adjoins your own in most convenient fashion."

"But there *is* no other bedchamber," Anthony pointed out equably. "Would you have me roust my mother from bed in the middle of the night and insist she change rooms? I shall certainly do so if that is your desire. However, I do fancy it would be somewhat less awkward if we were to postpone the exchange until tomorrow—"

"There need be no exchange!" Miranda snapped. She realized that the Earl had bested her once more, had made her appear irrational, ridiculous. "I daresay it little signifies precisely where Signorina Savino sleeps; it is sufficiently horrifying that she is in the house at all. I shudder to contemplate what will be said when the news circulates about."

"Perhaps it will be said that Lord Margrave was compelled to seek comfort when his wife began to dally with a Prussian officer."

It was, Miranda decided, a comment that did not warrant even the most contemptuous of responses. She whirled around and stalked toward her bedchamber.

"Permit me to mention one further matter." Miranda

stopped but did not turn back. "If your wardrobe is in such deplorable state that you must go about the house barefooted and in a woolen cloak, I shall be happy to authorize your return to Madame Leclair's."

Miranda rushed on into her room and slammed the connecting door with a resounding crash. As the echo died away, she thought she heard a short, sharp bark of laughter on the other side.

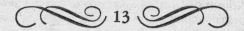 13

Miranda had not thought to consider the household's reaction to the arrival of Signorina Savino. Consequently, she was quite unprepared for the news Cassy delivered with her mistress's breakfast.

"Mrs. Horton resigned," the abigail announced, clattering a silver tray upon the top of the dressing table.

"Resigned?" Miranda gasped. "She is gone then?"

"Not exactly, but it did require Mr. Horton to put her straight."

"To put her straight about what?" Miranda asked, with dawning suspicion.

"Well, as I understand it, Lord Margrave summoned Mrs. Horton very early this morning. He told her that a guest had come during the night, a Miss Savino, and that Mrs. Horton was to appoint one of the maids to act as Miss Savino's dresser. I was just finishing my breakfast when Mrs. Horton flew into the servants' hall and told Mr. Morton that she would certainly do no such thing, that, in fact, she intended to leave at once. She said she would not continue to work in a—a—" Cassy stopped and bit her lip.

"A what?" Miranda pressed grimly.

"A—a brothel, ma'am."

Cassy blushed, and Miranda felt her own cheeks color as well. "Go on," she snapped.

"It was then that Mr. Horton said *his* piece. Lord Margrave's uncle had been a good master to them, he said, and after all they had endured with his present lordship, they were not going to give up their posts at *this* late juncture. Lord Margrave no doubt had a perfectly good reason for bringing a shameless actress un-

161

der his roof, Mr. Horton said, and they were not to question the matter. He told Mrs. Horton that she was to follow his lordship's instructions without further ado and assign a maid to attend Miss Savino."

"And did she? Assign a maid that is?"

"Yes, ma'am. Maggie."

Miranda bit back a smile. Maggie was, as she recalled, the homeliest and clumsiest of the scullery maids. "And then what happened?" she asked.

"Don't think I've forgotten your breakfast, ma'am. Sit down now before everything is cold. There. Well, just as Maggie was coming up the stairs, Miss Savino's trunks arrived."

"Trunks?" Miranda repeated sharply, strangling on a tiny sliver of egg.

"Yes, ma'am. As I understand it, Lord Margrave dispatched Pollard and Johnson—at the very crack of dawn, it was—to fetch Miss Savino's things from wherever it was she was staying before. They returned with four trunks. Please finish your egg, ma'am. Four trunks and any number of valises."

"Certainly enough to last for 'a few days,'" Miranda muttered, half to herself. "'A week at most.'"

"A week at the *least*, ma'am!" Cassy corrected helpfully. "I daresay Miss Savino could remain for *months* and never wear the same thing twice. I do believe that was what overset Mrs. Pennington so."

"Mrs. Pennington," Miranda sighed. She felt as though she were trapped in a very bad novel, the end of each chapter holding just enough promise to lure her to the next.

"Yes. She had rung for me, you see, directly before the trunks came. As it happened, I got behind the footboys on the steps, and she was waiting at the door of her bedchamber when I arrived. She demanded to know about the luggage, and I explained that it belonged to a Miss Savino, who had come overnight. Well, Mrs. Pennington seemed to *know* Miss Savino, and she was most distraught. 'He has moved her in?' she said. 'Anthony has moved the dreadful creature in, bag and baggage?'"

"I see. Thank you, Cassy. You—"

"'It is all due to Anthony's generosity,' Mrs. Pennington went on. 'Really, the boy has the charity of a saint. And dear Miranda has the *patience* of a saint to tolerate his kindness.'"

This was a peculiar pronouncement indeed, but Miranda decided not to pursue it. "Thank you, Cassy," she said again. "You may help me dress now. I fancy the situation will be resolved in very short order."

"I do pray so, for I feared Madam Dee would fairly have a stroke when *she* found out."

"Madam Dee."

"Yes, ma'am. I had just left Mrs. Pennington's room when Madam Dee opened her door and stepped into the hall. Bill, the footboy, was just bringing up the last trunk, and Miss Savino opened *her* door and looked out, and Madam Dee saw her and stopped dead in her tracks. 'Moan dew,' Madam Dee said; I don't know what it means, ma'am."

Miranda saw no reason to provide a translation, but Cassy, undeterred, rushed on. "She went on chattering in French, Madam Dee did, and finally she clapped her hands together and said 'Humphrey!' Then she raced down the steps, and I didn't actually *see* her go out, but I did hear the front door slam. So I surmise that Madam Dee went to tell Sir Humphrey about Miss Savino though why *he* should care, I can't imagine."

"No, indeed," Miranda choked.

She ground her fingernails into her palms, steeling herself for Cassy's next revelation. But the abigail had apparently finished her story; she proceeded to the wardrobe and plucked out a walking dress of biscuit mull. And what was left to tell? Miranda reflected despondently, as Cassy assisted her into the gown and began to dress her hair. As a purveyor of news, Sir Humphrey was just slightly more efficient than *The Times*; the tale of Lord Margrave's house guest would reach the remotest corner of London long before sunset. Miranda gazed sightlessly into the mirror, wondering what further misfortune could possibly befall her.

"Lady Margrave!"

It was a clear measure of Horton's distress that he had altogether neglected to knock. Nor did he look himself at all, Miranda observed: his normally immaculate shirt-points were hopelessly wilted, and his luxuriant white hair had formed a veritable jungle of damp, untidy tendrils about his face.

"Major von Rheinbeck has arrived," the butler panted. "He indicated that he is in a considerable hurry, but he did seem most eager to see you."

"The Czar!" Cassy hastily adjusted the last of Miranda's curls. "His Majesty no doubt has affairs of state to settle, ma'am; you'd best not keep him waiting."

"Perhaps he *is* the Czar," Horton murmured distantly. "Perhaps so; I shouldn't wonder at anything."

Miranda perceived no advantage in postponing her inevitable meeting with Rheinbeck, and she trailed Horton along the corridor. As they passed Signorina Savino's bedchamber, the butler glanced nervously sidewards, as though he feared the imminent emergence of some mythical monster, and he tripped twice on the stairs. At the drawing-room archway, he plaintively inquired if "His Majesty" would desire some tea.

"No, thank you, Horton," Miranda said gently. "You may leave us now."

"Yes, ma'am."

The butler retreated, stumbling once more before he reached the steps, and Miranda proceeded into the saloon. Rheinbeck, who had evidently been pacing a narrow path between the sofa and the hearth, rushed forward and seized her hand.

"I cannot stay, Lady Margrave; I am very shortly to ride with His Majesty in the park. But I did wish to stop, however briefly, to offer my sympathy."

"Sympathy?" Miranda echoed. She entertained a momentary notion that Anthony had met with a street accident of which she had not yet been informed.

"Yes. I can well conceive your dismay with regard to the shocking incident which occurred at the theatre last evening."

"Ah." Miranda attempted, unsuccessfully, to extricate her hand from the Major's grasp. "You witnessed the—er—incident then."

"As who did not?" Rheinbeck responded dramatically. "I daresay there were upwards of two thousand people milling about at the time." He seemed to realize, suddenly and quite belatedly, that he had said entirely the wrong thing. "However, I am certain that none of them actually *noticed*. You will recall that the crowd was distracted by the summoning of the carriages. The arrival of the carriages. The horses. And so forth. Far too busy to notice that Lord Margrave was fairly attacked by an opera performer."

"How comforting," Miranda said dryly. She tentatively flexed her fingers again, but the Major's grip had not loosened to any appreciable degree.

"And those few who did take note attached no significance to the matter at all," Rheinbeck continued. "I, for example, was conversing with Lady Sefton, and she commented that Lord Margrave has always had a host of female friends. She added that most have been women of very dubious reputation indeed—"

Miranda jerked her hand away, and the Major staggered backward, nearly falling over his sword. He caught himself up, biting his lip at the same instant, and Miranda thought she detected a drop of blood on his mouth.

"Pray forgive me, Lady Margrave." Rheinbeck licked his lower lip most gingerly. "I assure you I meant no insult. Quite the contrary: my hope was to encourage you to forget the incident altogether. I should not suppose you will encounter Signorina Savino—or so I believe she styles herself—again. Well. Good day."

The Major made his stiff little bow, and Miranda felt a flood of remorse. However inept in execution, Rheinbeck's intentions were unquestionably sincere; he, perhaps he alone, genuinely cared for "Lady Margrave." Miranda swallowed a maddening lump in her throat.

"Pray forgive *me*, Major," she murmured. "The fact is that I *have* encountered Signorina Savino again, indirectly at least." She did not know whether she was confessing the truth because she chose to or because he would inevitably find it out. "The fact is that my—that Anthony has brought her to live with us. Temporarily, at any rate."

"*Here?*" Rheinbeck raised his eyes, as if he expected to find the songbird flapping about the chandelier. "In this house? Lord Margrave has established his—his—" The Major bit his lip once more, winced, clicked his heels together. "It is not my affair, Lady Margrave," he concluded tersely. An unfortunate choice of words. "Such an arrangement would be quite unthinkable in Prussia, but evidently the customs in your country differ from those in my own. As I am a guest in England, I shall not presume to interfere. And I must be off in any event, lest I delay His Majesty's outing. I am to accompany His Majesty to Oxford tomorrow, but I hope to return in time for the assembly at Almack's. Good afternoon, Lady Margrave."

Miranda accompanied Rheinbeck to the top of the stairs, where the Major again tendered his abbreviated bow before descending to the foyer. Miranda proceeded slowly up toward the second story.

Rheinbeck had been far too kind when he had described Anthony's arrangement as "unthinkable," she reflected. And it was unlikely that London's *ton* would regard the matter as benignly as had the Major; no, Lady Margrave would soon be the butt of an endless repertoire of lascivious jests.

"*On dit* that the nightingale has befouled the head of the governess."

Miranda could almost hear the Duke of Clarence growling some such crudity, guffawing at his own wit, and she gritted her teeth. She was sorely tempted to pack her things and leave at once. In fact, the timing was ideal, for Anthony would have no difficulty explaining his wife's abrupt departure to Elizabeth, to the servants, to society at large. She would emigrate to Canada after all.

By what means? Lacking the Earl's promised bonus,

Miranda hadn't a feather to fly with; she could not purchase a seat on the mail, much less a transatlantic passage. And she did not believe Anthony would permit her to go even one day early; he seemed perversely determined to keep her on, to torment her, to hold her up to ridicule. Miranda's throat tightened once more, and she blinked back a tear of mingled outrage and self-pity. She had reached the top of the steps, and she vented her frustration, with a resounding kick, upon the newel post.

She started down the corridor, but the foolish kick had set her toe to throbbing, and she stopped and bent to massage it. When, at length, she straightened, her eyes strayed involuntarily to Signorina Savino's door, and at that moment the door opened, and the songbird peered into the hall.

Miranda could not decide which of them was the more surprised. Perhaps they were both startled literally to paralysis, for they stood for what seemed an infinity and simply stared at one another.

The Signorina *was* as small as she had appeared on the stage: inches shorter than Miranda and thin to the point of emaciation. Miranda observed that the songbird's gown—an elaborate creation of pale-blue jaconet —fairly hung upon her, suggesting that she had not always been so slight. Miranda raised her eyes and felt them widen with shock, for, upon close inspection, the Signorina looked quite ill. Her features were handsome enough: great dark eyes, a pert, uptilted nose, a slightly-too-generous mouth over a pleasant, rounded chin. But her complexion was fearfully pale, almost gray; her eyes seemed puffy, the lids swollen; and the lines about her mouth—new lines?—made her appear years older than her chronological age.

Miranda felt a surge of emotion and, with another stab of shock, recognized it as pity. "Good day," she said impulsively. "I am Lady Margrave."

The dark eyes narrowed until they were nearly invisible beneath the swollen lids, and the ample mouth twisted to a tiny slit. Without a word, Signorina Savino slammed the door with a crash that seemed to reverberate in Miranda's bones. She continued down the corridor, puzzling over the Signorina's expression, which was one she had not previously encountered. She had reached her own door when she realized, with a further rush of shock, that it was hatred she'd seen on the songbird's waxen face—pure, naked hatred. The doorknob rattled a bit in Miranda's hand, and she closed the door behind her with rather more force than absolutely required.

By mid-week, the household had returned to at least a semblance of routine. Miranda could not but notice that Mrs. Horton had adopted a severe, permanent frown; that Horton himself had developed a nervous tic near his right eye; and that Elizabeth had assumed the butler's former look of pained resignation. But even Cassy had evidently accepted the Signorina's presence to the extent that she no longer felt compelled to talk about it, for when she came to the Yellow Chamber on Wednesday afternoon, it was solely to discuss Miranda's attire for the evening's assembly.

The Midsummer Ball at Almack's, Miranda reflected wryly. A few short weeks before, she would have visualized such an event as the very pinnacle of her existence. Indeed, she now recalled, she had: she had pictured herself, in a gown of yellow lace, whirling across the floor in the Earl of Margrave's arms. But she had already worn the yellow lace, and the Earl was unable to dance. How wonderfully appropriate: her vision, like all her childish dreams, had turned to dust.

"It doesn't signify, Cassy," she sighed aloud. "Choose what you will."

"What you will" proved to be a dress of pale blue crape over a matching sarsnet slip. Miranda frowned at her reflection, initially unable to define what it was she disliked about the ensemble. Eventually it came to her: except for the difference in fabric, the gown bore a suspicious resemblance to Signorina Savino's blue jaconet. Miranda's frown deepened, but it was too late to change. Cassy adjusted the splendid sapphire necklace she had plucked from the jewel box and shepherded her mistress to the foyer.

Miranda had dreaded to confront Sir Humphrey, for whom they were to stop en route to King Street. However, the baronet seemed altogether to have forgotten the Signorina; he had no sooner taken his place in the landau than he began to chatter of a "Princess Claude." It was a mark of Miranda's distraction that some minutes elapsed before she deduced that *Princess Claude* was a ship rather than a woman.

"You are going abroad then?" she asked idly.

"Yes, I booked our passage today." Sir Humphrey smiled at the Comtesse. "We had hoped to leave tomorrow, directly after the wedding, but the *Princess* does not sail until Friday. Lord Margrave has very kindly offered the use of your home for our wedding night." Jeanne giggled, and the baronet patted her gloved hand.

"Tomorrow?" Miranda repeated. "You are to be married tomorrow?"

"I thought you were aware of that, Lady Margrave. I do believe I mentioned that we would be wed on the sixteenth, which, as it happens, is also dear Jeanne's birthday." Another pat, this one in the general vicinity of the Comtesse's knee.

"Yes, I believe you did," Miranda murmured. "How quickly time passes." For some reason, the notion prompted a flutter in her rib cage, and she began to study the blue-chenille rosettes on her slippers.

The confusion of the preceding days had driven all thought of Thomas and Martha from Miranda's mind, so it was with some surprise that she found them waiting outside the entrance to the assembly rooms. She then recalled Anthony's invitation to her cousins and collected that the Earl had arranged to meet them. But there was no time to confirm her conjecture, for the Cavendishes were fairly champing at the bit, eager to get on with the conquest of London's social citadel.

For her part, Miranda was not unduly impressed by the former gaming club, now converted to perhaps the most fashionable address in all the realm. She attended but vaguely her presentation to the patronesses of the establishment; indeed, she was subsequently unable to distinguish Princess Esterhazy from Countess Lieven. But she did take particular note of Lady Jersey, the rumored object of the Czar's affections, and the dowager Countess avidly returned her scrutiny.

"I must own Clarence quite right when he pronounced you far too comely for a governess, Lady Margrave. But then I always fancied it would take an exceptional sort to bring our wicked Anthony to heel."

Her ladyship tapped the Earl's arm with her silver-embroidered fan. She was still quite beautiful, Miranda observed, though she must surely be sixty. Lady Jersey's small mouth curved into a smile, and Miranda thought she detected a hint of malice round the edges.

"In truth, Anthony seems determined to convert all humankind to the domestic life, eh?" The tip of her fan grazed the Earl's chin. "*On dit* that you will imminently marry off your little French *amie* to Sir Humphrey Hammond. Do you seek a suitable husband for *la Signorina* as well? I do trust so, for I am told that she is now under your protection. Indeed, though I found it difficult to credit such an astonishing bit of information, I was given to understand that you have taken the nightingale under your very *roof*. I do fear, Anthony, that you are well in the way of eclipsing even Lord Byron's scandalous conduct."

"I do hope to locate a *parti* for Miss Savino," Anthony said politely. "I hold it altogether disgraceful when gentlemen drop their old friends without a crumb of recompense. Do you not agree, Lady Jersey?"

The Countess turned a most alarming shade of scarlet and snapped her delicate fan neatly in half. Miranda could only surmise that her ladyship was remembering, as Anthony had clearly intended she should, her ill-fated *affaire* with the Regent, who had jilted her quite shamelessly more than a dozen years before.

"I do indeed agree," Lady Jersey sputtered and, with a final nod at Miranda, spun about and flounced away.

Anthony and Miranda rejoined the rest of their party in the refreshment parlor, which—in view of the fact that said refreshments consisted entirely of bread and butter, stale cake, lemonade and tea—was hardly a scene of unbridled hilarity. Even as they entered, Thomas was lamenting the excruciating dullness of the beverages and wondering aloud whether any nearby gentlemen had thought to equip themselves with flasks of somewhat stronger spirits.

"You had quite enough in the way of strong spirits at Miranda's last week," Martha snapped. "Enough, I should say, to last you for some months to come."

Thomas gulped rather sheepishly at his lemonade, and Martha turned to Miranda. "I met Countess Lieven," she breathed, her small gray eyes aglow. "And Lady Castlereagh. I do believe, Miranda, that I could die happily. I can certainly return to Sussex happily, as we plan to do tomorrow. I—I wish to thank you for all your kindness."

Miranda felt herself dangerously, absurdly close to tears. A week since, she would have wished her cousins cheerfully at the devil; now they seemed a very underpinning of her life, soon to be lost forever. She took refuge in an elaborate fit of coughing and, fortunately, was rescued: the orchestra launched into a lively country dance, and Thomas tugged Martha out to the floor.

Miranda herself was invited to stand up with a young peer whose name she couldn't recall, and she danced several ensuing sets as well. But her feet were peculiarly leaden, her arms wooden; and at the first opportunity she slipped back into the refreshment parlor. She found Anthony and the rest of the group gone; except for half a dozen hatchet-faced matrons, the room was deserted. Miranda poured and sipped another glass of lemonade.

"Lady Margrave!" Rheinbeck rushed into the refreshment parlor, and the matrons peered over their cups and glasses with intense curiosity. "Thank God I have found you!"

The Major looked rather bedraggled, Miranda observed: his side-whiskers were damp, there was a spot of dirt upon his chin, and his boots were pale with dust.

"I have just ridden up from Oxford," Rheinbeck said, as though he had discerned her thoughts. "And I have received the most dreadful news." In quite uncharacteristic fashion, he ran one hand through his blonde hair, now somewhat limp and dark with perspiration. "I have been ordered back to Prussia. I am to leave on Friday, on the *Princess Claude* out of Dover."

Miranda entertained a fanciful, frightful notion that all her props were being snatched away, that she would soon be left, utterly alone, on a dark and empty stage. "What a coincidence," she said aloud, with brittle gaiety. "Some dear friends of mine will be traveling on the same ship. Sir Humphrey and Lady Hammond; she will be Lady Hammond by then, at any rate. Do allow me to present you to them, Major, for I daresay you will find them to be amusing shipboard companions."

"There is but one shipboard companion I would wish for, Lady Margrave."

Rheinbeck, in his extremity, had thrown all caution to the winds. He seized Miranda's hand and gazed down at her, his blue eyes glowing with unmistakable passion, and Miranda became uncomfortably aware of the fascinated scrutiny of their audience. She heard, as if from an immense distance, the strains of a waltz and judged the crowded dance floor the lesser of the available evils.

"I fancy we have never danced together, Major," she said brightly. "Come, let us avail ourselves of what may be our final opportunity."

She led him into the main assembly room and deliberately prolonged the selection of a vacant spot, hoping Rheinbeck would forget the nature of their interrupted conversation. But it was not to be; as the Major took her in his arms, the feverish light in his eyes seemed, in fact, to intensify.

"I pray you will forgive my frankness, Lady Margrave, but as you yourself point out, this may well be my final opportunity to speak. I am sure you have perceived my admiration for you, my deep, if recent, affection. I quite recognize the seriousness of the marriage bond, but it is not an indissoluble one. I am not without influence in my homeland, and in view of the shocking mistreatment you have been compelled to endure . . ."

Rheinbeck stopped, momentarily released Miranda and mopped his brow, apparently unable to voice the rest of his horrifying suggestion. As he tugged her again into motion, Miranda completed his statement for herself: in Prussia, in the shadow of the family castle, far from Lord Margrave's interference, the Major would no doubt be able to have her marriage annulled.

Miranda realized that she could not have dreamed a more opportune moment for confession. She had only to say that there *was* no marriage, no obstacle to the alliance Rheinbeck so desperately desired; and the Major, in his joy, would scarcely question her peculiar position in the Earl of Margrave's household. "I am not married." The words teased her tongue, but she could not say them after all, for she sensed that, wherever her future lay, it was not with Rheinbeck.

"I am exceedingly flattered, Major," she murmured gently. "However, you will understand that I cannot agree to any such endeavor."

"Not at *present*." It was part statement, part question, part plea. Rheinbeck pulled her so tightly against him that the buttons of his uniform cut quite painfully into her chest. "But circumstances change, Lady Margrave. If I may, I shall leave you my brother's address, by which you can always reach me if the need arises."

The waltz ended with a flourish, and Miranda attempted to break away. But Rheinbeck seemed entirely oblivious to this particular change of circumstances. He pressed her, if possible, even closer, and his breath stirred the curls below her *toque*.

"Promise me that you will do so, Lady Margrave. That you will advise me at once if your situation becomes intolerable."

"I—I promise," Miranda stammered.

She started once more to back away, and the Major's embrace loosened so abruptly that she lost her balance.

A strong hand caught her up at the very last instant, shook her, and she had scarcely registered the furious glitter of Anthony's green eyes when the Earl whirled on Rheinbeck.

"I must insist most strenuously that you cease annoying my wife, Lieutenant von Richter."

"Major."

Rheinbeck had evidently bitten his lip again, for he dabbed up a small drop of blood with the back of one hand. The sight of the wound, minuscule though it was, generated a ripple of excitement amongst sone dozen couples who had gathered round them.

"You may be a general officer for all it signifies," Anthony said coldly. "Whatever your rank, it does not entitle you to force your attentions upon respectable Englishwomen."

"I assure you that I did not intend to force my attentions on Lady Margrave." The Major spoke with great dignity, somewhat impaired when he was compelled to lick another drop of blood from his mouth.

"Indeed? Your implication, then, is that my wife invited your panting and pawing."

The crowd simultaneously, sharply, drew its breath, and one woman, looking quite faint, began to fan herself.

"Please, Anthony," Miranda hissed. "The Major meant no harm; he was, in fact, telling me that he plans to leave on Friday—"

"Leave?" the Earl interrupted loudly. "That is most fortunate because if Rheinhardt did not think to depart of his own volition, I should make every effort to arrange his expulsion from the country."

Rheinbeck drew himself up, his epaulets fairly quivering with indignation, and Miranda closed her eyes. She had stood thus for a few seconds when the crowd emitted a great gasp, and Miranda forced her eyes back open, shuddering to contemplate the mayhem which had apparently transpired. But their recent spectators were looking toward the door, and Miranda, following their direction, glimpsed the Czar striding into the assembly room. Even as His Majesty bowed to Lady Jersey, Rhein-beck clicked his own heels and slipped away. The orchestra struck up another waltz, the Czar swept Lady Jersey into his arms, and the floor around them came to frantic life. Anthony propelled Miranda through the whirling throng, holding her arm in a viselike grip, and when they had reached the fringes of the mob, announced that they would leave at once.

"You must locate Jeanne and Sir Humphrey then—"

"To *hell* with Jeanne and Sir Humphrey!" the Earl snapped.

He prodded her past Lady Sefton, but that august patroness did not notice them, for she was staring, with jealous rage, at Lady Jersey and the Czar. Anthony jerked Miranda on to the street and waved his cane imperiously at the waiting line of carriages. When the landau clattered up, the Earl shoved Miranda inside and fairly leaped in behind her, and Pollard, as though sensing his master's wretched humor, put the vehicle into motion with a fearful jolt.

They rattled on in silence, a silence so cold that it seemed almost palpable, as if a damp, chilly mist had seeped into the carriage. Miranda had, of course, witnessed Anthony's irritation on several occasions, but she believed this was the first time she had seen the Earl deeply, implacably angry. The awareness that his anger was entirely justified set her to squirming uncomfortably in her seat, and she cast rather desperately about for an appropriate apology.

However, the words did not immediately come, and as Miranda continued to grope, her guilt began to recede, and she felt the blossoming of her own anger. She had not, in fact, "invited" Rheinbeck's attentions, but Anthony's ill-chosen phrase suggested quite the contrary. The Earl's statement would be gleefully misconstrued, and the tale would soon be all about that Lord Margrave had publicly accused his wife of infidelity.

It suddenly occurred to Miranda that perhaps his lordship had deliberately contrived to create this "misunderstanding." His military training had no doubt included extensive instruction in the art of the diversionary tactic. What better way to deflect criticism of his shocking arrangement with Signorina Savino than to imply that his wife was dallying with a Prussian officer? Yes, she now recalled, the Earl had used those very words following the incident at the opera. And tonight he had literally dragged her out of Almack's, in full view of the *haut ton*, an action calculated to inspire all manner of sympathetic gossip. He had not even allowed her to bid her dear cousins a possibly final farewell.

Well, she would not permit him to best her so easily, Miranda decided; not again. She opened her mouth, unsure as to exactly what would emerge, but at that moment the carriage stopped. Anthony threw open the door, climbed out and, without a backward glance, marched toward the house. By the time Johnson had assisted Miranda down and she herself had raced through the front door, the Earl had disappeared.

Miranda dashed on up the steps, seemingly driven by demons of fury. Unnaturally quick as she was, she but narrowly overtook Anthony, who had already attained the second story when she reached the final flight of stairs.

"Milord!" she hissed.

He turned and gazed down the staircase, regarding her as if she were an exotic, mildly interesting insect the like of which he had not previously encountered. He waited for her nevertheless, and as she arrived at his side, he raised his uneven brows.

"Yes?" he said frostily.

"I would have a word with you." The unaccustomed exertion had rendered her whisper quite ragged.

"Certainly," the Earl said with frigid courtesy. "Though I cannot conceive of any matter we need discuss."

"No matter?" Miranda croaked. "I have never, in all my life, been so embarrassed, so humiliated as I was by your behavior this evening."

"What a remarkable coincidence," Anthony drawled,

"for I feel entirely the same. Now that we have shared our mutual displeasure, I propose we retire without further ado."

He bowed and started to step away, but Miranda clutched his sleeve. "No!" she rasped. "You will not put me in the wrong this time, milord. You will not escape by claiming your own discomfiture, for which there is no reason—"

"No reason?" The Earl yanked his arm away, and in the flickering lamplight, Miranda's falling hand did indeed resemble a giant, white moth. "I have been called many names, my dear, not all of them kind, not all of them warranted. But I daresay I earned, tonight, an appellation of which I never dreamed, that of cuckold."

"Cuckold!" Miranda gasped. Was there a slight creak at the far end of the corridor? If so, it but dimly penetrated her stunned senses. "You cannot be serious."

"I am most serious indeed. Once the novelty of His Russian Majesty's unexpected visit has run its course, I fancy our marital situation will become the *on-dit* of the Season. It makes for such a juicy tale, you see: Lord Margrave's bride of under a month entwined quite brazenly in the arms of a dashing foreigner."

"But you know very well that it signified nothing!" Miranda's voice had assumed an exceedingly peculiar timbre, something between a whisper and a screech. "You know that I have not spent a single private moment with Major von Rheinbeck—"

"And I can only assume, in view of your display this evening, that you bitterly regret the lack of opportunity."

It was suddenly, horribly quiet. Miranda could hear his breathing, could hear her own; she thought she could hear the hiss of the lamp. "I am leaving, Anthony," she said at last. "Tomorrow. And there is no means by which you can prevent me."

"I do not intend to prevent you." Did he sound tired or was that but a figment of her overwrought imagination? "I had hoped . . ." He stopped and shook his head, and his red-gold hair gleamed in the dancing light.

"Never mind; it is quite clear that our project has proved a dismal failure. As I do not keep a great deal of cash about, I shall be unable to provide any money until tomorrow afternoon. At that time, you will receive your due."

"I don't want your money!" Miranda spat. "I shan't accept it, not a groat; I should prefer to starve."

She dodged past him, fled down the hall and plunged into the Yellow Chamber. Cassy was asleep in one of the striped-silk chairs, and Miranda closed the door very softly.

She stripped off her *toque* and her jewelry and the hateful blue dress and crept toward the wardrobe. But Cassy sighed, stirred, and Miranda feared to wake her, feared to face her. She crawled into the canopied bed, still clad in her underthings, and burrowed beneath the bedclothes.

There, in total, blessed darkness, the tears came, and Miranda buried her head under the pillow and sobbed herself to sleep.

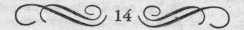 14

When Miranda woke, she initially fancied that she had
somehow fallen asleep in a cave. She then recalled the
wretched circumstances of her retirement, eased her
head from beneath the pillow and cautiously lifted the
bedclothes. Cassy was not in sight, and with a sigh of relief, Miranda sprang out of bed, hurried to the wardrobe
and donned one of her more modest peignoirs. She
crossed to the dressing table, thinking to straighten her
hair, and gazed at her reflection with shock.

She did not look like herself in the least, but the
woman in the mirror seemed tantalizingly familiar. It
was a moment before Miranda realized that her pale,
sunken cheeks, her red and swollen eyelids lent her an
astonishing resemblance to Signorina Savino. She rushed
to the washstand, splashed water upon her face and eyes
and dashed back to the dressing table, furiously pinch-
ing her cheeks en route. She was pleased to note some
slight improvement in her appearance, and just in time
at that, for she detected the rattle of the doorknob and
the squeak of the corridor door.

"Come in, Cassy," she called.

There was a slight delay, then another rattle, soon explained as Elizabeth entered the room bearing a silver
tray. She kicked the door closed behind her and flashed
an over-cheerful smile.

"I hope you do not object, my dear, but I insisted that
Cassy permit me to deliver your breakfast. I daresay you
are not at all hungry, but I did not wish to arouse
Cassy's suspicions." Elizabeth crossed the Brussels carpet
and set the tray on the dressing table. "The dear girl

does worry about you so; perhaps you might just spread the food around a bit as we talk."

"Talk?" Miranda echoed, her own suspicions rising. "Talk of what, Mother Elizabeth?"

"Of your quarrel with Anthony. Pray do not deny it, dear, for I could not but overhear you. I did not intend to eavesdrop, of course, but my ears chance to be exceedingly sharp."

And most particularly sharp when placed at the crack of a door, Miranda thought dryly, recalling the creak she had heard the night before. She stabbed her fork into a boiled egg. It was clearly pointless to deny an argument, but *she* would not be the one to inform Anthony's mother of their impending, permanent separation.

"We did have a—a minor disagreement," she said lightly.

"A disagreement so minor that you plan to leave Anthony." Elizabeth perched on the edge of the disordered bed and smoothed her skirt with remarkable unconcern. "Yes, I heard it all, my dear. I trust you will not take it amiss when I say that I was compelled to chuckle, for I was reminded of the occasions upon which I threatened to leave Anthony's father. It is an obvious mark of dear Anthony's generosity that he offered you a financial settlement. Peter invariably advised me that I should find myself walking the streets before he would give me a single shilling."

Miranda was so startled that she failed to blush at this latter comment. "You were once inclined to leave Anthony's father?" she gasped.

"Not *once*, my dear; many times. And if that surprises you, it shouldn't. There is not a living wife who has not thought, at some juncture, to escape her husband. Show me a woman who claims never to have entertained the notion, and I shall show you a liar. I fancy the same is true of men as well," Elizabeth added grudgingly. "The fact is that all of us have our faults. Peter's was that he gambled to excess; in truth, I often wondered how little Anthony and I were to obtain our next meal."

"But he died a wealthy man," Miranda protested. "Mr. Barham, that is."

"Yes, in time I was able to reform him," Elizabeth agreed airily. "As you will eventually reform Anthony."

"But Anthony is not a gambler," Miranda said. "I do not believe he has visited Brook's for several weeks—"

"You misunderstand me, Miranda," Elizabeth interrupted kindly. "I stated that all men have flaws; I did not suggest that all share the *same* failing. Anthony's defect is that of jealousy."

"Jealousy!" The word struck Miranda like a bolt of lightning.

"Have you not perceived that Anthony bitterly mislikes your slightest attention to another man? I collect that Major von Rheinbeck is the immediate target of his wrath though I can scarcely conceive a more improbable seducer. Be that as it may . . ."

Elizabeth chattered on, but Miranda did not attend her. Jealousy! she marveled again; was that not the same emotion which had plagued *her* these past weeks? From the very beginning, in the carriage driving up from Sussex, she had fretted over Anthony's "friends." She had resented the Hortons' unstated suggestions of earlier guests, had resented Anthony's previous patronage of Madame Leclair, had resented Jeanne. And she had fairly bristled at his lordship's relationship with Signorina Savino; the Earl himself had accused her of jealousy on that account. And where there was jealousy . . .

But the logical conclusion was too absurd to be admitted even in thought. "You must be mistaken, Mother Elizabeth," she blurted out. "Surely you are mistaken."

"I am not mistaken," Elizabeth said briskly, "for if I know nothing else, I do know a great deal about the nature of men. I must remind you, my dear, that I took my first husband at nineteen and my second when I was well into middle age. As I have pointed out, not all men share the same failings, but they all have common faults."

Miranda was uncertain whether this pronouncement made sense or not; she let it pass.

"One of these is pride," Elizabeth continued. "Men are ever persuaded that they are right in all regards, and women must ever yield to this fantasy. Consequently, and distasteful though the prospect may be, you must apologize to Anthony."

"Apologize!" Miranda screeched.

"It is not a defeat, Miranda." Elizabeth spoke with uncharacteristic gentleness. "Quite the contrary: a clever woman will always be victorious in matters of love because love is a condition men do not understand. Anthony is utterly besotted with you; that much is clear from his actions even were it not written in his eyes."

"His actions?" Miranda repeated. "One of his more recent *actions* was to establish his—his—to establish Signorina Savino not ten paces from his bedchamber."

"You must put Signorina Savino entirely out of your mind," Elizabeth said firmly. "I, too, was somewhat distressed when I first learned of her arrival, but after one close glimpse of the poor girl, I quite understand the situation. Have you not observed how very ill she appears?"

"Yes; yes, I have."

"She is not ill in the least," Elizabeth sniffed. "She is withering away as a result of Anthony's inattention. It is very clear that he terminated their relationship—whatever *that* may have been—as soon as he fell under your spell, my dear."

Miranda was fairly dizzy with confusion. "But if that is the case, why is Anthony so willing, nay, *eager*, to allow me to leave?"

"He wants to believe that he can live quite happily without you," Elizabeth responded. "And he *does* believe that you have wronged him. Consequently, he will not come to you—he would rather die—but he will seize upon your slightest gesture of atonement to effect a reconciliation."

Elizabeth stood and walked to the dressing table. "Naturally I shall not suggest precisely what that gesture should be for I have no wish to interfere in your marital affairs."

182

Elizabeth flashed her sunny smile again, picked up the tray and bore it triumphantly off as though it were the palm of the conqueror. By the time Miranda was sufficiently sensible to consider assisting Elizabeth with the door, Elizabeth had departed, and the door had clicked shut behind her.

Miranda gazed sightlessly into the mirror, reflecting on Elizabeth's observations, and could no longer deny the logical culmination of her earlier thoughts. She was in love with Anthony, and perhaps that sentiment, too, dated from the very start of their acquaintance. Indeed, she believed she could recall the moment of its birth, the moment when—persuaded that "Mr. Bartlett" was not, after all, a lunatic—she had leaned across the table at the Knight and Dragon, half-entertained by his predicament, half-horrified by his solution. An appropriate beginning, she now decided, for from that time forward the Earl of Margrave had alternately amused and annoyed, soothed and infuriated her. But she loved him, and she did not wish to go to Canada or to Prussia or to any other place in all the world because she could not conceive of a life without him.

She loved him; was it possible, as Elizabeth insisted, that Anthony loved her as well? He had played the role of jealous husband most convincingly, but Miranda well appreciated his thespian capabilities. Nevertheless Elizabeth had termed him "besotted," had claimed to find love written in his eyes.

Miranda sighed. Only one thing was certain: she would never know the Earl's true feelings if she departed; she must stay on until his anger had abated sufficiently to permit them a rational conversation. And, as Elizabeth had pointed out, his anger would *not* abate unless Miranda offered some gesture of atonement. But what gesture? She could not, *would* not, burst into his bedchamber and stammer a confession of love. She was still contemplating and discarding various alternatives when Cassy bounded through the door.

"Madam Dee and Sir Humphrey are off to the

church," the abigail announced. "Isn't it *romantic*, ma'am?"

Miranda had altogether forgotten the imminent wedding, and she chose to regard it as "romantic" indeed, perhaps a favorable omen for the general cause of love.

"Lord Margrave was to attend as a witness," Cassy continued, "but he nearly crossed them up, for he has been away all morning. At any rate, he returned just in time and left again at once. He desired me to bring you this, ma'am."

Cassy extended an envelope, and Miranda took it most gingerly, as though it might burn her fingers. The envelope was opaque, but Miranda well knew that it contained a sheaf of banknotes. She was sorely tempted to open it and count the bills so as to ascertain his lordship's estimation of her worth. But she refrained, for she suddenly glimpsed the envelope as a key: she would approach Anthony ostensibly to return his money. She placed the envelope in one of the dressing table drawers and allowed Cassy to help her dress.

Miranda paced the Yellow Chamber for the better part of the afternoon, rehearsing her discussion with Anthony. Eventually she decided that no rehearsal was possible: she would be compelled to deliver up the envelope, like the proverbial burnt offering, and play the rest of the score by ear. She then began to fear that Anthony would seek to avoid her; they had no plans for the evening, and he might well take the opportunity to return to Brooks's. But at half past six, she heard the jingle of harness, the clatter of hoofs in the coach yard, and she flew to the window and watched as his lordship's curricle halted below. A few minutes later, the doorknob rattled, and Miranda spun around, her heart crashing into her throat.

"Did I startle you, ma'am?" Cassy asked. "I can't seem to remember to knock. At any rate, Lord Margrave instructed me to tell you that he has ordered dinner for seven."

"Thank you, Cassy," Miranda murmured.

"Actually, he told me to tell you so if you were still here, ma'am. I was at the point of asking where *else* you would be. Men do say the oddest things, do they not?"

"Indeed they do," Miranda choked.

Anthony acknowledged her arrival in the dining room with an exceedingly terse "Good evening" and started immediately to wolf down his turtle soup. Miranda entertained a dismal suspicion that, were it not for Elizabeth, the soup, the wine, the very air would turn at once to ice. As it was, Elizabeth was able to sustain only the most clipped of conversations.

"How was the wedding, dear?" she asked brightly, finishing her own soup.

"Like any wedding," Anthony snapped. "One of the curates at St. George's performed the ceremony. Jeanne and Hammond are married."

"How nice," Elizabeth cooed. "And what did the dear Comtesse wear? Dear Lady Hammond, I suppose I should say."

"I believe it was yellow though it might have been almond. It was definitely not white, if that is the substance of your question."

"Well, I am sure my question had no *substance*, dear. I was merely curious. Weddings are such *happy* occasions, do you not agree?"

"Umm," Anthony growled.

"And where are they now? Sir Humphrey and the lovely new Lady Hammond?"

"They are partaking of a wedding dinner at Lord Crowley's. I daresay *he* is the happiest man in London tonight, faced with the welcome prospect of his nephew's permanent departure."

The footmen presented the entree, and Anthony attacked his rabbit as if he feared it might still be breathing. The Earl's black humor was sufficient to daunt even the gallant Elizabeth, and they consumed the rest of the meal in silence. Anthony devoured his pudding in two or three furious bites and flung his napkin on the table.

"As you are no doubt aware, I have invited Hammond and Jeanne to spend their wedding night here, and I propose to offer them maximum privacy. With that end in view, I myself shall retire at once. Good night."

He rose, bowed and stalked out of the room, and Elizabeth gave Miranda a look of great, piercing significance. Miranda, though her dessert was still but half-eaten, nodded and hurried up the stairs.

The second-floor corridor was still reverberating with the slam of his lordship's bedchamber door, a sound scarcely calculated to bolster Miranda's morale. She crept down the hall and into the Yellow Chamber, wondering if it might not be best to postpone the interview after all. Anthony was so *very* annoyed. There was a thud from beyond the connecting door, as though the Earl had thrown something upon a table or against a wall, and Miranda winced.

But she was not a procrastinator by nature, and she doubted that Anthony's mood would be improved by the mere passage of time. She strode to the dressing table, removed the envelope from the drawer and marched boldly to the connecting door. She had intended to tap very lightly, but her knock seemed to echo like the blow of a battering ram upon a castle gate. There was a creak of footsteps on the other side, and Anthony shoved the door open.

"Miranda," he said tonelessly. He sounded as though he had been altogether unaware of the identity of his caller and was intensely disappointed to learn it. "If you have come to say goodbye, I suggest you spare us both any final recriminations. You were quite adequately unpleasant last night, and I do not choose further to indulge your ill humor. Good evening."

The Earl turned and stepped back into his bedchamber, and Miranda bit her lip. *His* indulgence? *Her* ill humor? She recalled Elizabeth's advice, swallowed a furious retort and trailed Anthony into the room.

"I did not come to say goodbye, milord. I came to return your money."

She proffered the envelope, and the Earl frowned, as if puzzling over just what this peculiar article might be. At length he shrugged, took the envelope and tossed it carelessly upon his writing table, a splendid piece in black lacquer which looked to be genuinely Chinese.

"As you will, Miranda," he said wearily. "It appears you are determined to cut off your nose so as to spite your face. Determined, as I believe you phrased it last night, to starve. Very well. I wish you to understand, however, that once you have left my house, I shall take no further responsibility for your welfare. The matter will be entirely finished." Did his last word ring a bit hollow or was that merely her own wishful thinking? "You do understand, I trust."

"Quite so," Miranda said. She waited for him to provide an opening, a tiny chink, but the Earl began to untie his neckcloth, and she realized that she had been left entirely to her own devices. "As it happens, I do not intend to leave. Not right away, at any rate."

If she had expected this pronouncement to send his lordship into immediate transports of ecstasy, she was doomed to bitter disillusion. Anthony yanked off his neckcloth, flung it down beside the envelope and ran his fingers through his red-gold hair.

"Hell and the devil!" he hissed. "How long do you think to try my patience, Miranda? First you wish to go, next you agree to stay, then you resolve to leave again within the day . . ." He stopped, and his green eyes narrowed. "Perhaps you hope to reach a more advantageous financial arrangement. I assure you, my dear, that you will not. Had you counted the money you claim to disdain, you would have discovered the sum of six hundred pounds, and I shall never give you a farthing more. You may go tomorrow or you may stay until hell itself freezes over; it does not signify to me. I only request that you make a decision—a firm, *permanent* decision." His lordship started to unbutton his waistcoat as though, in truth, said decision did not signify a whit.

Her initial offering had been insufficient, Miranda reflected dryly; she would be forced to follow Elizabeth's counsel after all. "I know you are extremely overset, Anthony," she said, as contritely as she could. "And I must own that you have cause, for I recognize that I behaved somewhat indiscreetly last evening. I wish to apologize."

"Splendid," the Earl snapped. "You have done so. I therefore suggest that you retrieve your money and plan to depart tomorrow. I shall put a carriage at your disposal."

"Tomorrow," Miranda gulped. She had failed to prepare for such utter, such implacable hostility, and she cast about for an excuse to prolong her stay. "I hesitate to leave so precipitously, milord. I fear that Thomas and Martha might pose some exceedingly embarrassing inquiries."

"Your fears are quite groundless, my dear," Anthony said coolly. "Were you not aware that the Cavendishes returned to Sussex early this morning? They bade me a rather tearful farewell at Almack's. In fact, I now recollect that they requested me to relay their final compliments. You, as you may recall, were otherwise occupied at the time."

"Anthony, please—"

"Mrs. Cavendish indicated that she did not expect to see me again for some time." His lordship continued as though he had not heard her. "Consequently, it seems an ideal moment for your departure, does it not? Your cousins are unlikely to reappear for several months, and I daresay I can manufacture a credible explanation of your absence in the interim."

"I daresay you can," Miranda mumbled. The conversation was not following even the vaguest of her plans, and she began to grope again. "However, there remains the matter of your mother."

"Dear God, how your tune has changed!" Anthony laughed, but there was no hint of amusement in the short, sharp sound. "Have you become so fond of Mama that you cannot bear the prospect of her displeasure? If so, permit me to assure you that I shall explain your departure most chivalrously. I may well confess that I throttled you half to death and packed you off, bruised and bleeding, to contemplate your sins." He laughed again—the same bitter, mirthless bark. "So there is no reason for you to remain, is there? Quite the contrary:

you can at last make the escape you have so long and passionately desired. Take the money and go."

The Earl tore off his waistcoat, and Miranda felt the first flutter of panic. He was not only willing to let her leave, he was *determined* to be rid of her. She clenched her hands, vainly attempting to stop their sudden trembling.

"Where—where would you have me go?" she stammered.

"I should have thought you had settled on Prussia," his lordship said nastily. "Barring that, you will find that the Empire fairly spans the world." He stopped, and his eyes slitted again. "But I nearly missed the gist of your question, didn't I? You were remembering that I agreed to pay your passage to any site you might select. I must point out, my avaricious darling, that the additional hundred pounds I've furnished"—he nodded toward the envelope—"will see you to the moon if that is your preferred destination. And I must reiterate that I shan't provide another groat."

Anthony flicked an imaginary speck of lint from his waistcoat, and Miranda stared at him, unable to quell the impression that she was trapped in a nightmare. He did not care; he did not care at all.

"How long do you intend to stand there?" Anthony demanded. "I cannot suppose you have anything further to say, but if you do, say it. If not, please go and leave me in peace."

Go. Leave. Miranda willed herself to do just that, to turn and stalk regally out of his bedchamber. But her feet seemed rooted to the carpet, and her vision began to blur. She squeezed her eyelids closed and felt little rivulets of moisture coursing down her cheeks.

"Tears," Anthony sighed. "Woman's ultimate weapon. Pray be advised, my dear, that an emotional display will buy you nothing. You may sob to your heart's content, but I should vastly prefer you to do it elsewhere."

His words might have been a cue: Miranda's shoulders started to heave, and she was compelled to catch her breath in a great, choking gasp.

"Oh, for God's sake!" his lordship snapped. "Here; use my handkerchief."

Miranda, unable to open her eyes, waved her hand aimlessly about for a moment, and the Earl emitted another sigh. He pushed her hand away and dabbed, rather roughly, at her face and lashes. Miranda forced her eyes open at last, and Anthony stepped hastily back.

"Please let us have no more of that," his lordship said gruffly. "As I have stated, tears will avail you nothing, and I did hope we could part on amicable terms." He returned his handkerchief to the pocket of his waistcoat. "I suggest you get an adequate night's rest in preparation for your journey." He walked to the bamboo-legged chair in front of the writing table and draped his waistcoat over the back. "Goodbye, Miranda."

He fussed with his waistcoat, and Miranda watched him, as though he were demonstrating some unique physical talent. She would not see him again, never again. She licked the salty taste of tears from her lips.

"I should hate to have to bear you bodily out," the Earl said tiredly, "but if necessary, I shall. I therefore recommend that, unless you have a very good reason for lurking about, you exit at once."

He had nearly finished with his waistcoat. His red-gold hair was glowing in the candlelight, and shadows flickered across his lean, strong hands.

"Apparently you failed to hear me, Miranda. I asked you to leave or to furnish a reason for your continued, annoying presence. Do you have such a reason?"

"I—I—" She had started to cry again; the tears were trickling off her chin and splashing upon the front of her dress.

"Do you have a reason?" his lordship roared.

The last remnants of Miranda's control dissolved. "Yes, I have a reason!" she sobbed. "I wish to stay because I am in love with you."

The Earl seemingly turned to stone—an awkwardly sculpted statue with one arm still stretched toward the chair and the bulk of his weight on his good right leg. After an eternity he moved, whirled toward her, and

190

Miranda furiously brushed her tears away. She thought she would die if he laughed, would die or kill him, one or both. But Anthony did not laugh.

"As a former boxer, I am compelled to describe that as a blow delivered below the belt," he said tightly. "I had not supposed that you, *even* you, would employ such an underhanded tactic."

"It is not a tactic," Miranda insisted, gaining confidence from his obvious discomfiture. "Indeed, it's the one whole truth I've told for weeks: I love you."

She had stated her feelings, bared her soul, but there was no change in his grim visage. It occurred to her that she might have misread his unease, and she sought to provide herself a graceful retreat.

"I am sorry for my unseemly outburst," she said stiffly. "Evidently I have embarrassed you. I quite understand your reaction; you have demonstrated only too well that you do not reciprocate my affection."

"Not reciprocate?" Anthony bounded across the space between them with no hint of a limp and seized her in his arms so tightly that she feared he might crack her ribs. "Oh, Miranda, my dear, dear love." He buried his face in her hair for a moment, then thrust her away and gazed down at her, his green eyes glowing with a new, intoxicating light.

"I could not at first judge whether I was mad for you or merely mad. None of my old amusements proved in the least amusing; were it not for sheer good luck, I should have lost my entire fortune at Brooks's within forty-eight hours of our meeting. And the jealousy! Good God, if I could not bear to see you dancing with the eldest, homeliest swain in the land, to discover you serving tea to Hammond, how much less could I tolerate your entertainment of Lieutenant von Rechberg?"

Anthony took her face in both his hands, and Miranda counted it a most inappropriate time to correct him in the matter of Rheinbeck's name and rank.

"But I get ahead of my story, for it was long before Rechberg arrived on the scene that I found myself suffering another odd malady: a concern for the future. I, who had little worried whether I might be killed in to-morrow's battle, was contemplating events a year, five years, a decade hence! I soon realized that I only cared for the years ahead because I hoped to spend them with you."

He pulled her into his arms again and kissed her temple. A light kiss, casually placed, but Miranda's stomach constricted most painfully.

"It was at that juncture that I purchased the property in Hertfordshire," Anthony murmured, his breath ruffling her hair. "I persuaded Mr. Oakley, half-persuaded myself, that it was simply an investment. But I knew, in some corner of my mind, that I had bought the house for you, for us, for our children."

"Why didn't you tell me, Anthony?" Miranda drew a bit away and glared up at him, briefly, truly angered by the thought that he could have spared them so much suffering.

"I was at the point of doing so." The Earl pushed her head into his shoulder and left his fingers entwined in her hair. "But that was the very night you encountered your father's friend at the Turners' assembly and insisted you wished to leave at once. It was quite clear to me that you did not reciprocate *my* affection; it was all I could do to encourage you to stay on as my employee."

"I should hardly term it 'encouragement,'" Miranda snapped, her words muffled by his shoulder. "As I recollect the evening, you were exceedingly harsh, milord."

"You *must* stop calling me 'milord.'" Anthony's hand moved from her hair to the nape of her neck, and though his fingers were very warm, Miranda shivered. "Yes, I was rather harsh, and I immediately regretted my odious behavior. So you can imagine my delight when Mama arrived and provided me the perfect excuse to keep you on till Christmas. I was delighted still more when your cousins appeared, for I calculated that their involvement would compel you to remain indefinitely. I hastened to embroil them in our lives, and perhaps I succeeded too well: I wonder how we shall ever be rid of them."

Miranda tilted her face up again and frowned with as much severity as she could muster. "You stated, not five minutes since, that you could parry Thomas and Martha very credibly if I departed."

"Thank God I shall not be called upon to fulfill my boast." Anthony flashed his engaging grin. "No, if you *had* departed tomorrow, my love, I fear I should have been quite drowned in a sea of explanations."

The Earl lowered his head and kissed her squarely on the lips. Miranda had a nagging inkling that something had remained unsaid, and even as Anthony's lips gently parted hers, it came to her: they had yet to discuss his odd relationship with Signorina Savino. But could it matter? she wondered distantly. She seemed to be drowning in a sea of her own, aware of nothing but Anthony's mouth and his hands on her bare shoulders and the thud of his heart through the thin muslin of her gown.

Anthony's lips moved to her neck, and Miranda heard herself moan, deep in her throat, and began to sense that they were moving. Yes, Anthony was propelling her, as if to the strains of a waltz, further into his bedchamber, toward . . . Well, toward the bed, of course. Miranda stiffened. Despite that odd, momentary notion she had entertained at the opera, she was not Anthony's wife; they were not married. The Earl transferred his mouth to hers again, and she felt as if her bones had melted. Not married, she thought dreamily, but they would be soon, within weeks, days perhaps.

The backs of her knees met the edge of the mattress, her legs buckled, and Anthony deftly lifted them onto the bed. He stood over her, smiling—a different smile now, gentle—and began unbuttoning his shirt. One button, two—

"Am I so late that you had given up, Anthony?"

Miranda bolted up just as the third button flew off his lordship's shirt, and by some geometric quirk, the button bounced off her nose before coming to rest on Anthony's shiny left Hessian. Miranda whirled toward the voice and watched, paralyzed, as Signorina Savino closed the opposite connecting door and sauntered into the bedchamber. She wore a bold smile and an exceedingly revealing peignoir, a peignoir *exactly* like Miranda's lace.

"Mary Anne!" Anthony croaked.

His words cured Miranda's paralysis quite miraculously. She leaped out of the bed, and Anthony, seeking to dodge her, lurched to one side, stumbled into an occasional table and thudded to the floor. Miranda flew toward her own room, passionately praying that he was dead. Unfortunately he was not.

"Mary Anne!" he yelped again. "Miranda! Miranda, please permit me to explain—"

Miranda pulled the door to with a crash which, she had no doubt, resounded well into Berkeley Square.

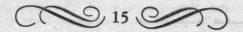

Miranda sagged against the door, gasping for breath, and detected a series of sounds beyond: a creak, a crash, a muffled curse. She gleefully surmised that the heavy, three-branched candelabrum had fallen from the occasional table and damaged some portion of his lordship's miserable anatomy. Which portion soon became clear as she heard the thud of uneven footfalls and an angry mutter: "Hell and the devil! My good foot at that . . ." The footfalls stopped, the doorknob rattled, and the knob on Miranda's side of the door thrust into her back. She whirled around and slammed the door shut again.

"Do not attempt to enter," she whispered furiously. "If you try to open the door, I shall scream. I shall scream to the very heavens, and then you will find yourself drowning in explanations indeed."

"Pray be reasonable, my love," Anthony said. "I assure you that I can clarify the situation to your entire satisfaction—"

"I shall not listen," Miranda hissed. "I shall never listen to you again. I suggest you get about your business at once, for the Signorina seemed exceedingly impatient."

"Miranda, please. I can well conceive your annoyance—"

"Annoyance!" she screeched. She attempted to slam the door again but, as it was quite firmly closed already, succeeded only in jamming the knob most painfully into her palm.

"Perhaps I should allow you to ponder the matter for a time," Anthony said. "I shall return when your wrath has cooled a bit—"

"Then, to quote yourself, milord, you can return when hell itself has frozen over."

"We shall see," the Earl said airily.

He limped away—*thud, THUD, squeak, SQUEAK*—and Miranda turned back round. The connecting door contained a keyhole, but insofar as she knew, there was no key; evidently Charles and Althea's marriage had been considerably more placid than her turbulent relationship with Anthony. Miranda fully intended to erupt into screams upon his lordship's slightest intrusion, but what if she fell asleep? In view of her chaotic emotional state, the possibility appeared remote, but the night was young; sleep might eventually come. Consequently, she must devise some means of protection.

Miranda peered about the room. Of all the furniture, the wardrobe stood nearest the door, but she could not possibly move that. She could, on the other hand, easily move one of the chairs, but she feared the Earl could just as readily dislodge it. The washstand seemed the best compromise, and Miranda walked to it and, pushing and pulling, panting and puffing, maneuvered it in front of the door. She frowned, still dissatisfied: if Anthony worked patiently, quietly, he could at length displace the washstand sufficiently to gain entrance. Miranda glanced around again and had a brilliant notion. She dashed across the bedchamber and plucked the candlestick off the writing table, raced back and placed it on the very edge of the washstand. Yes, upon the slightest movement, the candlestick would tumble to the floor.

Miranda performed a final inspection and belatedly considered the corridor door. Fortunately it *was* equipped with a key, and she hurried to the door and locked it. There. She was quite secure now unless his lordship attempted to come in through one of the windows. Which, in light of the fact that he had literally been left without a good leg to stand on, appeared most unlikely indeed.

Miranda was suddenly so tired that she could not walk as far as the bed, and she collapsed into the nearest of the striped chairs. She wriggled into a comfortable, highly unladylike position, laid her head back and discovered that her exhaustion was only physical; her mind was fairly spinning.

Perhaps she should have permitted Anthony to "clarify the situation" to her "entire satisfaction," she thought, for she could not but wonder what sort of inventive tale the Earl had concocted. The fact was, of course, that he had resumed his relationship with Signorina Savino, had retired early so as to spend a long evening and longer night in the songbird's eager arms. Miranda's interruption had caught him unawares, and in the heat of the moment, he had apparently forgotten his rendezvous.

That was the puzzling part, the heat of the moment. Miranda frowned and closed her eyes. Anthony had seemed so sincere; his words had rung so very true. She reviewed their conversation, and her eyes flew abruptly open. *What* words? He had not, she now remembered, stated that he loved her. He had called her "my love" even "my dear, dear love" but those were nothing more than expressions. No, he had left the important words unsaid.

Nor had he offered for her. He had dangled the future, like a great, golden carrot, before her, tantalizingly referring to "us" and "our children." But had he mentioned marriage? Proposed a time, a place? No, he had left that possibility to Miranda's keen, fevered imagination.

It was, in short, painfully clear that the Earl had identified and seized upon an opportunity to seduce her. Miranda could not begin to guess his motives; perhaps he had merely wished to add a conquered governess to his endless string of actresses and singers and demi-reps. Miranda shuddered to contemplate how nearly he had succeeded. Had it not been for Signorina Savino, barging in to keep the appointment his lordship had so carelessly overlooked . . .

But it was all in the past now, and she would not give Anthony another chance to humiliate her. She hoped, in

197

fact, to avoid even the most casual encounter, for she could well imagine his suggestive commentary, his smirk of triumph. She frowned again. The only practical way to avoid the Earl was to leave at once, perhaps tomorrow with the Hammonds. Yes; though Miranda had not yet determined her ultimate destination, she was suddenly overwhelmed by a desire to escape England. She would travel with the Hammonds to Dover, where, with luck, she might be able to secure passage on the *Princess Claude*. If the *Princess* was fully booked, she could soon embark on another ship; whether she landed on the Continent or in the New World made little difference.

Miranda rose and went wearily to the bed. She had already knelt and begun to draw her portmanteau from beneath the counterpane when she was struck by an appalling recollection: she had returned Anthony's money. Her financial situation could only be described as one of dire poverty, and—last night's rash pronouncement notwithstanding—she could not set out without a shilling to her name. Her eyes stole to the jewel box, and she could not suppress the thought that the sapphire necklace alone was surely worth six hundred pounds. But she would not add theft to dishonesty, and she shoved the portmanteau back under the bed. Trapped: she was still trapped.

Miranda heard a faint sound at the connecting door, and she leaped to her feet just as it cracked open. There was perhaps half an inch of space between the door and the washstand, and when the door met this latter obstacle, there was a moment of silence. Then Anthony pushed again at the door, very cautiously, and Miranda dashed across the room.

"I meant my warning," she rasped. "If you persist, I shall scream. I fancy Sir Humphrey has arrived by now, and I daresay he would cancel even his honeymoon in order to circulate the delicious news that Lord Margrave has taken to wife-beating."

"Miranda, please. If you will grant me five minutes, I shall tell you everything—"

"I do not wish to hear it!" she croaked. "Not every-

198

thing, not anything; your actions are far more eloquent than words, milord."

She was dangerously close to tears, and she stopped and bit her lip. She toyed with the possibility of requesting that he pass the envelope through the crack in the door, eventually shook her head. Her ill-timed declaration of love had been sufficiently degrading; she would not surrender the last shreds of pride.

"I perceive that you remain a trifle overset," Anthony said. "I shall return in an hour or so—"

"You may return in an hour or a day or a year," Miranda hissed; "my sentiments will not have changed. And in the event you think to come in when I am asleep, I must advise you most sternly to abandon any such notion. I have set a candlestick on the edge of the washstand, and I shall light the candle before I retire. If the fall of the candlestick awakens me, I shall scream. If it does not, the house may well be set afire. Good night, milord."

Miranda leaned across the washstand, slammed the door and was rewarded by a yelp. She could not determine whether the Earl was merely startled or had again been physically injured; she fervently hoped it was the latter.

Miranda stepped to the wardrobe, removed her dress and examined her collection of nightclothes. The lace peignoir seemed to mock her, and she quelled an urge to snatch it out of the wardrobe and rip it to tatters. Madame Leclair really should maintain records of some sort, she reflected grimly. She settled on a demure muslin nightgown, started toward the bed and paused to contemplate the candlestick. Wretched though she felt, she was not prepared to be literally incinerated, and she elected not to light the candle after all. She stretched out on the canopied bed but stuffed the pillows behind her head, resolving to stay awake as long as possible. She would watch the door, guard the door, and she would definitely scream if it so much as squeaked.

Miranda was later unable to reconstruct the events of the night, to distinguish sleep from waking, reality from dreams. At one point, she found herself in an Indian teepee, furnished with nothing but a black-lacquer writing table; certainly that was a dream. She was not so sure about the knocks. She thought there were several at the connecting door, thought she reared up in the bed, thought she ordered Anthony to go away. But maybe not; maybe those were dreams as well. She was more persuaded that Cassy rapped, at least once, at the corridor door.

"Are you all right, ma'am? I don't wish to interfere, but you've never locked the door before, and I only want to know that you aren't ill." Yes, it sounded just like Cassy, so that knock must have been real.

It was shortly after dawn, Miranda surmised, when she was definitely jarred awake. The room was still gray, but pink and gold tendrils of light were creeping round the drapes, and she eased herself into a sitting position, caressing her stiff, aching neck. She peered fuzzily about, attempting to recall the sound that had disturbed her, and heard it again. A rattle from the coach yard. Miranda leaped out of bed, rushed to the window and tweaked the curtain aside.

It seemed, for an instant, that she had been whirled back in time: Anthony's curricle, the matched grays hitched, stood in a circle of pale morning sunlight. Then the Earl and Signorina Savino, hand in hand, stepped out of the shadows, and his lordship assisted the songbird into the seat. The vehicle was extremely crowded, Miranda now observed. The box between the rear wheels was quite heaped with luggage, secured with ropes tied around the axle; two small cases were placed in the middle of the seat; and it appeared that the Signorina was herself perched atop a trunk. Even as Miranda watched, Anthony passed still another case up to the songbird, and she wrestled this one onto her lap. The Earl clambered rather awkwardly into the driver's position, and Miranda yanked the curtain shut.

Evidently Anthony and Signorina Savino were off on holiday, and Miranda could not but speculate as to how his lordship would have explained this turn of events.

Not that the Earl's departure troubled her a whit; quite the contrary, it came as a considerable relief. There could be no further confrontation as long as Anthony was absent, and, judging from the veritable mountain of baggage in the curricle, his absence looked to be quite prolonged. If only she could leave prior to his return!

Miranda turned away from the window, and her eyes fell on the connecting door. It could hardly be construed as theft if she took the envelope; the money was hers, her due. Miranda hurried across the Yellow Chamber, wrested the washstand sufficiently away that she could slip behind it and entered the Earl's bedchamber. She tried not to look at the bed, but she could not help noting, from the corner of her eye, that it was exceedingly rumpled, and she marched to the writing table.

The envelope was gone. Miranda pawed half-heartedly amongst the papers strewn on the surface of the table, but she had little hope of success. Anthony had taken the envelope with him, taken it or hidden it, his last and nastiest prank. She heard a noise in the corridor and rushed back to her own room, squeezed past the washstand and gently closed the door. She was again overcome by exhaustion, exhaustion and bitter defeat, and she returned to the bed and fell at once into a fitful sleep.

She was awakened, within minutes, it seemed, by a barrage of loud, determined knocks at the corridor door.

"*Please*, Lady Margrave," Cassy begged. "If you will only assure me that you're well, I shall go away and not come back till you ring. However, I do have a message."

Despite herself, Miranda's heart bounded, and she jumped out of bed and rushed across the Brussels carpet. "What message?" she demanded breathlessly, through the door.

"You *are* all right then, ma'am?"

"I am fine," Miranda lied. "What message?"

"Well, Sir Humphrey and Madam Dee—though I guess she is no longer Madam Dee, is she?—are preparing to depart for Dover, and they wish to say goodbye."

"That—that is all?" Miranda felt her knees sag with disappointment.

"Yes, ma'am. If you don't choose to see them, I shall inform them you're indisposed." She hesitated. "*Are* you indisposed, ma'am?"

"No," Miranda snapped; "no, I am quite well. I shall dress and be out directly."

"If you will just unlock the door, I shall help you." Cassy rattled the knob.

Miranda recalled the washstand, still situated in front of the connecting door. She doubted she had the strength to move it, and she was in no mood to cope with Cassy's inevitable curiosity. "That won't be necessary," she said. "I shall dress myself and come along shortly."

Miranda went to the wardrobe and peered inside. For some reason, she was inclined to wear one of her old gowns, but she had no desire to prompt Sir Humphrey's curiosity either, and she randomly selected a walking dress of blue jaconet with a white-lutestring spencer. Once dressed, she proceeded to the dressing table and attempted to rearrange her disordered hair, but it was an impossible task. She gave up and decided she looked much as she had upon her arrival in London. Perhaps that was appropriate: she had never been a countess, never would be, and she must learn to accept herself as she was.

Miranda opened the corridor door with trepidation, expecting to find Cassy lurking beyond, but the hall was empty. Miranda relocked the door from the outside and started toward the steps, and at that moment a small army emerged from the former Comtesse's bedchamber: Cassy, the three footboys, two footmen and even Horton, all encumbered with trunks and cases and valises. Miranda met the group at the top of the staircase, and Cassy, who was in the lead, paused to inspect her mistress with sharp disapproval. Fortunately Horton ordered the abigail to "Move ahead!" and the Hammonds' bearers proceeded down the steps.

Horton had just disappeared round the landing when

Sir Humphrey and Jeanne dashed into view. The baronet was carrying a small dressing case, his wife a jewelry chest, and though neither burden could have weighed more than half a stone, both of the Hammonds appeared quite flushed. Miranda could only collect that they had not yet recovered from their wedding-night endeavors, a notion she found inexplicably disturbing.

"Ah, Miranda." Jeanne started down the stairs, beckoning Miranda rather imperiously to follow, and Sir Humphrey brought up the rear. "I had hoped to speak with dear Antoine, but I am told he is gone. When do you expect his return?"

Miranda was most reluctant to confess that she did not know where her alleged husband *was*, much less when he might come back, and she decided that another tiny lie could scarcely damage her already riddled character. "Tomorrow," she gulped.

"*Quel dommage.*" They had flown along the first-floor corridor and were pounding down the final flight of steps. "I wanted to advise Antoine that Humphrey and I cannot fit all our luggage into the carriage. Consequently, we wish to leave a few items behind and send for them later, when we are settled. I do trust that *cher Antoine* will have no objection."

"I am confident that *cher Antoine* will not object at all," Miranda said dryly.

They had reached the foyer, and Miranda began to understand the magnitude of the Hammonds' difficulty. There were bags scattered all about the entry hall and a stream of servants bearing luggage out to the street, from which direction emanated a constant shout of instructions, punctuated by the occasional curse.

"I also wished to thank Antoine." Jeanne seemed entirely oblivious to the general chaos she had fostered. "To thank him for all he has done in my behalf. And you as well, of course," Lady Hammond added quickly. "In any event, I hope you will relay my sentiments when Antoine returns."

She paused to supervise the removal of her largest trunk, sternly reminding the footboys that its contents were *"très fragile."* She then turned back to Miranda with a pretty frown. "But if Antoine is to be away until tomorrow, perhaps you might drive to Dover with us. I understand that Monsieur Pollard is to spend the night and bring the carriage back tomorrow. Antoine would scarcely miss you, eh?"

Miranda doubted that "Antoine" would miss her for many days to come, and she impulsively decided that the proposed outing might be just the thing to boost her dismal spirits. "I believe I *shall* go with you to Dover," she said. "However, I've nothing but a trunk—"

"You may borrow one of my cases," Jeanne offered generously. "The one immediately inside the bedchamber door contains only spare underthings. Dump them out and use the valise for yourself."

"But you must hurry, Lady Margrave," Sir Humphrey said. "We are behind schedule as it is: the *Princess Claude* sails at five, and it is nearly nine already. I fear both Jeanne and I were *dreadful* lie-abeds this morning."

They giggled, and Miranda, overset again, closed her ears and raced up the stairs. She located Jeanne's case, emptied it and wished she had the time to count Lady Hammond's "spare underthings"; she estimated a supply sufficient to last for several months. She galloped to the Yellow Chamber, unlocked the door, packed the minimum essentials, jammed on her leghorn hat, relocked the door and rushed back down the steps. She thought the entire effort had required under ten minutes, but the Hammonds were already seated in the landau, and as soon as Sir Humphrey had dragged Miranda in, the carriage set smartly out.

The first quarter-hour of the journey was devoted to a precarious reorganization of the baggage. After much standing and crouching, Miranda eventually found herself crammed into the rear-facing seat, her feet resting on a trunk, four valises piled beside her and her own borrowed case in her lap. She could not but recall Signorina Savino's cramped circumstances, and she gazed studiedly out the window.

It was a beautiful day, a perfect English summer day, and Miranda attempted to store every detail in her mind. Perhaps the memory of the blue sky, the green trees, the soft, warm breeze would prove comforting during the course of a frigid Canadian winter or a stifling Indian summer. These thoughts reminded her that she really must make a decision as to where she would go. She must swallow her pride and demand that his lordship return the envelope, for it was quite out of the question for her to remain with Anthony a day longer than absolutely necessary. Not now; not since he had come to regard her as another of his multitudinous playthings.

Miranda felt an infuriating prickle of tears behind her eyelids, and she snatched a linen handkerchief from her reticule and dabbed discreetly at her eyes. She chanced to glance across the carriage as she did so and realized that the Hammonds, their passionate interest in one another notwithstanding, were regarding her with intense curiosity.

"I—I fancy there is something in the air this time of year that causes my eyes to water," she said brightly. Neither of the newlyweds appeared entirely to accept this explanation, and Miranda judged it best to change the subject at once. "I do not believe I was told exactly where it is you are going. Do you plan to live on one of Jeanne's estates in France?"

The Hammonds burst into merry laughter, as though Miranda's inquiry had been enormously witty, and she studied them with considerable puzzlement. The baronet recovered first.

"You needn't maintain any fictions on our account, Lady Margrave," he said, still chuckling a bit. "I know the truth about dear Jeanne, and she about me. The most amusing aspect of the matter is that we determined, in retrospect, that neither of us actually lied about our circumstances. I simply *assumed* that Jeanne was wealthy, and she assumed the same of myself."

"It was not until the night at the opera that the truth was revealed." Jeanne took up the story. "You will recall that I overheard *cher* Humphrey telling your cousin, Mr. Cavendish, of my riches, and on the following day I set him smooth. He then confessed that he, also, was poor as a church rat."

Jeanne laughed again, and Miranda was compelled to smile as well at Lady Hammond's confused English idioms. "But what will you *do*?" she asked, sobering once more.

"Why, we shall make our way, of course," Sir Humphrey said firmly. "Now that Jeanne and I have each other, nothing is impossible."

The baronet took his wife's hand, and they exchanged a long look which could not be misread. It was clear that they had fallen deeply, sincerely, in love, and Miranda could not but contrast their happiness to her own shattered dreams.

The Hammonds began to giggle and chatter again, utterly lost in their private world. Miranda laid her head against the seat, closed her eyes and, mercifully, drifted to sleep.

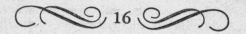 16

They stopped only once, and for under a quarter of an hour, to wolf down a cold, wretched lunch. Nevertheless it was after four when they reached the Dover docks, and Miranda, who had slept intermittently throughout the journey, shook herself and peered fuzzily about. She might, in fact, have been able to sail today, she thought, for there were perhaps a dozen ships moored in the harbor, and the wharf was a sea of carriages, a beehive of activity.

They clambered rather stiffly out of the landau, and Pollard began at once to search for porters. The coachman eventually collared an ancient, wizened little man who looked as though, under the best of circumstances, he was unlikely to survive the day. The porter, with Pollard's assistance, piled Lady Hammond's trunk and several cases into his sagging cart, then announced that he could not possibly manage the rest of the baggage.

"Send one of your fellows along then," Pollard instructed.

"If ye had eyes in ye're head, ye'd see that me mates is occupied," the little man snapped. "Ye'll have to fend a bit for yereselves."

"And so we shall," Sir Humphrey said cheerfully, as the porter tottered away. "You and I shall take the heavier items, Pollard; the ladies can carry the smaller pieces."

The baronet started to divide the remaining luggage, whistling tunelessly under his breath, and it occurred to Miranda that he seemed a new person. He had unbuttoned his waistcoat and loosened his neckcloth, his shirt-points had wilted most alarmingly, and his strawcolored hair was tumbling into his face. Ah, the power of love, she reflected; she wanted to laugh but somehow couldn't.

At length, the baronet separated the baggage into four stacks, each of which he assigned to one member of the party. Miranda tucked Sir Humphrey's dressing case under one arm, picked up the two valises that had fallen to her and set out beside Pollard and the Hammonds.

Perhaps the crowd was larger than Miranda had estimated; perhaps, burdened as she was, she simply fell behind. In any event, she soon found herself toiling along quite alone, the cases growing increasingly heavy, rivulets of perspiration trickling from beneath her leghorn hat and into her eyes. She surmised that she had traversed half the distance to the gangplank when she was compelled to stop and rest. She set the valises down, and, having left her reticule in the carriage, mopped her brow with one sleeve. She was just completing this indelicate activity when she was assailed by a voice at her left.

"Lady Margrave!" Major von Rheinbeck literally hurdled the luggage cart between them and panted to her side. "Lady Margrave," he repeated. "I spied you from the deck—at least I thought it was you; I *prayed* it was you—and I rushed down to see." He examined her with growing shock, sighed, shook his head.

"It is clear that you are exceedingly distressed," he continued kindly, "but your lamentable appearance merely enhances my admiration. A woman cannot, *should* not, casually leave her husband, no matter how deplorable his behavior may have been." The Major seized her hand and dared to plant a kiss upon her damp, grimy palm. "You will not regret your decision, my dear Lady Margrave; I promise you that. Once we have reached Prussia, we shall put your brief, tragic marriage entirely behind us; indeed, it will soon seem that there *was* no marriage."

Miranda's training in the classics had imbued her with a great respect for Fate, and she now wondered if it was not destiny, cleverly disguised as a Prussian officer, which stood before her. She had only to board a ship, the *Princess* or another, and, as Rheinbeck had suggested, the past would soon be entirely behind her. She was still pondering the situation, the Major still clutching her hand when, to her astonishment, she glimpsed Anthony and Signorina Savino not ten feet away.

Miranda initially fancied that they were a mirage brought on by heat and exhaustion. However, as the Earl approached, she noticed that neither of his legs seemed sound; and when he halted just beside Rheinbeck, she observed that his right forefinger was bandaged, as though it had been smashed in a door.

"Margrave," the Major snapped, confirming the reality of Miranda's vision.

"Yes, it is I," his lordship snapped in turn. "And not a moment too soon, it appears. I collect, Sergeant Rosenheim, that you are well in the way of adding *ab*duction to your previous attempts at *se*duction."

"My name is Major von Rheinbeck," the Major corrected frostily.

"Ah, yes, I believe you so counseled me at Almack's," Anthony retorted, with equal frigidity. "I believe I advised you that you might be a *prince* for all it signifies." Miranda did not believe this was what Anthony had said at all. "Whatever position you may claim, it is quite clear that you are bent not only upon alienating my wife's affections but upon spiriting her out of the country."

"Please, Anthony," Miranda said, "there has been a fearful misunderstanding—"

"Hush, Miranda. This does not concern you. I very much fear, Lieutenant, that honor compels me to demand that you go out with me at your earliest convenience."

The Earl slammed his walking stick on the ground, as though proposing that the duel take place at once, and Miranda stole a terrified glance at Rheinbeck's sword. "Please, Anthony, if you would only listen for a moment—"

"Pray allow me to respond to your husband's allegation, Lady Margrave." The Major drew himself stiffly up. "As it happens, sir, I did not plan to meet your wife today, and I in no way influenced her decision to leave you, a decision, however, with which I am entirely in sympathy. Be that as it may, I shall be delighted to go out with you at any time, though I find it ludicrous that *you* should prate of honor."

Rheinbeck stared pointedly at Signorina Savino, and Miranda herself examined the songbird for the first time. She was clad in a demure gown of apple-green mull and a matching bonnet, and she carried a small valise. The Signorina was returning the Major's look with considerable interest, and even as Miranda watched, the songbird's pale cheeks flushed most fetchingly.

"If you refer to my presence here with Miss Stephens, I must take grave exception to your implication," Anthony said. "Miss Stephens is a dear friend of mine, and, as a friend, I escorted her to Dover today where she is to sail upon the *Princess Claude*. You may know Miss Stephens by her professional name, Captain; as Signorina Savino, she is an opera performer of wide renown. Due to certain—ahem—difficult circumstances, Miss Stephens has elected to pursue her career on the Continent."

"Miss Stephens." Rheinbeck clicked his heels and tendered his prim bow, but his eyes did not leave the Signorina's rosy face.

"Little did I think to discover my own wife upon the docks, at the very point of being smuggled off to Prussia by a—"

"I am not being smuggled off to Prussia!" In her eagerness to be heard, Miranda fairly shrieked the words, and a passing party stepped hastily away so as to give their own group a wide berth. "I am not *going* to Prussia," she hissed. She would have preferred to break Rheinbeck's heart in gentler fashion, but she observed, with some annoyance, that the Major was still gazing at Signorina Savino. "These are not my bags." She kicked one of Lady Hammond's valises with rather more force than

210

absolutely required. "They are Jeanne's bags, and I was merely assisting her, carrying them down to the ship."

"I see." Anthony coughed, and Miranda was reminded of the first day of their acquaintance. "It seems I have done you an injustice, Rothburg." The Major tore his eyes from the Signorina, but evidently he was not sufficiently sensible to note this latest distortion of his name. "Since the *Princess* will be departing momentarily, I suggest we forget our differences. If you, Colonel, would assume responsibility for Lady Hammond's luggage . . ."

"Yes, yes, of course," Rheinbeck mumbled. "And I do wish you the very best, Lord Margrave. Lady Margrave."

The Major picked up Jeanne's cases but managed, nevertheless, to offer one gallant arm to Signorina Savino. They threaded their way through the crowd, chatting animatedly, and Anthony shook his red-gold head.

"I predict that Mary Anne will not sing another note," he said. "I daresay she will settle down in Prussia and produce a veritable platoon of stiff, Teutonic officers."

Miranda was inclined to agree, for she had surmised early on that Rheinbeck was ripe, passionately ready, to find the woman of his dreams. She hoped that Signorina Savino would not disappoint him. She peered sharply up at Anthony.

"Do you not regret it, milord? Regret the loss of your songbird?"

"Regret it!" The Earl's green eyes widened, and his crooked brows raced up his forehead. "My dear, obtuse darling, do you not perceive that I have tried to rid myself of Mary Anne from the moment I met you? I did not choose to disclose my deception to her; I merely informed her that I had found it expedient to marry. In the very same breath, I assured her that my marriage would not affect our relationship—hers and mine."

Anthony flashed his engaging grin, and Miranda was pleased to note a distinct sheepishness about the edges. "In fact, our relationship was affected at once. I was to meet Mary Anne on your second night in London, but, as you may recall, I elected to return to Brook's

211

instead. And I did not see her again until the night at the opera—"

"At which point you brought her to live with us," Miranda interposed coolly.

"*Will* you stop interrupting!" his lordship snapped.

Miranda was again reminded of that first day, that first, magic day; and she began to hope, began, at least, to dare to hope. She felt a grin tickling the corners of her own mouth, and she bit her cheeks against it.

"I allowed Mary Anne to stay with us," his lordship continued, "because, as I stated to Lady Jersey, I felt I owed her nothing less. I *was*, at one time, fond of Mary Anne—I shan't deny that—and I believed it my obligation to assist her in her hour of need. I explained to her, in no uncertain terms, that my gesture was merely one of friendship and that she must not suppose our liaison would be rekindled."

The Earl appeared to have paused, and Miranda risked a comment. "How unfortunate that you did not explain the situation, in similarly uncertain terms, to *me*," she said.

"There was an excellent reason for that omission," Anthony said airily. "You had, in the interim, taken up with Rothburg, and I fancied that a bit of competition might do you a great deal of good."

He was beginning, as he so often did, to irritate her. "I presume that was also your reason for the disgraceful scene last night?" Miranda inquired icily.

"That *scene*, as you phrase it, was not of my doing," his lordship replied. "I had informed Mary Anne, quite candidly, that I was in love with my wife." Miranda's heart crashed into her throat, and she lowered her eyes. "She stormed about a good deal and then wept quite a lot, after which she seemed to conceive an intense hatred for you. Why women react so *emotionally* to such circumstances, I cannot comprehend." Miranda stifled another grin.

"At any rate, I collect that Mary Anne was listening at the door and decided to intrude and create the impression that we—she and I—had previously arranged a rendezvous. I determined that she would have to leave immediately, and I drove her to Dover this morning. I hoped to purchase passage for her on the *Princess Claude*, and, as you have no doubt inferred, I was successful. The bulk of Mary Anne's baggage had been removed to the ship before I encountered you, and you know the rest."

"Not all the rest," Miranda demurred sternly. "Last night—" Her cheeks grew warm, and she fastened her eyes on the shiny toes of his lordship's boots. "Last night did not *begin* with Signorina Savino's intrusion; it ended there. Prior to that . . ." But she could not go on.

She waited for the Earl's customary glib retort, but to her surprise, he was silent for a moment. "Ah," he said at last. "You thought I wanted only to seduce you then. That was not the way of it, Miranda."

He tilted her face up, and his green eyes seemed to devour her. "Every word I spoke last night is true: I love you, and I have from the start. You have become so much a part of my life that perhaps I felt we *were* wed. Although, now that I think on it, seduction would not have proved a bad notion at all."

His eyes had begun to twinkle again, and Miranda could not suppress a smile.

"In any event," he continued briskly, "we *shall* be wed at once. I should have explained my plans quite fully last night had you not barred me from your bedchamber. As it was, I tossed and turned in my lonely bed and knocked at least a dozen times, and you ordered me off in most uncivil fashion. Which, I must add, I shall not tolerate again; the next time I shall batter down the door and, if need be, the whole house with it."

Miranda doubted his lordship would ever be put to any such trouble, but she decided not to mention this shameless opinion to him.

"As a result of your stubbornness, I was compelled to take the damned envelope with me when I left," Anthony continued. "I judged you quite capable of snatching up the money and escaping in my absence. Really, Miranda, I fear it may be some years before I am able to make of you a proper, docile wife. Therefore, as I indicated, I intend to undertake the task immediately."

"What do you mean by 'immediately'?" Miranda asked, as docilely as she could.

His lordship coughed. "Since the wedding will have to be rather—ahem—discreet, I propose we go to Scotland. We shall return to London tonight and pack up tomorrow; we shall tell Mama and the servants we are off on a brief holiday." The last lie, Miranda thought, the very last lie. "I shall visit a jeweler and select a somewhat more imposing ring—"

"No!" Miranda said firmly.

She twisted the plain gold band on her finger, for it seemed symbolic. She had dreamed of being a countess, but that dream, she now recognized, was hollow. She wanted only to be a wife, a wife to this irrepressible, impossible man who would comfort and amuse and annoy her through all the years they might be given.

"No?" Anthony barked. In his astonishment, he neglected to glower at her interruption. "You will not marry me?"

"Oh, I suppose I shall be forced to marry you," Miranda replied, "for you have already promised Mother Elizabeth a tribe of grandchildren. But I do not wish any other ring."

The Earl pulled her against him and kissed her quite enthusiastically, quite shockingly, on the mouth, and Miranda could only shudder at the public spectacle they were creating. But she would not draw away, for she suspected that Anthony's behavior would always be slightly horrifying, and she would have him no other way. Nor, she vowed, would she lie, even by implication, ever again. Her arms stole round his neck, and she heard a thud, and his lordship abruptly lifted his head and grunted with pain.

"It is Sir Humphrey's dressing case!" Miranda stooped, plucked it off Anthony's most recently injured foot and whirled around. But it was too late to think of returning it: the *Princess Claude* had raised her sails and was easing into the Channel.

"I daresay Hammond will fairly die without it," Anthony chuckled.

"No, I fancy Sir Humphrey will manage very nicely," Miranda said.

Anthony did not understand her, of course; as Elizabeth had said, men never did comprehend the nature of love. But Miranda observed, as the Earl took her hand and led her away from the sea, that he was swinging his walking stick quite jauntily and not limping at all.

About the Author

Though her college majors were history and French, Diana Campbell worked in the computer industry for a number of years and has written extensively about various aspects of data processing. She had published eighteen short stories and two mystery novels before undertaking her first Regency romance.

Recommended Regency Romances from SIGNET

Buy them at your local

bookstore or use coupon

on next page for ordering.

More Regency Romances from SIGNET